SHUTOUT

SHUTOUT

A MYSTERY

David F. Nighbert

• • •

St. Martin's Press
New York

This is a work of fiction. Names, characters, places, and incidents are either the product of the author's imagination or are used fictitiously. Any resemblance to events or persons, living or dead, is entirely coincidental.

LIBRARY OF CONGRESS CATALOGING-IN-PUBLICATION-DATA
Nighbert, David F.
    Shutout: a Bull Cochran mystery / David F. Nighbert.
      p.   cm.
    ISBN 0-312-11890-2 (hardcover)
    I. Title.
PS3564.I363S58   1995
813'.54—dc20   94-42078
                                        CIP

First Edition: March 1995

10 9 8 7 6 5 4 3 2 1

FOR MY BROTHER, DANNY ALLEN NIGHBERT,
KILLED BY A DRUNK DRIVER ON MARCH 13, 1994.

Acknowledgments

I have many people to thank. My editor at St. Martin's, Gordon Van Gelder, for supplying the title and for suggesting that I set the story in my hometown. David and Barbara Wesner for the loan of their last name. My parents, Herbert and Jeanette Nighbert, for their generosity and hospitality. My brothers, Danny and Joe Nighbert, and Sandra Doyle, for reintroducing me to Knoxville. And to all of those who contradicted Thomas Wolfe by showing me that it was possible to go home again.

For technical help, I want to thank Lt. Robert B. Sexton, Jr., of Support Services, Knox County Sheriff's Department, Detective Mike D. Freeman of Major Crimes, and all the other members of the "Green Lamp Squad"; Foster D. Arnette, Jr., of the Knoxville Police Department; Larry D. Rowlette, Center Manager, Magnetic Resonance Imaging, at St. Mary's Medical Center; Rev. A. J. Henkel, pastor of Holy Ghost Catholic Church, and Rev. Xavier Mankel, Vicar General, Roman Catholic Diocese of Knoxville; as well as Ellen Beason, Melody Sharp, and Lora Burney of Ridgeview Psychiatric Center. These people did their best to help me get it right. Any mistakes or liberties are entirely my own responsibility.

the dead are gentle to us
we carry them on our shoulders
sleep under the same blanket

Zbigniew Herbert
"Our Fear"

SHUTOUT

1

Coming down off the Cumberland Plateau, East Tennessee looked like Eden. I should have known there was a snake waiting for us somewhere, but all I could see was the end of the road.

Molly had called the evening before to tell me she had to go home to Knoxville. That was Molly of the freckles and the auburn curls, the bottle-green eyes and the badge: Detective Sergeant Emily Louise Flanagan of the Galveston Police Department. Her uncle Dewey had had a nervous breakdown, which was bad news for her whole family because he ran the family business, and Dewey's wife, Helen, had called Molly for help. Ordinarily, Helen would have called Molly's father, Dewey's brother Donald, but Donald was too sick to make such a trip, so Molly got the call.

She'd taken emergency leave from the Galveston PD and had asked me to drive up with her. The timing was bad for me because I'd promised my editor a draft of my second mystery by the end of the month. On the other hand, I knew I wasn't going to make the deadline anyway, and I could rationalize this as a good excuse. As an added benefit, I could still blame Molly for taking me away from my work. Pretty slick, huh?

My name is William Heyworth Cochran. I prefer Bill, though everybody, including Molly, calls me Bull. I got the nickname as a hot young pitching prospect in the Boston Red Sox organization, and it seems a little silly on a forty-five-year-old never-was, now eighteen years out of the

1

game. In sportspeak, I had "failed to live up to my potential," that most dreaded of career epitaphs, and after five and a half seasons in the minors and one brief, embarrassing stint in the majors, my only claim to fame was that I was the first pitcher since Carl May to kill a man with a fastball. The name "Bull" was a reminder of all that, but I was learning to live with it.

Molly insisted on driving to Knoxville, explaining that she wanted to see how her new Celica took to the road. Truthfully, she hated flying, but she didn't like to admit it. We were supposed to take turns at the wheel, but because the hum of tires on pavement worked on Molly like a sleeping pill, I ended up doing most of the driving. I knew about this tendency going in, which was one reason I'd suggested air travel. It wasn't that driving bothered me—I would rather drive than be a passenger—it was the principle of the thing. Because Molly insisted on going by car, I ended up chauffeuring her halfway across the country. And because I couldn't resist remarking on this irony, we ended up riding in silence, even when she was awake, all the way from Tyler, Texas, across the northwest corner of Louisiana, well into Arkansas.

Ten hours after leaving Galveston, we crossed the Mississippi River into Tennessee, and I thought to myself, *That wasn't so bad.* But the joke was on me, of course. If I'd paid more attention back in eighth grade geography, I would have known that Tennessee stretched five hundred miles east to west and that most of it still lay between us and Knoxville.

As Molly explained it to me, during one of those periods when we were talking, a native wasn't from Tennessee; he was from East, West, or Middle Tennessee. I figured all states were like that to some degree, but I could see that the physical differences between the regions might aggravate the problem. West Tennessee was flat black bottomland tangled with rivers; Middle Tennessee was rolling hills and woodland climbing into the Cumberlands; and East Tennessee was a great green valley enclosed by mountains.

An hour after sighting the Tennessee Valley from the crest of the Cumberlands, we got onto the 640 bypass, which arced around to the north of downtown Knoxville. Though 640 was eventually intended to make a full circle around the city, so far only the northern half had been completed, finished in time for the '82 Knoxville World's Fair. The highway curved through rolling hills, then straightened out between facing ridgelines. It was the tail end of summer, so the leaves hadn't yet started to turn, and the ridges rose green on green on green. Topping the one to the right, as we approached I-275, was a row of radio towers, flashing their warning lights even in the late afternoon sunshine.

We took the Broadway exit off 640 and got onto Tazewell Pike. It ran north for about a hundred yards between strip centers, then made a sharp turn to the east at a vegetable market. The market sat across from a gas station and a snow-white Baptist church. The pike led past a well-tended cemetery into the shade of great oaks, past more churches—half a dozen in the first mile—past large old homes set well back from the road and smaller new ones that crowded the pavement. Homes *and* churches thinned out gradually, giving way to green fields that glowed in the slanting, late afternoon light. Much of the land looked good for farming, but I saw little sign of it, just a few truck gardens and lots of fallow fields. For the son of an Illinois farmer, it was a sad sight, but I knew it was hard to make a living out of the soil anywhere these days.

I saw scattered signs of poverty, a few crude shacks and shotgun houses tucked into odd little nooks and crannies, but prosperity seemed to be the norm. Elegant old country homes sat atop rolling stretches of lawn, or rested half-hidden in the trees, and even the new subdivisions with their treeless expanses of red dirt generally featured large

3

homes meant to imitate those of their wealthy neighbors.

As Black Oak Ridge closed in from our left, the pike veered toward it and followed a steep winding grade up its side. Halfway up, I caught sight of the hazy blue Smoky Mountains off to the right, about forty miles away, successive ridgelines mounting higher and fainter with distance. The pike passed through a gap in the ridge and wound down the other side. At the foot of the hill, it cut left at an old red barn. As it cut back to the right, I saw black horses in a green field, standing stock-still, as though posing for a painting.

Ridges again rose to both sides: Black Oak Ridge, now to our right, and what Molly said was Beaver Ridge to our left.

"Almost home," she said. A moment later, as we passed a dense stand of pines, she added, "Just ahead to the left, turn in at the gate."

A twelve-foot redbrick fence hid what lay beyond, and black wrought-iron gates guarded the entrance. Cameras looked down from columns to either side, and visitors used an intercom on a black metal post to request entry. But somebody was watching for our arrival, because the gates swung open as I pulled to a stop.

The driveway was bordered by black oaks and flanked by wide expanses of jade-green lawn. It led straight up a gentle incline to a handsome redbrick, white-pillared mansion no roomier than the Pentagon. I knew Molly's family was wealthy, but until that moment, I hadn't realized *how* wealthy. I was eager for a peek inside, but she told me to veer left at the top and directed me onto the gravel road that ran past the house.

"Your aunt doesn't live here?" I asked.

"Yes, but she moved back to the summerhouse after Dewey . . . was taken away."

Dewey was Molly's favorite uncle, and she didn't like to talk about his breakdown. She was well into the denial stage now and had told me several times that he was the sanest man she'd ever known. But she'd also told me that he'd been hospitalized after taking some potshots at his brother Darrell, which on the surface didn't sound like the behavior of an entirely stable individual.

The gravel road passed between the house and several acres of grape arbor—long rows of trellises stretching off to the left, supporting leafy green vines, heavy with purple grapes.

"Muscadines," said Molly with a smile. "Helen loves her muscadine wine."

The house was even bigger than it looked from the front, running much deeper than expected. Once past it, I could see that it was U-shaped, enclosing a tree-shaded garden between backward-thrusting wings. More trees were scattered about the huge backyard, along with a swimming pool, a tennis court, and a multilevel tree house half-hidden among the leaves of an ancient elm.

I stopped and pulled over to get a better look at the tree house.

"Built and improved by three generations of Flanagans," said Molly. "It was my favorite place in the whole world when I was a kid. Great for hiding and thinking about things." Green eyes glimmering, face glowing with memory, she looked impossibly beautiful to me at that moment. After giving the tree house the once-over, she said sadly, "Been neglected lately. No kids around here now."

"Who takes care of all this?"

"Uncle Cyrus and Aunt Ida do most of it."

I groaned. "Don't tell me you have more aunts and uncles I don't know about!"

She laughed. "And we've hardly discussed my mother's side of the family." Seeing my expression, she quickly added, "But you don't have to worry about them this trip. They mostly live down around Nashville."

"Thank heaven for that," I said. "But what about this Uncle Cyrus and Aunt Ida?"

"They're not really my aunt and uncle; we've just always called them that. Cyrus and Ida Wesner have been looking after this place since before I was born."

Beyond the tree house was a horse corral and a jumbo-sized, red-roofed barn. Past that, the road entered the woods and started to climb. As the slope steepened, the road began to cut back and forth across the face of the hill. After the third cutback, Molly told me to pull over.

I eased into a gravel parking space and killed the engine, then sat there for a moment, body still vibrating, mind half-hypnotized by the road. We'd driven from Galveston to Knoxville in nineteen hours, halting three times for food, once for gas, several times to find a rest room, and once just for the hell of it. Not only did Molly insist we drive, we had to drive straight through. We had the time to travel by car, but no time to pause for a brief snooze along the way.

Feeling stiff and numb from sitting too long in the same position, I opened the door and swung my feet to the ground, then craned myself out of the car with my arms. Rubbing my buttocks to restore circulation, I took in a breath of warm air that smelled of damp, loamy soil, decaying leaves, and the sharp scent of pine.

Starting around the car, I asked, "Where's this summer-house?"

"Top of the hill," she said.

The hill was steep and crowded with trees, more jungle than forest. Uprooted trees lay at all angles, caught as they'd fallen, all shrouded in leafy vines. Through this tangle, I caught glimpses of a log cabin about a hundred feet above.

I heard the pellets rattling in the trees an instant before I heard the blast. Then I was on the ground with Molly on top of me.

Spitting out leaves and dirt, I asked, "Wha—?"

"Shotgun," she said. When I started to raise my head, she shoved it back down and snapped, "Crawl over behind that rock!"

The rock was a gray granite boulder striated with veins of white quartz and big enough to shield both of us. Once

6

safely behind it, I asked, "Does your family always greet visitors this way?"

"Hang on," she said. "Back in a second."

She scrambled toward the driver's side of the car and disappeared. The door opened. A moment later, it closed, and she came crawling back with her Glock 9-millimeter semiautomatic.

She pulled the revolver I'd been using for target practice from the waistband at the small of her back and handed it to me. She ejected the clip from her Glock and made sure it was fully loaded, then dry-fired it to test the action, slapped the clip back in, and chambered a round.

"Wait here," she said.

"You're going up there?"

"Just want to take a look."

"Maybe I should go with you."

She smiled and gave me a quick kiss. "I can't take you into this, Bull. I shouldn't be doing it either. I should drive to the nearest phone, call the Sheriff's Department, and let them handle it. But my aunt's up there, and I have to do something. So just do me a favor, and watch my back from down here. Try not to shoot anybody unless you have to. But if you do, remember what I taught you."

Feeling useless, I said, "I'll remember, Teach."

"Sure you will," she said. "You're my best student."

"I'm your *only* student."

"That, too."

As she turned to go, I added, "Be careful."

She glanced back, grinned, and said, "Always." Then she was up and running in a crouch off to the left. She turned right and disappeared up into the trees, and after a few seconds, I couldn't hear her anymore.

Minutes passed. Cicadas resumed their chorus, and I started to worry. I knew Molly was good at her job and experienced with this sort of situation, but I didn't know what was happening, and not knowing was the problem.

I stared at the gun in my hand with mixed feelings. It was

a handsome, well-made weapon: a classic Smith & Wesson .38 service revolver, the preferred handgun of generations of police officers. The customized grips filled my fist nicely; the weight of it felt important; and once you got past the noise, firing it was a real kick. But I'd seen the kind of damage such a weapon could produce, and a big part of me wanted nothing to do with it. On the other hand, I'd been shot at a few times, and an equally big part of me wanted to make sure I was prepared in case it ever happened again.

In an effort to overcome my distrust of guns, Molly was putting me through the basic F.B.I. revolver course, featuring techniques developed by a Southern California police officer named Jack Weaver. In the Weaver position, you stood (or kneeled or lay) at a slight angle to your target, to avoid having to bend your wrist when aiming the weapon. Right shoulder back (for a right-hander), left shoulder forward, left hand cradling the right. The gun was held chest-high in ready position, and firing position was reached by punching the gun up to eye level with the right hand, while pulling back with the left to create an isometric force that steadied the weapon. The technique seemed to work, at least on the firing range, but I'd never actually tried it on a live target, and I wasn't anxious to start.

At the sound of the second shotgun blast, I nearly dropped the gun. I heard Molly yell something, followed by two shots from a smaller-caliber weapon, then nothing for several minutes. I wanted to call out and ask if she was all right, but I realized she might not want to reveal her position right now, and I knew she'd yell if she needed me. My pride took a severe beating, but I stayed where I was.

If you want to know what kind of man would sit in hiding and let his woman take all of the risks, the answer is a man whose woman knows a hell of a lot more about the ways and means of violence than he does.

I was about to risk it anyway when she finally yelled, "Come on up, Bull!"

"You okay?" I yelled back.

"Yeah! Bring the first aid kit!"

"You *hurt?*"

"No, it's not for me, dummy!"

2

A t the place where Molly had vanished into the trees, I found a flight of brick steps leading up the hill. Many of the bricks were cracked and worn, broken or missing, but they'd been laid down a long time ago by somebody who knew what they were doing, and there was grace in the way they wound upward through the trees. They curved out of sight about twenty feet above, so I couldn't see the top.

I started up with revolver in hand, feeling self-conscious, like I was acting out a scene from a movie or one of my stories. I held the gun down at my side, so it wouldn't be too conspicuous, but I didn't even think about leaving it behind.

The log cabin wasn't actually at the top of the hill, only at the top of the rise, backed up against a craggy cliff face of granite. The cabin looked old, but well cared for, constructed of stout logs a foot thick, the logs blackened with creosote to preserve the wood, the connective mortaring painted white for contrast. The house was only one story and not very deep, but nearly a hundred feet long, with a screened-in porch running all the way across the front. It was surrounded on three sides by a freshly cut lawn, and shade trees pressed against the sides. A stream ran down from the ridge on the west side and cut a diagonal across the front, and I had to cross a wooden bridge to reach the house.

I didn't see Molly, but an old man sat on the porch steps. He was small and wiry, with hands that looked too big for the rest of him. Those hands were now clasped on top of his head, spatulate fingers pressing down on his thin gray hair as though trying to hold his skull together. A pump-action 10-gauge shotgun leaned against the step railing beside him.

Although clearly in pain, he looked up at my approach and managed a smile, as he said with a nasal twang, "You mus' be Mister Cochran."

When he started to rise, I told him, "Don't get up. You look hurt."

"Some," he acknowledged, one hand still pressing down on his skull. "I'm Cyrus Wesner," he said, and reached out his other hand for me to shake. The hand was roughly callused, the grip firm.

"You're the man who looks after all this," I said.

"Leastways I try," he agreed with a grin. "You know, my wife'll be plumb tickled to meet you, Mister Cochran. She tole me all about your books and said you was a professional baseball player."

"Once upon a time," I said. "Mostly in the minors."

"Ain't that sumpin'," he said, more impressed than he needed to be. "You know, I listen to the Braves play whenever I can."

"Good team," I said, staring up at the porch. "But even with McGriff, they're going to have a hard time catching the Giants this year."

"Yep," he seconded, "that Bonds is somethin', all right."

"You know where Molly is?"

"She went in to see about Miz Helen."

"Anything I can do for you?"

"Not 'less you got a aspirin handy."

Reaching for the first aid kit under my arm, I said, "Matter of fact, I probably do."

"That'd be a godsend," he said.

The kit was brand-new, and the aspirin was easy to find. Cyrus accepted the foil-wrapped tablets with trembling fingers. "Much obliged, Mister Cochran."

"Need some water to wash that down?"

"No, sir, I reckon it'll do me as good dry as wet. You go on in. I'll just sit here and give it a chance to work."

I felt cool air on my face as I opened the screen door. The porch was ten feet deep, and French doors stood open to the house all along its length, two to my right and five or six to my left. A couple of metal gliders sat among ranks of rocking chairs, and two settees hung from chains at opposite ends of the porch.

The front door stood open, and it was even cooler inside the house. At the other end of the entry hall was a dark archway that Molly later explained led directly into the hillside. The house was cooled with air from the caves that riddled the ridge, brought into the rooms by fans and ducts. The system was developed by Sean Michael Flanagan, the first of the East Tennessee Flanagans, who'd built the summerhouse as a gift for his new bride, Katherine Eliza Flanagan, a hundred years ago.

The entry hall was paved in flagstone and scattered with rough hemp mats for cleaning shoes. Several pairs of rubber boots stood against the walls, under racks of raincoats and jackets and hats. Other racks held fly rods, a fishing net, and a couple of badminton rackets. An axe leaned in the corner beside the door.

Archways led into the dining room on the right and the living room on the left. Both rooms were large, the furniture sturdy and comfortable-looking—a heavy oak table and chairs in the dining room, slipcovered chairs and couches in the living room. Watercolors and photographs dressed the pine-paneled walls, and throw rugs were scattered about the hardwood floors. Seemed like a pleasant place to spend the summer.

Molly was in the living room bent over an older woman lying on a couch. Aunt Helen, I assumed. She was slender, dressed in a burgundy blouse, a gray skirt, and sturdy black pumps. She appeared to be sleeping.

Molly glanced my way and walked over.

"What happened?" I asked.

"Found her unconscious on the porch with a lump on her head," she said absently, her mind elsewhere. "Woke her up and helped her inside."

I'd seen Molly like this before, when she was preoccupied with a case, and I knew she was capable of answering simple questions. "Mister Wesner was knocked out, too, wasn't he?" I asked.

She nodded. "Found him outside, on the ground."

"Is that his shotgun leaning against the steps?"

"Yeah."

"I take it he didn't use it to shoot at us."

"Of course not." She looked at me directly for the first time since I'd entered. "I saw somebody in a denim jacket," she said. "A man, I think. I didn't spot him until he fired at me, then he dropped the shotgun and took off. I told him to halt and put a couple of shots over his head, but it didn't slow him down."

"Now, what does the book say about warning shots?" I asked, using my most patronizing elementary school teacher's voice.

" 'Warning shots are wasted shots,' " she said. "And don't be a smart-ass. I'm the one who told *you*, remember? But here I am, a thousand miles outside my jurisdiction, and I don't know what's going on, just that somebody's shooting at me. For all I know, it could be one of my relatives. What am I going to do, *wing him?*"

"Guess not," I had to agree. "Maybe Mister Wesner got a better look at him."

"Maybe," she said. "Let me call the cops and an ambulance, then we'll ask him."

13

* * *

The first thing Mr. Wesner wanted to know was if Miz Helen was all right.

"She's okay, Cyrus," said Molly.

After we helped him onto the porch and into a rocking chair, Molly took the first aid kit from me and started cleaning the wound on the back of his head. When he flinched, she asked, "That sting?"

"Jus' cold," he said. "But it feels good, miss. Don't stop."

"What happened, Cyrus?"

"Got bushwhacked, miss."

"Did you see who did it?"

"Nope," he said, sounding ashamed, "he caught me from behind."

"How do you know it was a *he?*"

"Well, I guess I don't *know*," he admitted. "I jus' natur'ly figgered it for a man. Wudn't no love tap he give me, I'll tell you that."

"But it could've been a woman?" Molly asked.

"Reckon it *could*," he agreed. "Is Miz Helen really all right?"

"She'll be okay, Cyrus. She was just knocked out, like you." When he started to get up, she held him firmly in place. "I've called an ambulance, but you know it usually takes them at least twenty minutes to get here, so that gives you plenty of time to tell me what happened."

He frowned and shook his head. "It's all kinda hazy to me."

"Then tell me what you can," she said.

"Well," he began slowly, "I wuz . . . I wuz workin' on the plumbin'. You know that's always been a problem up here." To me, he added, "Dewey's daddy had it put in on the cheap, Mister Cochran, and it never has worked right. I been sayin' for years that we should jus' tear it out and start all over again, but Dewey keeps tellin' me to patch it up, so that's what I do. Only now, it's more patch than pipe."

14

Molly smiled. "Dewey inherited a good deal of Grampa's tightness with money."

Cyrus nodded. "That's the God's truth, miss. Neither of 'em'd part with a buck without an argument."

Molly laughed, then glanced at something over my shoulder, and I turned to see a Sheriff's patrolman in a navy-blue uniform crossing the wooden bridge. "Hold on, Cyrus," she said. "I'll be right back."

She went out and spoke to the patrolman, who stood about six feet tall, had a miler's slender build, and looked too young to be a cop. After Molly had told him what he needed to know, he started talking into his hand-held radio, and she came back to us.

She opened the screen door and said, "Units are closing in to cut off the perp's escape, and the officer's putting out the description. Anyway—" She turned to Cyrus. "You were working on the plumbin', and then . . . ?"

He stared at her blankly for a moment. "Oh, yeah," he said. "Miz Helen come to tell me they was somebody outside, and for me to go out and shoo 'em off. So, I got my shotgun and—"

"Why?" asked Molly.

"What's that, miss?"

"Why'd you get your shotgun just to go out and chase this person off?"

"I never thought about it," he admitted. "But I guess it was on account of the trouble we been havin' here lately. The break-in and all."

"Break-in? Up here?"

"Down at the bighouse, Thursday night. Dewey caught somebody in his study. Then, last night, Helen tole me she heard somebody on the porch up here. So I guess I jus' felt safer with a gun in my hand, and I . . ." He sat there for a moment, mouth open, then shook his head and said, "Done lost my place again."

Molly smiled. "You were going out to chase off this stranger."

15

"Yeah," he said. "So, anyway, I went down off the porch and stood there lookin' around for a minute or two, not seein' nobody and not knowin' which way to turn. Then I heard sumpin' off to the side a the house and went over that way. But"—he sighed again—"I reckon whoever it was was just a-layin' for me."

"Then you didn't see anybody?" she asked.

"Nope," he said, shaking his head. "Sure wish I had."

"Can you guess who it might've been?"

He squinted at her. "Guess?"

"You don't stumble over this place by accident," she said. "So odds are it was somebody you know."

He thought about it, but finally said, "I just don't know who it could be, miss."

She gave him a reassuring pat on the shoulder and said, "That's okay, Cyrus."

We helped him into the living room, so he could see that Helen was still breathing, then we left him there and went back outside.

3

As we stepped onto the porch, another officer was crossing the bridge, this one in dark pants and a white dress shirt, a gold badge clipped to his belt. He was a big man with the look of a former athlete, just starting to show a belly. I knew how that went. You reached a point at which fending off the fat was a full-time job, especially after going through high school and college and, in my case, five years of pro ball eating all you wanted at the training table. He wore a navy-blue baseball cap with two lines of white printing above the brim, saying *Sheriff's Dept.* on top and *Major Crimes* underneath. The brim sat low over his eyes, so I didn't get a look at his face until he stopped to stare up at us from the foot of the steps. He was a handsome fellow with a square face and a Kirk Douglas–type dimple in his chin.

Molly walked to the screen door and said, "Tim?"

The detective took off his cap and grinned up at her. "That you, Molly?"

She smiled. "Yes, Tim, it's me."

"Well, I'll be galldurned." I swear that's what he said.

She went out the screen door and down the steps to give him a hug, triggering in my mind an unwelcome flash of some long-ago drive-in movie, the two of them dimly visible through the steamed-up windows of a '62 Chevy. Then I saw them looking up at me and realized I'd probably been introduced. *Try to pay attention, Bull.*

"Sorry," I said, as I followed Molly down the steps. "Guess I zoned out there for a minute. Long drive." Stick-

17

ing out a hand, I added, "I'm Bill Cochran."

"Bill, I'm Tim Deets," he said, trying to pulverize my metacarpus, "and I wanta thank you for bringing this young lady back to see us."

The "young lady" in question crossed her eyes at me behind his back and asked, "Is your brother around, Tim?"

"No, Lonnie was down in Florida the last I heard."

"See much of him?"

"Not in the last few years," he said, then got down to business. "What happened up here? I was on my way home when I heard the call about a shooting."

"Somebody fired a shotgun at us as we got out of the car," she said, "and I came up to investigate."

Tim shook his head disapprovingly. "You should've called *us*, Molly, first thing."

"My aunt was up here," she said, "and by the time you people showed up, it might be too late."

"Okay," he said with a judicious nod. "I suppose I'll go along with that."

"When I got to the top of the steps," she went on, "I cut into the trees and worked my way around toward the west side of the house. I didn't see anybody, but whoever it was must've heard me coming, because he let off another blast in my direction. As I dove for cover, I saw a man in jeans and a denim jacket under the tree at the end of the porch. I think it was a man. He was turning away as I caught sight of him, and I didn't get a look at his face. Long dark hair— long for a man—average height, or a little above, slender build, weight about one fifty. He dropped the shotgun and took off for the pine stand at the base of the cliff." She made no mention of warning shots, I noticed. "I found Cyrus on the ground where I saw the shooter. He was out cold with a lump on the back of his head, and I found Helen on the porch in the same condition."

"They all right?" asked Tim.

"I think so, but I'm no doctor. Cyrus seems okay, but

18

Helen only came around long enough for me to get her into the living room.''

"You call an ambulance?" he asked.

"Yeah, about fifteen minutes ago.''

"Too soon to expect it, then," he said. "Why do you suppose the shooter dropped the shotgun?"

"Don't know," she said. "Maybe he was afraid it would slow him down."

"It's a handy weapon," he said, "and he might've needed it if you'd gone after him."

"Probably had a handgun," she said.

"Probably," he agreed, "but it still seems odd. Was he wearing gloves?"

"Didn't notice, but I'd say he was."

"So he wouldn't be worried about leaving prints on the shotgun."

"That's right," she said. "Cyrus said there'd been a break-in down at the bighouse."

He nodded. "Thursday night. The security company phoned in the alarm. When the patrolman got there, he found the French doors to Dewey's study standing open, but no sign of a forced entry. It appeared that the alarm had been set, but the doors hadn't been locked. Nothing was stolen, or even disturbed, as far as Dewey could see. He claimed to've scared the burglar off, but he couldn't give us a description, and he finally admitted that he hadn't actually seen anybody. I offered to stay a few nights and see if the guy came back, but Dewey wouldn't hear of it. He told me he could protect his own damn home, thank you, and if he saw the bastard, he fully intended to shoot him dead."

"That's Dewey," Molly agreed fondly.

Tim nodded and looked away.

She stared at him. "Were you called in when he was . . . ?"

"Yep," he said, looking back. "I was there when they took him away."

"What happened, Tim? Helen was too upset to give me

all the details. I know Dewey took some shots at Darrell and—"

"Six shots," said Tim.

"*Six?*"

"Uh huh. Chased him out of his office and down the stairs."

Rebounding like a champ, she said, "Well, that proves Dewey wasn't trying to kill him. If he was, he wouldn't have needed six shots and Darrell would be dead."

Tim nodded. "That's the way I figured it, too," he admitted, "but things have a way of getting complicated when your family's involved."

"I've noticed that," Molly agreed.

"I mean, this was basically a simple matter." Tim had been holding his cap in deference to Molly, but now put it back on his head and squared it up, formally resuming his professional guise. "Shots were fired," he said, "but nobody was hurt. The gun was registered, and Dewey has a carry license. At most, he gets a slap on the wrist. Maybe he has to go downtown and get fingerprinted. *Maybe* he spends an hour or two in a holding cell before seeing the judge, then makes bail and goes home. And that's only if the cops can't talk to the brothers at the scene and get them to kiss and make up. Either way, it's simple. Or it's supposed to be. But, as I say, things have a way of getting complicated when it comes to your family."

"Don't rub it in," she said, meaning it.

He took the hint. "Well, anyway, when the detectives arrived, Darrell insisted that they arrest Dewey on the spot."

Molly shook her head. "That doesn't sound like Darrell. He was always the dignified one in the family, the one most concerned about the family's image and our place in the community. You wouldn't think that having his brother thrown in jail would improve his standing at the Rotary."

"Guess he just didn't take to bein' a target," said Tim.

"He made it real plain that he thought Dewey was too dangerous to be runnin' around loose."

"Can't say that I blame him," I said. "He was shot at, and his life was threatened."

"I know that," Molly replied, "and I'm not saying it's right, but—"

"No, you're saying it was only one of Dewey's pranks and that Darrell should have just smiled and turned the other cheek. But I have to say that I'm with Darrell on this. If somebody shot at me, I'd want to be damn sure he couldn't do it again."

Tim conceded the point with a shrug, but Molly got tight around the mouth. "I'm just saying that this was a family matter," she said, "and it could've been handled within the family."

"You make your family sound like an independent state," I said.

Tim grinned. "That's pretty close to the truth, Mister Cochran."

"Are you saying they're above the law just because they're rich?" I asked.

"I wouldn't say *above* the law," he replied, "but rich folks do have a way of standing *outside* of it."

Well, I realized, the country boy wasn't as dumb as he looked.

Molly said with a hint of impatience, "So Darrell told the cops he wanted Dewey arrested. Then what?"

Tim shrugged. "The detectives explained that they couldn't just arrest Dewey, that Darrell would have to go before a judge and swear to the facts of his charge before a warrant could be issued and served. But they said they'd be happy to talk to Dewey for him. They asked where he was, and Darrell told them to look in Dewey's office. You know how it's raised up high in the middle of the main building, so he can see all around."

She nodded. "I used to go up there all the time when I was a kid."

"Well, the two detectives go climbing up the steps with Darrell yelling instructions at them from the floor, telling them to keep low and warning them that Dewey could open fire at any moment. They do their best to ignore him, as they climb to the upper landing, then knock on the office door and identify themselves. The office has windows all around," he explained to me, "but the blinds are drawn, and they can't see inside. Getting no response, they knock again, and ask Dewey to open the door. Soon they're pounding on it, demanding that he open up immediately. When that doesn't work, they try the doorknob and find it locked. They ask for a key, but nobody has one, so they stop to discuss whether to go for a warrant before breaking the door down. But at that point, one of the workers yells out that Dewey isn't there, and that shuts them up long enough for him to explain that Dewey had left the plant while Darrell was in the business office calling the police. So the detectives are embarrassed and angry at Darrell, and Dewey is suddenly a fugitive from justice.

"Then somebody—we don't know who—calls Helen to warn her that Dewey's about to be arrested. Helen calls her lawyer and tells him she doesn't want her husband going to jail. The lawyer calls Doctor Matthews, who promptly signs the emergency commitment papers, and the lawyer trades for his client two or three hours at the police station for seventy-two hours of observation at a private mental hospital. When Darrell agrees to this compromise, the lawyer figures he's earned his retainer. Only there's one little hitch. Dewey doesn't want to go."

He grinned and shook his head. "When I got here, a couple of EMTs were taking cover behind their ambulance, and Dewey was wavin' that big Colt around like he thought he was Wyatt Earp. Helen was hangin' on to him trying to get the gun away, so I couldn't risk a shot, even if I'd taken the notion. But Dewey was a wild man, threatening to shoot anybody who came near him. I never saw him like that before and never want to again. But I'll tell you one thing: If Helen hadn't talked him into giving up that gun when she did, somebody would've got hurt."

"She said they took him to a place called Riverside Center."

"It's fairly new," he said, "down below I-Forty on the Holston River."

"You get off our property!" a voice demanded, and we looked up to see Helen standing in the doorway, supported by Cyrus.

Tim ducked his chin and said quietly, "Just doin' my job, ma'am."

"I'm amazed you have the gall to show your face around here!" she said. Her dialect was closer to Rosalynn Carter's than Tammy Wynette's, and it turned out that, like Rosalynn, she was from Georgia. "Helping them drag my husband off like that," she went on, "after all that man has done for your family! I want you out of my *sight!*"

I thought she was being unfair, since Dewey had been committed to the hospital at her insistence, but it wasn't my place to call her on it. I wouldn't have had a chance anyway, because at that moment, she coughed, choked, and slumped against Cyrus.

He held her up until I could get there, then we carried her into the living room. As we laid her back down on the couch, I noticed a crystal carafe of red wine on the table at her head. Muscadine, I wondered?

Molly and Tim followed us.

"I'm sorry," he said to her. "But I don't reckon Helen'll ever forgive me for being one of the ones who took Dewey away." He shook his head. "Guess strangers are better for some things."

"You were only doing what you had to do," Molly told him. "I don't blame you for it, and when Helen calms down, I'm sure she won't blame you, either. But you could do me a favor."

"Anything," he said, giving her a meaningful glance and me another flash of that '62 Chevy.

"The man I saw must've left some sign out there, and I'd appreciate it if you'd take a look around."

He nodded and said, "You got it."

The ambulance arrived as Tim left the porch. The paramedics carried Helen down the hill on a stretcher, and Cyrus went with her to be checked for a concussion. It was getting dark as Molly and I followed them down the steps, and I looked back to see Tim and a patrolman searching the ground on the west side of the house with flashlights.

4

Helen and Cyrus were taken to St. Mary's Medical Center in North Knoxville. After examining both of them in the emergency room, the doctors decided that Cyrus could go home, but they wanted to keep Helen for a few days. Visiting hours were over by the time they finished with her, but Molly persuaded them to make an exception for us, explaining that we'd traveled thousands of miles to see her.

Helen had a tiny private room with a view through the window of more windows. It was an odd little room stuck into an odd little corner, so small and cramped that one door had to serve for both the room door and the door to the bathroom. When you pushed the room door wide open, a complex hinging mechanism allowed it to click into place over the opening to the bathroom. It meant you could never close off both the room and the bathroom at the same time, but when I thought about it, I realized that having *two* doors that close together would have been impractical, possibly even dangerous. The room was in the purple wing and had far too much purple trim, but mercifully the decorators had settled on white curtains.

Cyrus' wife, Ida, had brought Helen some clothes and makeup, and she was sitting up in bed when we arrived, her face restored, her silver hair brushed into place, wearing a navy-blue robe over a white silk nightgown. At seventy-two, she might have passed for fifteen years younger. Once a great beauty, she was still a handsome woman, and she held herself like a queen. Only the slight Parkinsonian tremor in her head and hands betrayed her age.

"It's an honor to meet you, Mistuh Cochran," she said. "I've had the pleasure of reading both your works of non-fiction. Having once harbored dreams of being a writer my-self, I confess to being envious of your gift."

"You're very kind, ma'am," I said modestly.

"I have yet to sample your fiction," she went on, "and I'm not especially fond of the mystery genre as a rule, but Ida has assured me that your mystery is 'a real dilly,' so I suppose I shall have to give it a try." She blessed me with a smile nearly as gratifying as a rave in the *Times*. Well, maybe not *nearly*, but closer than you'd think.

"I'll send you an autographed copy," I promised.

"If I may suggest an alternative," she said, "perhaps I could purchase a copy and have you autograph it."

"If you want."

"I do," she declared. "I suspect it's royalties you need, far more than idle praise."

"How true," I agreed.

"I understand that Ida rode over here with you."

"That's right."

"If you don't mind my asking," she said, "what was your impression of her?"

"A very plain-spoken woman," I said, and Helen smiled. "She kept insisting that Cyrus' injury was 'his own fool fault.'"

"She'll say worse to his face," said Helen, "and Cyrus will nod and say, 'Yes, Ida.' She's been bullying him for as long as I've known them, but I've actually seen him smile in admiration when she's at her sharpest. Marriage, you see, is the art of complement and contrast."

"I don't know," said Molly. "You and Dewey always seemed well matched."

"But never alike," Helen insisted. "I assure you that we've had our differences, though we made every effort never to let you children see us argue."

26

Molly smiled wickedly. "Yes, but you know how well sound travels in the bighouse."

"Are you implying that you *heard* us?"

Molly nodded. "And *saw*. We—Dick, Bobby, Sarah, and I—would hide in your dining room and watch through the crack between the doors as you and Dewey fought it out in the parlor. And I have to say you usually gave as good as you got."

Drawing herself up, Helen declared with unconvincing sternness, "You should be ashamed of yourself, young lady, spying on your elders in such a calculated fashion."

"Begging your pardon, Auntie," said Molly, "but since we had to hear it anyway, it only made sense to get the details."

Helen resisted a smile, but when Molly leaned down to give her a hug, she returned it with vigor. "I'm so glad you came," she said in a trembling voice. "You've been gone too long, and your father should never have taken you so far away. Now this—" She shook her head. "I just couldn't handle it alone."

"You don't have to." Molly sat on the bed and put an arm around her. "Bull and I are here now, and we'll get through this together."

Helen patted her hand and smiled at me, saying with evident relief, "Yes, I believe we will."

"Have you spoken to Ruth and Rachel?" Molly asked, referring to her daughters.

"I phoned Rachel right after they took Dewey away," she said. "She wanted to fly down, but she's tied up testifying before some Senate committee. And Ruth,"—she glanced away—"hasn't returned my call."

Hmmm, I thought, *more family conflict.*

"So tell me what happened today," said Molly.

"There's little to tell," said Helen. "I saw somebody crossing the yard and sent Cyrus out to chase him off."

"Did you recognize him?"

"No."

27

"Did you see his face?"

"No, he was walking away from me."

"And then?"

"I went back to the book I was reading. When I realized that Cyrus hadn't come back, I stepped out to see what had happened, and I suppose someone hit me."

"You suppose?"

"I have no memory of it."

"Is that . . . usual?"

"According to the doctors," said Helen, "it's not uncommon."

"Then you didn't see who did it?"

"No."

"Same as with Cyrus."

"How is he?" Helen asked.

"He has a headache, but no cracked skull or concussion."

"Thank heaven for that."

"Who would *do* this?" Molly asked.

"I don't know."

"You know *something*," she declared. "What're you holding back?"

Helen blushed. "Nothing. I'll tell you anything. I *want* to tell you everything. It's just that there's so much . . ." Her hand rose to her face, but she saw it trembling and quickly tucked it back with the other one in her lap. As long as she kept them clasped, the shaking was hardly noticeable.

"If you're too tired, we can talk tomorrow," said Molly.

"No." Helen reached out, then pulled back in embarrassment. "I don't want you to leave," she said quietly. "Ask your questions, please."

"All right. Why did Dewey shoot at Darrell?"

"He didn't shoot *at* him," Helen said stiffly. "He fired into the air."

"Why?"

Helen sighed. "When Dewey came back from lunch on

28

Friday, he found Darrell going through his desk. He ordered him to leave, and when Darrell refused, he chased him out of his office with his daddy's Colt forty-five."

"Six shots," said Molly.

Helen nodded wearily. "He might've gotten away with one or two, but emptying the gun *was* excessive."

I had to bite my lip.

"What did the witnesses say?" asked Molly.

"Only two people saw anything, and they don't agree about what they saw."

"Figures," said Molly.

"I know how this sounds," said Helen, "and it's fair to say that Dewey is overly fond of the dramatic gesture. But he's no madman. He was furious when they took him away, but it was only anger, not insanity."

"Anger at what?" asked Molly.

"At being dragged away from his home."

"Sounds like he was pretty angry at Darrell, too."

"Yes," Helen agreed with a sigh. "They've been feuding over Shamrock for years, and you know what a disaster this past year has been."

Shamrock was Shamrock Coffee, the original source of the Flanagan wealth, founded more than a century ago by Sean Michael Flanagan, Molly's great-grandfather and the man who built the summerhouse. Most of the family income now came from other sources, such as the leasing of properties and real estate handled by Dewey's brother Darrell, and the wide-ranging investments managed by their brother Duncan. For some time now, the coffee company had constituted more of a financial drain than an asset.

"Nobody but Dewey thinks it can be turned around," Helen went on, "and everyone knows that any plan to save it is going to be expensive. And now this buyout proposal from Lester Prine has really stirred up the fire. For Dewey, it couldn't have come at a worse time."

"Lester Prine," Molly explained to me, "is a developer

from Knoxville, who's built most of his projects down around Atlanta." She asked Helen, "How much is he offering?"

"Twenty-three and a half million for the plant and all our downtown real estate."

Molly whistled. "Sounds more than fair."

"I thought so, too," said Helen, "but you know how much Dewey dislikes Lester."

Molly smiled. "Because of you."

Helen lowered her eyes. "All because I accepted a date with the man fifty years ago." Looking back up, she added, "Which is not to say that Dewey doesn't have other, better reasons for rejecting the offer. He sincerely feels that it would be a betrayal of the Flanagan name to give up Shamrock without a real effort to save her. And when he says he has a plan for turning her around, I believe him. But in all honesty, I think he'd sell out to anyone else. He's convinced that Lester's trying to cheat him."

"What do *you* think?"

"I think the offer is so generous because Lester anticipated Dewey's resistance, and because he desperately needs our land for his New Knoxville project. His plans had to be scrapped when the World's Fair Committee turned down his bid to purchase a piece of the Fair site, and if he doesn't get the land he needs very soon, he may lose his support in the City Council. But regardless of what I believe, I support Dewey's decision. It may be out of fashion, but I was brought up to believe that a wife stands by her husband. Even if it means facing this kind of physical attack."

"From the burglar, you mean?" asked Molly.

"If he *was* just a burglar."

"What else could he be?"

Helen shook her head. "The break-in at the bighouse, Darrell going through Dewey's desk, and now this . . ."

"You think they're connected?"

"Yes, I do."

"Then why were you attacked?"

30

"I'm not sure," she admitted. "Maybe he wanted something in the house, and we were in the way."

"What could he have wanted?"

"I don't know."

"But you think Darrell is behind it?"

Helen tossed her elegant head. "Darrell hasn't the gumption to arrange something like this," she said scornfully. "If he's involved, as I believe he is, then somebody else made the arrangements."

"Who?"

She pursed her lips. "Duncan might be capable of it."

"Duncan?" asked Molly in surprise. "I didn't think he and Darrell got along. Since when do they work together?"

"Since they joined forces to sell Shamrock."

Molly shook her head. "I always liked Duncan, and I find it hard to picture him being involved in something like this."

"You may be right," Helen conceded. "There could be somebody else behind it."

"Who?"

She turned to Molly. "You must promise not to laugh."

"I promise."

Helen took a deep breath. "I fear that the mob may be involved."

Molly didn't laugh, didn't show any facial reaction at all. "The mob," she repeated.

"To be accurate, I should say 'a mob.' I'm not suggesting that one of the New York crime families has established a southern auxilliary, but Darrell has a gambling problem, you know."

"I've heard it mentioned a few times," Molly agreed.

Helen nodded. "He's always gambled, but his losses have rarely been more than he could afford. However, that changed about a year ago. He came to me one afternoon, while Dewey was at the plant, and begged me to ask Dewey for a loan of twenty thousand dollars. His bookie, whose identity he stubbornly refused to reveal, was demanding his money and was threatening Darrell with bodily harm if his demand wasn't satisfied within a week. Darrell hadn't spoken to Dewey in months and was convinced that Dewey would turn him down if asked directly. But in fact, Dewey would never allow any of his brothers to be hurt if it was in his power to prevent it. And needless to say, Darrell got his money."

I said, "It sounds like he owes your husband a debt of gratitude."

"No one likes to be in debt, Mistuh Cochran," said Helen, "and gratitude all too easily subsides into resentment."

"But Dewey saved Darrell from possibly serious injury."

"The greater the debt," she said, "the stronger the resentment."

I shook my head. "It's a wonder the human race has survived."

"An endless source of amazement," Helen agreed. "As for Darrell, he underwent psychological counseling for his gambling problem and claims to have been cured, but," she added with a wry smile, "I'm always skeptical of miracles, aren't you? Dewey is convinced that Darrell has suffered a relapse and is pushing to sell Shamrock because he needs his share of the proceeds to pay off his new debts."

"Will it be sold?" asked Molly.

"Darrell and Duncan would sign the papers tomorrow," said Helen, "and the last time Dewey spoke to your father, he seemed inclined to side with them as well. Dewey was very discouraged by that. You know he's always been closest to Donald."

Dewey, Donald, Darrell, and Duncan. Sounded like the Disney Duck family.

"The board meets in a month," Helen went on, "and the buyout will be voted on at that meeting."

"And what happens if Dewey isn't there?" I asked.

"Ordinarily, he could file a proxy," she said, "but not

from a bed in a mental hospital. There's a 'sound mind' clause in the corporate charter."

"Then *you* would vote the stock?" I asked.

"Yes," she said.

"Then maybe it really was an attack," said Molly. "Maybe they were trying to scare you, hoping to influence your vote."

"Perhaps," said Helen. "Though anyone who knows me has to know I would never give in to such pressure."

"How much of the Shamrock stock does Dewey own?" I asked.

"Forty percent," she said, "and the other three have twenty percent each."

"So he only needs the support of one of the three to reject the buyout, and it would take all three of the others to sell it?"

"That's right."

"But Darrell and Duncan only have to talk Donald into voting their way?"

"Yes," she agreed. "And Donald is already leaning in that direction."

"The twenty-three and a half million would be divided between the four brothers?" I asked.

"Excluding lawyer's fees and guaranteed contributions to the company pension fund, but that still leaves nearly twenty-two million dollars."

"Divided according to their percentage of holdings?" I asked.

"That's right," Helen agreed. "Dewey would get forty percent, or just under nine million, and each of the others would get better than four."

Molly shook her head. "Motives galore."

5

I da Wesner stood half a head taller than Cyrus and was so thin that she looked even taller. I figured her for her early sixties, but the dowdy clothes, the spinster's bun, and the rigid bearing couldn't hide the fact that she was still easy to look at. Not a classic beauty, by any means—her face was too long, her nose too prominent, and her mouth too generous for that—but the sum was nonetheless pleasing. It was her manner that put people off.

"I don't want Helen going back up the hill," she said flatly, as Molly eased the car to a halt in front of the big-house. "Keepin' this barn open all year round makes twice as much work for me and Cyrus during the summer months. And 'cept for what happened to Dewey, we'd've closed the summerhouse up by now. I just cain't take good care of her with two houses to look after, and this whole mess might not a happened if I'd been there to see to things." Nobody argued the point. "So you'd be doin' ever'body a favor by stayin' here tonight. Once you move in, Helen cain't rightly head back up the hill when she gets home."

We agreed, and I finally got to see the inside of the big-house. Some shack. A more tasteful Tara; no gilt or red velvet in sight. The entry hall was a little cozier than the Cis-tine Chapel and a whole lot cleaner. Ida obviously had to have some help with this, but she clearly earned her keep. The white marble floor glistened like a sheet of ice, and the dark wood stair railings glowed like banked fires. As with the Cistine Chapel, the entry hall had a painted ceiling, this one featuring a pastoral scene of green fields, forested hills, and misty mountains. The staircase split in two at a landing halfway up and climbed right and left to the east and west sections of the main house.

Sean Michael Flanagan had wanted to keep all three of his grown sons in the house, where he could watch them. So he'd moved into the east section of the main house and had handed over the western half to his eldest, Francis Eugene Flanagan, Molly's grandfather. He had intended that his other two sons would raise their future families in the two new backward-jutting wings that flanked the garden at the back, but tragically, neither of them lived to have families of their own. One was thrown from a horse on his wedding day, and the other was killed in a boating accident on his honeymoon.

Francis Eugene's sons—the four Ds—had made their homes in the bighouse for a period after their father's death, but they had started moving out in the late fifties. Darrell had gone first, then Duncan, and finally, when Molly was twelve, a year after her mother died, she and her father, Donald, had moved to Houston.

Not only was the house big as a hotel, it was even set up like one—a luxury hideaway that catered to rich clientele and had only suites instead of rooms. Our suite was in the west section of the main house, where Molly had lived as a child. We had a bedroom, a sitting room, and a large bathroom with *two* toilet chambers. They sat on either side of a long vanity table, each containing a commode, a bidet, and wide range of reading matter. Now, *that* was luxury.

As we were unpacking, Molly said, "Tomorrow I have to talk to Dewey."

"If he's able."

She stopped to look at me. "You really believe he's crazy, don't you?"

"Disturbed, anyway," I said. "And with all the trouble at Shamrock, it's no wonder."

Still fighting it, she said, "You heard Helen. He was *angry*. And God knows he had reason."

"Reason to shoot his brother?"

"Of course not," she said. "But he didn't *shoot* Darrell, and I don't even believe he shot *at* him. I know he sounds out of control, but—"

"He sounds dangerous," I said.

"Dewey was always a wild man," she said, "especially when he was drinking. He'd have everybody laughing at his jokes one minute, and the next he'd have some drunk pinned against the wall, giving him a lecture on social etiquette. It's common to hear people threaten to throw somebody out of their home or place of business, but it wasn't just a figure of speech for Dewey. I actually saw him do it once. Saw him pick a man up and throw him out the front door." She shook her head. "One way or another, Dewey gets your attention."

"Sounds like he's getting more than he wants this time."

"True enough," she said. "And I'm not condoning what he did. I'm just saying it doesn't necessarily mean that he's crazy."

"Well, if he really believed shooting up the place was an appropriate response, then he might be in need of psychological counseling."

"He might," she conceded. "But we don't really know what prompted the shooting, do we? And you, of all people, should know that the truth isn't always obvious. When the Houston cops thought Joe Ahern had killed that woman, you *knew* Joe couldn't have done it. Well, *I* know Dewey, and I tell you he isn't just some wacko. I'll believe he's crazy when I see it for myself. But even if he *is* crazy, there has to be more going on here than we've been told."

"I'll go along with that," I said. "And you're right about Dewey: I don't know him, and I have no right to express an opinion about his sanity."

She nodded and said, "Good enough," then resumed her unpacking.

"Does that mean we're still friends?"

She went on emptying her bag, making me wait for it.

"Molly?"

Catching my eye in the dresser mirror, she allowed with a grin, "Guess I'll have to let you slide this time."

By the time we finished unpacking, it was twelve-thirty, and I'd been awake for almost forty hours. I was exhausted, but more hungry than sleepy. Fortunately, Ida had anticipated this.

French doors opened from the bedroom onto the veranda, where she set us a late supper of cold fried chicken and assorted trimmings. For nonsoutherners, "veranda" is another word for porch—this one on the second story of the bighouse overlooking the front lawn. Clouds had moved in, and there wasn't much to see, which was just as well, as the mosquitoes soon drove us inside anyway.

After supper, we made love in the king-size four-poster. Then I pulled the sheet over us and lay with Molly's head on my chest, letting the breeze cool us and listening to the faint tapping of mosquitoes hurling themselves against the screens.

"Go ahead and ask," she said.

"Ask what?"

"You know what." She propped her chin on my chest. "You've been wanting to ask about Tim ever since I gave him that hug."

"How do you *know* that?"

She tapped the side of her nose.

"What does that mean?" I asked. "That you can smell jealousy?"

"Women have a sixth sense about this stuff." Seeing my skeptical look, she asked, "Am I right?"

"Assuming you *are*. What about it?"

"What about what?"

"You and Kirk."

She laughed. "That *is* some dimple, isn't it?"

"You won't tell?"

"Sure," she said. "All you have to do is ask the question."

"*The* question?"

"That's right," she said, enjoying herself a little too much, I thought.

"Okay," I said. "Did Tim own a 'sixty-two Chevy?"

"I—well . . . no." She looked perplexed. "I think he was always a Ford man, but—"

"Good," I said, "that's all I wanted to know." With that, I nuzzled up close, gave her a buzz on the ear, then turned over and switched off the light.

I felt her looking at me, but I didn't budge. You don't catch Molly off guard very often, and when you do, you have to savor it.

We were back on the veranda for a late breakfast on Sunday morning. The sky was clearing after a night and morning of rain, and the grass glittered like emeralds. The eye swept easily over the lawn and fields and woods, through a gap in the ridge, to the hazy blue mountains beyond. The sunlight had chased off the mosquitoes, so we only had to worry about flies and gnats and midges and one or two adventurous wasps that settled briefly on my slice of watermelon for a drink. Like Southeast Texas, East Tennessee was heaven for bugs.

Tim Deets arrived while we were eating, and Ida showed him up. He was accompanied by an older, balding, sad-eyed man. Both were in suits and ties, but Ida didn't seem impressed. She delivered them to us without a word and tossed Tim a withering glance as she turned to go.

Molly gave me a surreptitious wink and said, "Morning, Tim."

He said, "Mornin', Molly," then tore his eyes away from her long enough to add, "Mornin', Mister Cochran." Jutting his dimpled chin at the older man, he said, "This is my partner, Detective Rooker."

We shook hands. "Detective."

"Mister Cochran." Very low key.

Tim added to his partner, "And this is my friend, Molly Flanagan."

Rooker shook her hand, too. "Tim tells me you're a detective down in Galveston."

"That's right."

At that point, a beeper went off, and all three cops reached for their hips.

Tim shook his head. Molly laughed, and Rooker said, "It's me." He asked Molly, "You got a phone up here?"

"Sure," she said, and pointed. "Through that door, in the sitting room, on the table to the right."

"Thanks."

As the screen door closed behind him, Molly asked Tim, "How long have you been partners?"

"Little over a year now."

"Looks like a pro."

"The best," he said.

Deciding to be adult about this, I said, "Have a seat, Tim. Want some coffee?"

He took the seat, but said, "No coffee, thanks." To Molly he added, "I wanted to tell you that we followed your man's trail as far as we could last night. His boots had a distinctive sole pattern, and we should be able to identify the maker." He added with a grin, "For what little good that'll do." Molly nodded, and they shared the grin—fellow officers who knew how rare it was that such evidence proved useful. "We followed his trail back to Pond Gap Road and the dirt pull-off where he probably left his car. There were lots of tire tracks, but we couldn't say which were his. We had somebody on that road a few minutes after you called us, but it wasn't soon enough."

"Did you print the shotgun?" she asked.

"Yeah, but you know how that goes. They'll all probably turn out to be Cyrus', or . . ." He looked from her to me.

39

"We didn't touch it," she assured him. "Cyrus brought the shotgun back up to the porch."

He nodded. "Like you said, the guy was probably wearing gloves anyway. If you can get Helen's permission, we'll put somebody up at the summerhouse to watch the place for a few nights."

"I'll talk to her," she said.

"Good," he said. "We're gonna drive up there now and see if there's any sign that he came back last night. I doubt it, but we should check it out."

"Good idea," she said.

"Call you later," he promised, letting his eyes linger on hers for a moment. Then he got to his feet, said, "Mister Cochran," and left, picking up his partner on the way out.

The hell with being adult, I thought. If he made eyes at Molly again, we'd have to tangle.

6

Riverside Psychiatric Center was just inside the Knoxville city limits, on the edge of an older, upper-crust development called Holston Hills. There was nothing particularly fussy about the structure—two three-story boxes of green-glazed brick connected by a glass atrium—but the setting was handsome. The lawn sloped gently down through a glade of oak, maple, redbud, and dogwood to the front of the building, then continued down the hill to the sluggish green water of the Holston River.

We parked in a visitor's space and went inside. Mid-morning sunlight poured into the atrium from the direction of the river. Brick walkways wound through stands of newly transplanted birch saplings and circled the mature redbud, maple, and two dogwoods around which the atrium had been built. Shiny metal stairs crisscrossed straight ahead, leading to upper stories in opposite wings.

We spoke to a studious-looking young woman behind the reception desk, who took our names, then made a call and told us that the Director would be out in a moment.

I waved at the trees. "Mind if we walk around?"

"Please," she said with a smile. "That's why they're there."

As we strolled along a brick path, we saw patients enjoying the dappled sunlight. An elderly man in a wheelchair sat under a maple tree in an embroidered robe and pajamas reading his Bible. A skinny teenage girl in a Grateful Dead tee shirt and faded jeans was huddled on a bench, staring at

41

nothing and talking to herself. Other patients wandered, or stood, or sat among the trees in their street clothes, all watched over by two young male attendants, also in street clothes, but wearing green name tags.

After a moment, a chubby, pink cherub in a doctor's smock emerged from an office on the left and jogged up to us on tiptoes.

"You must be Miz Flanagan," he said breathlessly to Molly.

"Yes," she agreed, "and you're"—she consulted his green name tag—"Doctor Fredericks."

"Indeed," he confirmed with a puckish grin. "I have the honor of being both the administrator and chief resident psychiatrist of this facility."

"This is Mister Cochran," Molly told him, and the doctor took my hand. His grip was stronger than expected, his palm dry as dust.

"Mister Cochran," he said.

"Doctor," I replied.

"Welcome to Riverside Center," he told us, making a sweeping gesture at the atrium and catching a birch sapling on the backswing. He snatched his hand back, grimacing in pain, then clasped it behind him and gave Molly a strained smile.

I bit off a laugh, as she patiently began, "My uncle—"

"Yes, your uncle," the doctor agreed. His face shifted from glee to a mask of seriousness, as he added in a conspiratorial whisper, "I'm afraid he's had something of a difficult morning."

"Difficult, how?" she asked.

Looking around to see that no one was listening, the doctor continued in a whisper, "He attacked one of our maintenance men and had to be restrained."

"Attacked?"

Another glance to right and left. "Your uncle was waiting behind the door when the man entered his room. He hit him with his breakfast tray several times, then ran out of the room and down the hall before he could be restrained."

"I don't understand," Molly said. "Sounds like Dewey was trying to escape, but why would he do that when he'll be going home tomorrow?"

"Perhaps he realized that his stay might be extended," the doctor suggested.

"Why?"

"I'm afraid we're having trouble balancing his medications."

"What medications?" she asked. "I thought he was only here for observation and evaluation."

"Your uncle," he patiently explained, "was admitted in a highly agitated state, a possible danger to himself and others. So we were compelled to sedate him, and further observation persuaded me that he would benefit from a course of psychotropic drugs. But psychopharmacology is still as much an art as a science, and it's often difficult to discover the correct medications and dosages. In your uncle's case, the matter is complicated by his age and by the variety of medications he's already taking for ailments ranging from high blood pressure to inner ear trouble." He concluded with a grin, "I concede that our efforts suffered a setback this morning, but I assure you it's merely temporary."

"What are you giving him?" she asked.

"On his arrival, we administered a ten-milligram injection of Fluphenizine, the generic form of Prolixin, as a sedative. Saturday morning, we started a regimen of twenty milligrams of Prozac, an antidepressant, each morning and one milligram of Xanax, a tranquilizer, every four hours, as needed. But this morning, after his attack on the maintenance worker, he was given a five-milligram injection of Haldol and put into a restraint bed, where he's currently under observation."

"Can we see him?" she asked.

He rubbed his hands together, making a faint rasping sound. "Ah, well, yes, you can *see* him, but I'm afraid you won't be able to speak to him, as he's still sleeping off the effects of the sedative."

Molly clenched her jaw. "Can he be awakened?"

He shook his head. "I would advise against it at present."

"You knew I wanted to speak to him today," she said coldly.

"Yes, I did," he agreed calmly, "and I can only offer my apology for this delay. However"—he shrugged in helplessness—"such acute episodes are highly unpredictable, and until he's properly medicated, there's little that we can do to prevent them."

I asked, "What's your diagnosis?"

He gave me the condescending smile physicians reserve for overly inquisitive laymen. "I fear it's too soon for anything but the most preliminary diagnosis, Mister Cochran."

"Is he psychotic?" I asked, earning a sharp glance from Molly.

"For that as well," the doctor said, "I fear it's simply too soon to tell. However, although the term 'psychotic' is currently out of favor in more progressive circles, there's little doubt that Mister Flanagan has recently experienced one or more of what might be described as psychotic episodes, including the one this morning. He appears to be manic-depressive, and he exhibits the classic symptoms of paranoia, specifically the fear that others are trying to rob him, or wreck his life, or steal his business."

"In his case," said Molly, "somebody really *is* trying to take away his business."

The doctor nodded. "Yes, I realize that your uncle is facing some very real business pressures at this time. As Freud said, 'Even paranoics have enemies.'" He smiled. "But Mister Flanagan's responses have been out of all bounds. He has quite simply lost control of his behavior. I could attach a label to his present state, such as paranoid schizophrenic, but labels are merely conveniences. The important thing to remember is that his condition is probably treatable. With therapy and proper medication, he should soon be back with his family."

Molly still didn't like it, especially the part about medications, but all she said was, "I'd like to see him."

"Yes, of course," he unctuously agreed. "I'll take you myself." On the way up the stairs, he said, "I should add that I have not yet ruled out the possibility of a physiological basis for your uncle's erratic behavior. His skull X rays were inconclusive, but in one exposure, I saw what I thought might—and I emphasize *might*—be a growth."

"A tumor, you mean?" asked Molly.

"Possibly," he said carefully, "though the two specialists I consulted were unconvinced. One thought it might be a flaw in the X ray, and the other suggested it could be a minor cerebral hemorrhage. However, both agreed that he should have an MRI exam as soon as possible, and I heartily concur with that recommendation. It's the only way to be sure."

On the second floor, we stopped at locked double doors, and the doctor swiped a plastic ID card through a scanner. Then he tapped a code into a keypad and pulled the door open when it buzzed.

The corridor beyond gave an impression of restful calm. Low, indirect lighting, pale green walls, dark green carpeting, and some tastefully subdued paintings on the walls. It could have passed for a corridor in a good hotel, except for two features. There were too many doors, and there were no locks on them.

Doctor Fredericks nodded at the woman behind the counter at the nurses' station. She wore street clothes, and I realized that the doctor's lab coat was the only hospital-white I'd seen so far.

"We're going in to take a look at Mister Flanagan," said the doctor.

The woman said, "Yes, Doctor," then pushed a concealed button, and the door we were approaching buzzed faintly.

Doctor Fredericks pushed through, into a small, semi-darkened room like a walk-in closet. The light came from a slightly tinted window to the right.

"A one-way mirror," said the doctor.

The room beyond was larger, maybe twelve feet by fifteen. The walls were covered with glossy, cream-colored tiles, and the light level was just bright enough for us to see the two occupants clearly.

A young man held a penlight in one hand as he made notes on a clipboard with the other. An older man in dark blue pajamas lay under a sheet on a bed with a heavy metal framework, bound to it by padded restraints at the chest, waist, wrists, and ankles.

The patient was a tall, raw-boned man with a striking profile and thinning, sandy gray hair. He had freckles, like Molly, and the good Flanagan bones, but age spots mixed with the freckles, and the flesh was sagging a bit, especially under the eyes and along the jawlines. He appeared to be sleeping and seemed physically well cared for. His hair was combed, his face shaved.

"How long will you keep him here?" asked Molly.

"If he's reasonably calm when he awakens," he said, "he may be allowed to return to his room, but he'll be kept under observation for another twelve hours."

From there, we went to see Dewey's room. Grass-green walls, forest-green drapes, and more low-level indirect lighting. In addition to a regular hospital bed, there was a couch, an armchair, and a rocking chair near the windows.

On our way out of the room, I said, "I never saw a rocking chair in a hospital room before."

"I suppose not," he agreed with a pleased smile, "but we've found that rocking often has a soothing effect on the disturbed patient."

Molly said, "I saw that you had surveillance cameras as well." I hadn't noticed. "One aimed at the bed," she said, "one at the door."

"That's right," he agreed.

"One in the bathroom, too?"

"Yes."

"How did Dewey catch the maintenance man off guard with cameras watching him?"

The doctor shook his head. "Sadly, it's not economically feasible to hire people to do nothing but watch the monitors, and it seems that your uncle made every attempt to fool the casual observer. He stuffed pillows and blankets under the sheets to make it appear that he was still in bed, then stood in a poorly lit corner of the room at the edge of the camera's field of view. So, unless someone was watching him the whole time, they would have assumed that he was in bed and might well have missed the shadowy figure in the corner."

Molly had nothing to say to that. She was quiet on our way downstairs, and the doctor respected her silence. When we reached the floor of the atrium, she told him, "I'll be back tomorrow, at the same time."

"By all means," he said graciously. "With luck, your uncle will be awake and lucid." Molly's glance set him back a step. "And I assure you," he quickly added, "that we'll do all we can to see that he is."

"Thank you," she said.

She was silent again on our way from the building to the car, and I left her to her thoughts. She drove us away from Riverside Center and got back on the 640 bypass, again arcing around to the north, this time from the eastern end of town. The highway ran through green hills, grassy fields, and stretches of woods, with the occasional gas station, subdivision, or shopping mall only seeming to accent the natural beauty.

After taking in the scenery for an appropriate length of time, I asked, "Where're we headed?"

Keeping her eyes on the road, she said, "I'd *like* to ask Darrell why he was so anxious to see Dewey locked up."

"I thought it was to keep him away from the board meeting."

47

"But why *now?*" she asked. "The board doesn't meet for a month, and Dewey will be out of the hospital long before then."

"I don't imagine they picked the time," I said, "and I doubt they planned on Dewey shooting at Darrell, but they couldn't have asked for a better setup for putting his sanity into question."

She nodded, still looking ahead. "I'm not ready for Darrell yet, anyway. I'd like to look around the plant, but there won't be anybody there on a Sunday, so we'll have to wait till tomorrow for that."

"So where to now?"

"Time for another talk with Helen."

That sounded like a good idea, but we arrived as she was being loaded onto a stretcher. A young man in green surgical scrubs explained that she was being taken down for a new series of CT scans. The doctor, it seemed, wasn't satisfied with the first set. We accompanied her downstairs and watched her disappear through a door with a bronze plaque that said SISTER MARIA MOORE, RSM, and below that, CT SUITE.

The whole procedure took only about forty-five minutes, but afterward, she seemed too tired to answer questions. Molly asked for her permission to let the Sheriff's Department keep an eye on the summerhouse for the next few nights, and perhaps because no mention was made of Tim, Helen went along. Molly also suggested that she hire some private security for the gate and the bighouse, but Helen said she didn't like the idea of strangers prowling around her property.

On our way out of the hospital, I said, "She has a real thing about privacy, doesn't she?"

"Yes," said Molly, "but she would have put on the added security if it'd been free."

"Is that why she agreed to have the Sheriff's Department watch the summerhouse, in spite of her feelings about Tim?"

Molly nodded. "As long as it doesn't cost her anything, Helen can put up with a lot. Dewey wasn't the only thrifty one in the family."

We headed down the hill from St. Mary's and took Broadway north into a section of Knoxville called Fountain City. After stopping to pick up sandwiches and drinks at a deli, we drove a few blocks to a duck pond with a fountain in the middle and ate our lunch at one of several covered wooden picnic tables, watching ducks swim in lazy patterns about the pond. Then we went back to the bighouse.

7

W e took a swim, then headed for the barn to saddle
up. I was still new to horses, so Molly checked the
cinches on my saddle before letting me mount. My ride
was an aging mud-brown mare inappropriately named
Frisky—a sad-looking animal that seemed ready to drop at
any moment.

"Think she'll make it?" I asked.

Molly chuckled. "I'd say she's good for another trip or
two. Actually, she's always looked like that, even when she
was a filly. She has only one gait, a slow walk, but she'll go
where you aim her, and she'll keep going till you say,
'whoa.' "

Frisky stood with her head down, looking half-asleep,
and didn't so much as twitch when I climbed into the saddle. She could have been a wooden horse for all the impression I made.

By contrast, Molly's mount, a speckled gray filly named
Stormcloud, had energy to spare, and she was allowed to
run some of it off while Frisky and I watched. After Stormcloud sprinted back and forth a few times, tearing up the
turf with her flashing hooves, Frisky sighed and looked
away, exhausted from the sight.

We took the winding gravel road up the hill, past the
brick steps that led to the summerhouse, then got onto a
narrow trail that continued at a shallow angle up the slope.
Frisky plodded along, and Stormcloud danced ahead, peri-
odically forcing Molly to pull up and wait for us.

At Pond Gap Road, we turned right and rode along the gravel verge until we came to a muddy pull-off area, big enough for maybe four full-size cars to parallel-park.

"This is where the shooter left his car?" I asked.

"Apparently," she said.

I looked on down the road. "This goes through the gap?"

"That's right," she said. "And the other way, it goes back to Tazewell Pike."

"Then the shooter could have gone almost anywhere from here?"

"Almost."

"How much of this belongs to your family?" I asked.

"Everything on this side of the road, from the other side of the ridge back to the pike. About four hundred and fifty acres."

"Nice spread."

"Yeah," she agreed. "We've been buying up land around here for a hundred years. Whenever a neighboring farm goes broke, the family snaps it up."

The pull-off was backed with a wall of trees, but there was an opening to a half-overgrown trail on the left.

"That leads back to the summerhouse?" I asked.

"Uh huh," she said. "Want to take a look?"

"Why not?"

Frisky and I followed Molly and Stormcloud onto a stretch of trampled grass, littered with beer cans. After the first thirty feet, the grass grew higher, and a wooded slope rose to the left, broken by an occasional gray outcropping of granite. Then trees crowded in to steal the light, and the grass gave way to a layer of leaves and pine needles. The going was easy and quiet under the trees, but intruding limbs finally forced us to climb down and lead the horses.

Frisky scarcely seemed aware of the change, though I imagined she must prefer having less to carry. She plodded along behind me, showing little enthusiasm—*none*, actually—but she would go wherever I wanted, as long as I wasn't in a hurry to get there. But Frisky's pace was too

51

slow for Stormcloud, who also didn't like being pulled. She fought the reins until Molly jerked her close, held her head still, and whispered in her ear. The filly seemed to listen and nodded, as though she understood, then blew through her nostrils and allowed herself to be led onward.

Around the next bend in the trail, Molly stopped and knelt beside a patch of mud. As I stopped beside her, I saw the tracks.

"They look like hiking boots," she said.

"Yeah," I agreed, staring at the deep tread marks. "You can almost read the maker's name."

She indicated two separate sets of tracks. "They run in both directions, so he came and went this way."

"Then it's a given that he parked at the pull-off."

"If he had a car," she said, "that's where he left it."

It was a minor detail, and Detective Tim had already told as much, but we both liked to see these things for ourselves.

I followed Molly through the rich, dark odor of damp earth and sweet pine resin, the sharp tang of cedar and a faint whiff of horse sweat, feeling contented with the company, pleased by the day, and unreasonably excited by the faint hint of trouble in the wind. And I wasn't even stoned.

When we reached the summerhouse, we dropped the reins and sat in the grass by the stream under a maple tree, letting the horses drink and graze. Molly stretched out and put her head in my lap, and I ran my fingers through her hair.

"That feels good," she said, and closed her eyes.

I went on combing her hair, relieved to see her relaxing for the first time since we'd arrived. I knew she hadn't forgotten about Dewey and Helen, but she'd tabled their troubles for now. I'd seen her do this before, and I admired the ability. Twenty years of being a cop had taught her that there were times when you just had to save your strength.

The day was warm, but the humidity was low, and a

cooling breeze stirred the grass and rustled the leaves. As the pale blue sky gradually darkened, Molly curled up on her side and dozed off. She slept half an hour, then sat up and rubbed her eyes. She smiled at me and gave me a kiss, then crawled to the stream and washed her face. Blotting the water on her shirtsleeve, she looked at the sky and said, "We should get back."

We retraced our steps to Pond Gap Road, then turned back toward the pike along the verge. The road ran flat and straight for about a hundred yards, then curved down and away to the right. We cut left and picked our way down through a pine stand, coming out at the edge of a sloping green meadow. We rode along the tree line until the big-house came into sight, then veered between the rows of a pear orchard, pulling off ripe pears and munching on our way to the barn.

What a way to live. I'd dreamed of having a place like this when I was a ballplayer, and I'd planned to spend some of my big bucks building such a home for myself and my family. Except it never happened. I was in the majors barely long enough to qualify for a pension, and if I hadn't killed Juan Domingo Sanchez, nobody would have remembered I was there.

How depressing! It was being exposed to such conspicu-ous evidence of her family's accomplishments that did it, and I couldn't help but wonder what the hell Molly was doing with a notorious screwup like *me.*

"What's the matter?" she asked, as we pulled up at the barn.

"Nothing," I said with a grin. "This is great."

I unsaddled Frisky and brushed her down, then parked her in her stall and gave her some feed. She yawned to show her appreciation, and I bid her, "Night-night."

We went back to the house for a shower and dressed. Then, with a sighing breeze keeping the mosquitoes away, we had dinner in the garden.

It was full dark by the time Molly decided to show me the tree house, and I said, "Maybe we should wait till daylight?"

But she assured me, "We don't have to. Come on, I'll show you."

She led me to the tree and around the thick trunk until she found a fold of twisted bark and reached inside. I heard metal scrape on metal, then a click, and lights sprang on over our heads. I stepped back and saw that the whole tree was lit up: spotlights on ladders and stairways, strings of Christmas lights outlining platforms and tree limbs.

"Wow," I said.

"Pretty, isn't it?" she agreed. "We were always playing in it after dark, and Dewey put up the lights after Darrell's daughter, Sarah, fell out and broke her arm."

Molly led me to the other side of the trunk and up a ladder to the first platform. From there, more ladders and steps spiraled around the trunk toward the top of the tree, sixty feet above. Halfway up, we stopped at a square platform about eight feet on a side. Molly pulled some blankets out of an old cedar chest and made a pallet on the wooden deck. Then she turned off the lights, and for the first time in my life, I made love in a tree.

Monday morning, on our second visit to Riverside Center, we found Dewey in his room. He was awake this time— barely—sitting in the rocking chair by the window, staring at his lap and slowly rocking.

Molly stopped in front of him. "Dewey?"

The sound of her voice took a moment to sink in, and it took another for him to recognize his name. Then his head came up, eyes trailing behind. When they settled on Molly, it took a beat or two for him to place her. Then the lower lip trembled, and the eyes began to water.

"Do you know me?" she asked him.

He nodded carefully, as though his head was too heavy for sudden movement.

"What're they doing to you, Dewey?"

"Molly," he said.

"Yes, Dewey, it's me. Tell me what's happening to you."

"Oh, Molly," he said, tears brimming.

"What's the matter?" she asked.

"He . . ." He faded out, licking his lips.

"Who?"

"Molly?"

"Yes, it's Molly, Dewey. Talk to me."

"He's making me crazy," he said blurrily.

"*Who* is?"

"You're *here*," he seemed to realize for the first time, weakly reaching out a hand.

She took it in both of hers. "You have to talk to me, Dewey."

Tears oozed over his eyelids and ran in rivulets down his face. "You're really *here*."

"Yes, I'm here," she said, "and you have to tell me what's going on."

"I want to go home," he said.

"I know you do," she said, "and I'll do all I can to help you. But you have to help me, too." But he'd already faded out on her, chin dropping toward his chest. "Dewey?" she said, and reached out to shake him. "Dewey?"

"I think that's all you're going to get," I said.

Doctor Fredericks spoke from the doorway. "I'm afraid Mister Cochran's right, Ms. Flanagan. You can see that we're still having problems with his medication."

"You're turning him into a vegetable," she said angrily.

"That's not our intent, I assure you," he said.

"You're overmedicating him," she declared. "Anyone can see that."

"As you say," he replied with a cherubic smile, "*anyone* can see it. This sort of reaction sometimes occurs with Haldol, and we've already discontinued its use."

"Is that it?" she asked in disbelief. "You work by trial and error?"

"It's the only method known to us, I'm afraid, as no two individuals have identical responses or tolerances."

"What if you accidentally kill your patient along the way?"

"Safe levels have been established," he said, "and dosages are altered in careful increments." He added with a kindly expression, "I assure you we know our business, Ms. Flanagan, and it's only a matter of time before we solve this problem."

"He said somebody was making him crazy."

The doctor smiled politely. "Did he say who?" No urgency, just curiosity.

"No," she said, "he could hardly finish a sentence. But why would he say that?"

"Disturbed patients often express such beliefs," he said. "In your uncle's case, it would appear to be an obvious, even textbook, symptom of his paranoia."

Doctor Fredericks seemed more sure of himself today, and Molly allowed herself to be persuaded that he was doing all he could.

We weren't due at Shamrock until sometime after eleven, so we stopped by to see Helen on our way. She seemed better. Like Dewey, she was out of bed when we arrived, sitting in a chair by the window.

She took both our hands and greeted us happily, "I'm so glad to see you two!" She asked Molly, "How's Cyrus?"

"He's fine," said Molly. "Says the headaches are gone."

"I just hope he's telling the truth," Helen said. "He always was a stoic."

"What about you?" asked Molly. "What do the doctors say?"

"That I can probably go home tomorrow."

"Probably?"

"If I'm strong enough."

"They don't like to commit themselves, do they?"

"Of course not. It's too likely to reveal their fallibility."

56

We laughed, and she asked, "Did you see Dewey today?"

"Just came from there," Molly said, looking away.

"What is it?" Helen asked her.

"He's not well, Helen."

"What do you mean?" she asked stiffly.

"I mean he may be sicker than we thought."

"If you mean *mentally* sick, I don't believe it. I know Dewey's been under a lot of pressure lately, but he's always thrived on it."

"Maybe it finally added up to more than he could take."

"I still don't believe it," Helen insisted.

"I'm not sure I do, either," Molly agreed, "and it's possible that what we saw was merely an effect of the drugs, but—"

"What drugs?" asked Helen.

"He had a bad reaction to something called Haldol."

"Who's treating him?"

"A Doctor Fredericks is in charge."

"Call Doctor Matthews, and ask him what he knows about this Doctor Fredericks."

"I will," Molly promised.

"Do it now," Helen said, and started to push herself out of the chair.

But Molly held her in place. "I'll call him," she promised quietly, "but first I have a question."

Helen sat back. "Of course, darling. What is it?"

"You said Darrell was looking for something in Dewey's desk. Do you know what it was?"

Helen shook her head. "No, I'm afraid not."

"Could it have been his plans for rebuilding Shamrock?"

She thought about it. "I suppose that's possible."

"Is there a safe at the summerhouse, or any other hiding place you can think of?"

"No," she said. "Except the caves, of course."

Molly nodded and glanced at me.

Caves? The notion of searching through caves didn't appeal to me.

Molly walked to the phone. "What's Doctor Matthews number?" Helen told her, and she placed the call. She gave her name and asked for the doctor. "Yes, thank you, I'll hold." She waited a moment, then said, "Yes, Doctor . . . Yes, it has been a while. I—no, just for a visit. I . . . Oh, I love Galveston. You should come down sometime, maybe in the spring, before it gets too hot. Yes, I—I certainly will if I can, I promise. The reason I called: Helen wanted me to ask your opinion of another physician." She laughed. "I won't tell anyone, honest. It's Doctor Fredericks, the chief psychiatrist and administrator at Riverside Center. I—" She listened. "I see. Uh huh. Yes." She laughed again. "Well, I don't think they'll kick you out of the AMA for that recommendation. I will, and thanks again. Goodbye."

She hung up and reported with some regret, "Doctor Matthews has nothing but good to say about Doctor Fredericks. Said he sent Dewey to Riverside Center entirely because of the doctor's reputation."

"Well, he must be all right," Helen said with relief.

"I hope so," said Molly, still not completely convinced.

She kissed her aunt on the cheek, then I gave Helen's hand a squeeze, and we left.

8

"Caves?" I asked Molly, on our way downtown.
She laughed. "I could tell you didn't like the sound
of that."

"I've never gotten into caves," I admitted.

"But you've been into some, haven't you?"

"Not unless you count a New York subway tunnel. All I
know about caves is that they're dark, and bats live in
them."

"What've you got against bats?"

"Well, for one thing, they carry rabies."

"So can any other mammal," she pointed out, "and I've
never heard of anyone contracting rabies from a bat in
these parts. What we have around here are mostly fruit
bats, and they'd only bite if you covered yourself in apple-
sauce."

"I'll try to avoid that," I promised.

Approaching downtown from the northwest on I-275, I
could see the copper globe of the Sunsphere straight ahead,
sitting atop its blue elevator tower. The Sunsphere had
been the symbol and centerpiece of the '82 Knoxville
World's Fair, but oddly enough, it had been built in a low-
land area, considerably reducing its visibility. The downtown hills rose to the left, covered with mostly four- and
five-story buildings, the skyline dominated by the city's
twin skyscrapers, the Plaza Tower and the Riverview
Tower, standing side by side atop high ground to the left.

59

The towers were built in their better days by the Butcher brothers, the older of whom, Jake, had served a term in prison. Both enterprises had gone belly-up after the World's Fair, then the buildings, the bank, and the S & L had all been taken over by the FDIC and sold to the highest bidder. I got all this from Molly, of course, who enjoyed filling me in on her hometown lore.

We had to cut back to the northeast on I-40 to reach the Shamrock plant, and I smelled roasting coffee beans while we were still on the highway, long before I could see the plant. It was out of sight, somewhere below us, shaded by the snarl of interstates and exit ramps.

The plant was in a low-lying area at the base of the downtown hills near the old Southern Railway depot and freight yards. It was located in Knoxville's "historic warehouse district," on the edge of an area called Old City, where decaying nineteenth-century buildings, including several former warehouses owned by the Flanagans, had been renovated to create a trendy shopping and entertainment district. There were bars and clubs, restaurants and coffeehouses, clothing boutiques and antiques stores, a hair salon and a barbershop, all with easy access to parking.

The Shamrock plant looked slightly disreputable by comparison—a lopsided structure of interconnected, soot-darkened brick buildings with incongruously bright lime-green trim and a huge, lime-green shamrock sprouting from the roof.

As we climbed out of the car, a stocky middle-aged man in a lime-green baseball cap came out to greet us. He shook our hands and said, "I'm John Borland, the foreman."

"Oh, I know you, Mister Borland," Molly said with a smile. "You used to let me work the line with you when I was a girl."

He blushed and looked down at his feet. "I didn't think you'd remember," he said quietly.

"I'll never forget it," she assured him.

The blush darkened, but he got very serious and formal

as he said, "I jus' wanted to tell you they ain't a one of us here don't know that, if it wudn't for Dewey, we'd been out of a job a long time ago. So you tell him we're all pullin' for him."

"I'll tell him," she promised.

Mister Borland led us into the main building, where coffee was being roasted, ground, blended, and packaged. The smell had been strong in the parking lot, but inside it was so thick, you could almost see the caffeine hanging in the air.

The main building was a cavernous space full of gleaming machinery, conveyor belts, catwalks, and overhead tracks. The building hissed and hummed, screeched and whined, whirred and clattered. Hoppers rattled along overhead tracks and clanged into huge stainless steel roasting vats. Belts moved product through its paces, and people stalked purposely here and there, or worked with practiced movements where they stood.

"Decaf over there." Mister Borland gestured to the right. "Original blend over here."

"Were you here the day of the shooting?" Molly asked him.

"Sure was," he said. "Matter of fact, it was me tole the police that Dewey had left the plant."

"Did Dewey get any sort of delivery that morning?" she asked.

"No, I don't believe he did."

"Maybe a visitor?"

"Not that I recall," he said. "But he showed up late."

"He *did?*"

"Yeah, and you know how unusual that is. I cain't remember him ever bein' late before."

"How late?"

"Well, he's usually here by seven-thirty at the latest, half an hour before work begins. But on Friday, he didn't drag in till I was ready to start the line."

"What time was that?" she asked.

"Right at eight o'clock."

"Half an hour late," she said thoughtfully.

"Yeah," he said, "but for Dewey, that's somethin'."

She nodded. "When did he leave for lunch?"

" 'Fore twelve."

"How long before?"

"I guess maybe ten minutes."

"Then he wasn't going far, was he?" she said. "Not if he had an appointment for twelve o'clock."

"Don't guess so," he agreed uncertainly.

"When did Darrell show up?"

" 'Bout half an hour later."

"And how long after that did Dewey come back?"

"Wudn't long," he said. "No more'n five minutes."

"Five minutes," she repeated. "How long after Dewey went up the stairs did the shooting start?"

"Not a minute, I bet."

"Did you see any of it?"

"Well, no, ma'am," he admitted. "I was tryin' to reseat the drive chain on the decaf line when I heard the shots. And you don't run *toward* a shootin', if you're smart."

"No," she had to agree.

"So me and the others just sorta squatted down behind anything solid we could find. With all this metal in here, you gotta be careful 'bout ricochets."

"Who saw it?"

"Bert and Bart was the only ones who saw anything, and they wudn't much help."

"Why not?"

" 'Cause they saw it different," he said. "Sorta canceled each other out, if you see what I mean."

Bert and Bart were identical twins, Bertrum and Bartholomew Coonts. Stocky, balding, round-faced, and slightly cross-eyed, both wearing the same bib overalls, sweat-stained tee shirts, and black clodhopper work boots. I was never clear about which was Bart and which was Bert, but I figured they wanted it that way, or they wouldn't still be dressing alike in their forties. They maintained identical grins throughout, while politely begging to differ about everything.

"Dewey was aimin' to kill him," said one.

"Jus' puttin' a scare in him," said the other.

"Had murder on his mind," said one.

"On'y wanted Darrell outta his office," said the other.

"Wanted him dead, you mean," said one.

"Nah, jus' a prank," said the other.

Both of them grinning all the while.

We left them to discuss the matter and looked over the scene of the crime. Dewey's office stood in the middle of the room, elevated atop a thirty-foot framework of girders. A steep flight of metal stairs climbed to a small landing halfway up, then did an abrupt one-eighty for the final ascent. It was easy to see that anyone on those stairs would have been exposed to a shooter on the upper landing the whole way down. Dewey would have needed to be very disturbed indeed to miss Darrell six times, if he'd really wanted to hit him. It might seem like a slim point to belabor, but it was the difference between reckless endangerment and attempted murder.

All the blinds were closed in Dewey's office, and it was dark in there until Molly turned on the lights. The office was roomy and cluttered: a table and four chairs to the left of the door, armchairs and couches to the right, the desk straight ahead. Behind the desk was a row of low filing cabinets under the windows, the tops crowded with trophies and books and knickknacks. Newspapers and magazines were scattered over every available surface, and a pillow and blanket had been left haphazardly on the sofa, as though Dewey had just finished his nap.

"Nobody's been in here to straighten up since Dewey left," I said. "Doesn't that seem strange to you?"

Molly shrugged. "Maybe he doesn't allow anybody in here when he's away. We'll have to ask Mister Borland about that. But we know the police came in."

"We do?" I asked.

She pointed out two bullet holes in the acoustical tile ceiling, circled in red Magic Marker.

"Then he wasn't shooting at Darrell," I said.

"Not on these two shots." She walked over for a closer look at the second bullet hole. "You notice this one blew out a larger chunk of the ceiling tile, and there're powder burns all around it, so I'd say he had the gun raised over his head when he fired."

"That still leaves four shots unaccounted for," I said.

She nodded as she stepped out onto the landing. "And finding the slugs in all this would be a challenge for the F.B.I., let alone the two of us."

We talked to the workers in the main building, where the shooting had occurred, ignoring for now the salesmen, drivers, and the people who loaded the trucks. The workers were mostly older men, many of them approaching retirement age. Only two were under thirty, and one looked like he was hardly out of high school. The business office, which we'd passed on our way in, was run by a woman named Mrs. Witherspoon with the help of three other women, the youngest of whom could have been the youngest male's date to the prom. All of them, male and female, genuinely seemed to like Dewey, and all repeated the sentiments that Mister Borland had expressed in the parking lot. They knew their jobs depended on Dewey's continued health and well-being, and nobody but Bert and Bart admitted to seeing anything during the shooting.

On our way out, Mister Borland confirmed that nobody was allowed inside Dewey's office when he was away.

"Then you weren't surprised when he chased Darrell out of there, were you?" asked Molly.

"Well, no, miss," he agreed. "Don't guess I was. Course, I never counted on gunfire, but I knew it was trouble when I saw Darrell climbin' those stairs."

"Was the door locked?" she asked.

"I doubt it. Never is. It's just understood that nobody goes in there unless Dewey invites you in."

"But it was locked when the police arrived," she said.

"Yeah," he agreed with a grin, "I figgered Dewey done it just to make it hard on 'em."

She nodded, then grinned at him. "Why did you take so long to tell the detectives that Dewey had left the plant?"

"Well, they didn't ask me," he said, "and Darrell wouldn't let nobody get a word in edgewise anyway. But when they started to talk about warrants and breakin' down the door and such, I figgered it was time to speak up."

She smiled. "With Dewey gone, who takes care of the business end of things?"

"That would be Missus Witherspoon," he said. "Dewey made her business manager when he was in the hospital some years back. He give her the power to write checks and all that, so she does most of it."

We thanked him and shook hands.

As he turned to go, Molly said, "One more thing, Mister Borland. You said you saw Dewey leave the plant on Friday afternoon."

"That's right, miss."

"Do you recall if he was carrying anything?"

He cocked his head. "Far as I can remember, he jus' had his briefcase, like always."

Molly nodded. "Well, thanks again for showing us around."

"Anytime, miss."

9

Having viewed the scene of the crime and established the facts, Molly decided it was time to see Darrell. His offices were about five miles west of downtown, occupying the top floor of a five-story building of dark glass off a busy four-lane commercial strip called Kingston Pike.

The tinted glass entryway to Darrell Flanagan & Associates was modern, but beyond that, the scene was strictly Victorian. The decor was a tad spare, with a notable shortage of bric-a-brac, but the furniture and layered Oriental rugs looked genuine. Tall, potted aspidistras stood in the corners, contributing a fresh green scent to the hushed air.

The receptionist had her hair piled up in something vaguely resembling a Victorian do, but the plunging neckline of her black silk blouse was decidedly inappropriate for the period, not to mention the office. Seeing a flashy number like her out front, I had to wonder about her relationship to the boss. Ms. Markham (according to her nameplate) ignored Molly and concentrated her attention on me, so she looked a bit confused when Molly spoke, as if she thought I might be throwing my voice.

"I'd like to see Darrell," said Molly.

Finally looking her way, Ms. Markham said in a breathy twang, "Yes, ma'am. Do you have an appointment?"

"No, but if you'll tell him his niece is here, I'm sure he'll be happy to see me."

"His niece," the woman repeated, mustering an uncertain smile. "I didn't know, I'm sorry. And you're—"

"Molly," she said.

"Thank you," the woman said. "Would you wait just a moment, please." She picked up the phone, pressed a button, then paused a beat and said, "Molly is here to see you, Mister Flanagan." She glanced at us. "Molly, sir, your niece?" She listened, nodded, and said, "Yes, sir." Then, with a bright smile, she waved at the double doors to the inner sanctum and told us, "Go right on in."

The doors were jerked open as we approached, and a man stood there smiling at us. A younger, shorter, pudgier version of Dewey—the same freckles, fewer age spots, a thicker plot of the same sandy gray hair, and the same good bones beneath a modest layer of fat.

"Molly, child!" he exclaimed, and rushed out. I expected him to hug her, but at the last moment, he settled for patting her hand. "Good to see you, so good, and how you've grown, into quite a beauty, I see, and this must be Mister Cochran." He shook my hand, *then* patted it. "Come in, come in, please," he said, tugging us into his office. "And here's Duncan. Duncan!" he proclaimed. "Here's our prodigal niece, home at last!"

Duncan, the youngest of the four brothers, walked over from the window smiling widely, looking fit and trim in his late fifties. I was ten years younger, but found myself envying his flat stomach and easy, athletic walk. And there was so little sag to his facial muscles that I had to assume he'd had a lift. He gave Molly a fond peck on the cheek and me a firm handshake.

Molly smiled at him with restraint, obviously wondering what he and Darrell were up to.

"Sit down, sit down, please," Darrell urged us. "Like old home week, isn't it, Duncan?"

Duncan nodded and told her warmly, "It's good to have you back, Molly."

The office was done up as a Victorian study, in green leather and dark mahogany, walls lined with book-filled shelves, volumes bound in dyed leather. Law books, mostly, though the classics were well represented as well. I wondered, unkindly, how many of them Darrell had actually read.

As Molly and I settled into comfortable leather armchairs, she got right to the point. "We've been to see Dewey."

Darrell shook his head as he lowered himself into his desk chair. "An unfortunate situation," he said.

"How is he?" asked Duncan, perching on the corner of the desk.

"Not well at all." She asked Darrell, "What do you know about this Doctor Fredericks?"

"A respected psychiatrist," he said, "or so I understand."

Duncan nodded. "Said to be very progressive."

"He may not be releasing Dewey on schedule, you know."

"I'm not surprised," said Darrell.

"No," Duncan agreed, "I'm afraid he's seriously ill, Molly."

"They're drugging him," she said.

"That's standard procedure in such cases, isn't it?" asked Duncan.

"In *what* cases?"

The brothers shared a look, and Duncan went on in a gentle tone, "You do understand what's happened here, don't you, Molly? I mean, you do realize that Dewey has had a nervous breakdown?"

"I'm not convinced of that," she said.

Darrell shook his head in disbelief, and Duncan assured her, "You will be."

She asked Darrell, "Do you honestly believe that Dewey belongs in a place like that?"

Darrell responded defensively, "If you think I enjoy seeing my brother thrown into a mental hospital—"

"Of course she doesn't think that, Darrell," said Duncan. "She's only concerned about Dewey. And so are we," he assured her.

Duncan had the gift of sincerity, but Molly persisted, asking Darrell, "Couldn't you have worked this out between you?"

"Not with him shooting at me, I couldn't!"

Duncan agreed, "You just can't talk to him anymore, Molly. Even your father called the other day to discuss Dewey's state of mind, and you know how close they've always been." He shook his head. "We all resisted the idea, but it finally became clear that it was time to seek professional help."

"Even if that's true," she said reluctantly, "I don't trust this Doctor Fredericks."

"Why not?" asked Duncan.

"He seems too drug-happy for my taste," she said.

"I'm sorry you feel that way," said Duncan. "He's supposed to be very capable."

"Highly respected," Darrell concurred. Leaning over his clasped hands, he added, "I assure you, Molly, that none of us wanted to see Dewey locked up, but—"

"And yet you insisted on it," she said.

"I had no choice," he said. "He was trying to kill me."

She shook her head. "He was firing into the air. You can see the bullet holes in the office ceiling."

Darrell sat back, spread his hands, and said dryly, "I was too busy ducking and running to check his aim."

"He's too good to miss six times," she said, "and he had a clear shot at you the whole way down the stairs."

Darrell again just shook his head, but Duncan said quietly, "Even the best shot can be affected by their emotions, Molly. And it sounds to me like Dewey was just too mad to shoot straight."

Darrell nodded. "He was out of control."

"Was he drinking?" she asked. "Did you smell it on him?"

"He doesn't drink anymore. Been going to AA twice a week for twenty years. No, I didn't smell any liquor on him, and I don't believe he was drunk. He was just a wild man." Darrell shook his head. "In your work, I'm sure you've faced gunfire many times, but for me, it was a first, and," he said plaintively, "you don't know how scared I was."

Molly softened a bit. "I *do* know, Darrell," she said. "It's not something you forget."

"No, it isn't," he agreed with a nod.

"I'm sorry you had to go through this," she said. "Dewey had no right to shoot at you."

"No, he didn't."

"Just tell me one thing," she said. "Why were you looking through his desk?"

He threw up his hands. "Not that again! That's all I hear from Helen!" He glanced at Duncan for support, then back at Molly. "*I—wasn't—looking—through—Dewey's—desk*," he said, emphasizing each word. "I was just waiting in his office for him to come back from lunch."

"Why?" she asked.

"I wanted to talk some things over with him."

"I thought you two weren't talking."

He looked down at his hands. "I felt it was time we tried." He glanced at his brother, who nodded encouragingly. "I was hoping to patch things up with him, like I did with Duncan. I thought I might catch him in a good mood and see if we could hash out some things."

"Anything in particular?"

"Business matters."

"Such as selling Shamrock?"

He winced. "That was part of it, of course. I thought that, if I could talk to him in private, I might be able to make him see our point of view."

"Yours and Duncan's?" she asked.

"And your father's," Darrell insisted.

"The last time we discussed it," she said, "Daddy hadn't made up his mind."

Duncan said, "He may have been closer to a decision than you realized, Molly."

"What is there to decide?" Darrell asked impatiently. "We should have sold out fifteen years ago, when we had the offer from that company in New Orleans. If we try to hang on now, it'll put us all in the poorhouse."

She said, "I understand that Dewey has been covering cash shortages out of his own pocket."

"He can't keep it up forever," said Darrell. "Sooner or later, we'll all end up paying our share, and for nothing."

Duncan nodded. "It really does seem hopeless, Molly."

She asked Darrell, "Do you know where Dewey went for lunch on Friday?"

"He was supposed to meet Duncan."

"When?" she asked.

"At noon, I believe."

"That's right," Duncan agreed. "We were supposed to meet at Regas Restaurant, but he didn't show up."

She asked Duncan, "Any idea where he went?"

"Not a one," he said.

"And you, Darrell?"

"No idea."

She nodded and asked Darrell, "If you knew Dewey was meeting Duncan for lunch at twelve o'clock, why did you go up to his office at twelve-thirty?"

"Oh, I didn't know about his meeting with Duncan at the time," he said smoothly.

"You didn't?"

"No, but we've discussed it since then, of course."

"Didn't they tell you that Dewey wasn't there?" she asked.

"The foreman may have said something about it when I came in."

"And you knew Dewey didn't allow anyone in his office when he was away?"

"Well, yes, I knew that, but I wanted some privacy and a little time to think about what I was going to say to him."

Molly nodded. "So what happened when he came back? You say you were sitting down when he arrived?"

"Well, no, I guess I was actually leaning over his desk at the time."

"Why?"

"I was phoning to cancel a lunch reservation."

"Well, if Dewey caught you leaning over his desk, that might explain why he thought you were searching it."

He asked sharply, "Does that mean he had the right to shoot me?"

"No, of course not," she said. "I'm just trying to get an accurate picture of what happened. You were leaning over his desk with the phone in your hand, and then what?"

"The door was open," he said, "and I didn't hear him come in. He made me jump when he snarled at me to get away from his desk, and before I could move, he hit me."

"Punched you?"

"Well, I suppose it was more of a push than a punch."

"Trying to get you away from the desk."

"Trying to get to his *gun*, you mean! He said he'd blow my head off if I didn't get out of there, and when I tried to reason with him, he started shooting! And he didn't stop till he ran out of bullets!"

Molly sat back and shook her head and said in quiet disgust, "I just can't believe that either of you could let it come to this. How did it all get so ugly? What kind of family is this?"

Darrell looked to Duncan, and Duncan said wryly, "Just your typical American family, Molly. No more dysfunctional than most."

On our way out of the building, I asked Molly, "You think he was telling the truth?"

"Darrell?" she asked with a grin. "Oh, occasionally."

"I mean about not looking through Dewey's desk."

"No, he was looking, all right. The question is, for what?"

"I don't think you'll find out from him or Duncan."

"Not yet, anyway," she agreed.

10

B ack at the bighouse, we went looking for Ida and Cyrus. We found her in the back parlor vacuuming the carpet, and we could see him outside washing the windows.

Ida shut off the vacuum and said, "Help you?"

"Sorry to interrupt, Ida," said Molly, "but I was wondering if you'd seen Dewey's briefcase."

"It's on his desk, where he left it."

"Thanks, I—"

"I never move his things," she stated for the record. "Dewey don't like me to move 'em."

"No," said Molly. As Ida reached for the switch to her vacuum cleaner, Molly asked quickly, "Do you remember what time Dewey left for work on Friday morning?"

"Same time as always."

"What time is that?"

"Never leaves here later'n seven."

Molly nodded, and Ida switched the vacuum back on, so Molly had to yell, "One more thing!"

Ida switched off again and sighed. "Yep?"

"Do you recall if Dewey went up to the summerhouse when he came home on Friday?"

"No, I don't rightly recall—Cyrus!" she bellowed, making us both jump.

Cyrus opened one of the French doors and poked his head in. "Yes, Ida?"

"Did Dewey go up to the summerhouse Friday?"

"Sure did," he said. "He nearly run me down with his car when he went tearin' up the hill."

Molly asked, "How long did he stay up there?"

"Couldn't tell you that," he said. "Didn't see him come back. But he was down here when they come for him."

"Well, thanks, both of you."

Cyrus said, "You're welcome, miss."

Ida nodded and hit the On switch on her vacuum cleaner.

"Okay," I said, as we stepped into the study, "Dewey left home at his usual time on Friday morning, and Mister Borland said he was half an hour late getting to work, so whatever he did took half an hour."

"And wherever he went had to be fairly close to Shamrock."

"Or he didn't spend much time there."

She nodded. "Length of stay would also be a factor."

The decor in the study was French. I'm not sure about the period—I'm not good on periods—but it was elegant. Lots of inlaid woods, intricate carvings, painted panels, and a desk that looked to be worth as much as a corporate jet.

The briefcase was on the desk, as Ida had said, but it contained nothing unexpected. Business papers—contracts, memos, some correspondence—ballpoint pens clipped to accordion pockets in the lid, a collection of credit card receipts, a calculator, and an appointment book.

Molly turned to the previous Friday in the appointment book. "The lunch with Duncan isn't listed."

"Wonder when the appointment was made."

"I should have asked Duncan," she said.

"Well, we know Dewey didn't go to the restaurant," I said. "So where did he go?"

"Maybe he didn't go anywhere," she said.

"What?"

"Mister Borland said Dewey came back five minutes after Darrell went up to his office."

75

"Right."

"So maybe he just moved his car out of sight and watched for Darrell to show up, then gave him time to start his search before going in to catch him at it."

"You think he knew it was a setup?"

"Well, he didn't make his appointment with Duncan," she said, "so he must have been suspicious."

"Then Duncan was purposely drawing Dewey away from his office?"

"That's my theory," she said.

I watched over her shoulder as she went through the desk drawers. Finding nothing of any apparent significance, she finally got up and said, "Let's go take a look at the summerhouse."

I hadn't had a chance to explore the place on my first visit, so we started with a quick tour. The floor plan was unusual: The rooms all sat in a row, each running the full depth of the house, most only connected by the porch. On the east end of the house, there was a big country kitchen with screens running from waist level to the ceiling on both the end wall and the wall facing the porch, to allow the heat of cooking to escape. The kitchen was equipped with an old wood stove, which appeared to get some use—judging from the kindling stacked beside it—as well as a modern gas range, a two-door refrigerator, and lots of white Formica counter space. The walk-through cupboard between the kitchen and the dining room was well stocked with canned goods, stacks of rice and beans, bins of potatoes and onions.

Swinging doors led from the cupboard into the dining room, and open archways allowed free passage between the dining room and the living room by way of the entry hall. But to reach the other rooms, you had to go out onto the porch. There were two pairs of bedrooms, each sharing a connecting bath, and a storage room on the end.

The storage room contained three Coleman lanterns and

a gallon of fuel, an assortment of lawn chairs and a portable barbecue grill, plus cardboard boxes of old toys, books, and Mason jars.

Only the bed in the first bedroom was made up—Helen's, I assumed. The room was furnished in black cherry: a four-poster, a chest of drawers, a dressing table, and a chifforobe instead of a closet. A chifforobe is a wardrobe with shelves on one side.

"What are we looking for?" I asked.

"Whoever attacked Helen and Cyrus must have been after something."

"Like whatever Dewey brought home in his briefcase?"

"Smart lad."

"So we're looking for a hidden safe, maybe, or a secret panel?"

"Either would be acceptable," she agreed. "But I'd settle for one of those fireproof storage boxes. Try to keep an open mind," she cautioned me. "Narrow your focus too much, and you might miss something. Anything unusual could be important."

We searched behind watercolors and photos looking for a safe. We tapped the wainscotting for a secret panel and dumped out canisters of flour and cornmeal and sugar onto waxed paper searching for emeralds or a safe deposit key. But whatever we were looking for, we didn't find. Or we did find it and didn't recognize it, which is another problem when you don't know what you're looking for. We did, however, make at least one discovery that might qualify as unusual.

In the bottom drawer of the chest of drawers in Helen's bedroom, we found a cracked leather portfolio of very old, yellowing eight-by-ten photographs. I saw no copyright date, but the settings and attire were turn-of-the-century, and the photos looked like they might actually be that old. They featured a woman with long dark hair and a heart-shaped face in a series of erotic vignettes, sometimes working solo, sometimes with a man. The man first appeared in white tie and tails and a Lone Ranger mask. Later, he appeared in just the mask. He was chubby and soft-looking and not particularly well endowed, but then the woman was no airbrushed sex goddess, either. Her flesh was too pale, her breasts too small, her hips too wide, and her pubic hair too plentiful for any of the major modern skin mags. No neat, carefully trimmed Playboy Bunny muff for this woman. Her pubic hair grew thick and dark at the source and spread thinly across her lower belly and down her inner thighs. And you can call me kinky if you like, but I found it a whole lot sexier than any Miss August.

When I mentioned this to Molly, she said flatly, "A pervert. I always suspected it."

"Nothing wrong with pubic hair," I insisted.

"Consider yourself an authority on such matters, do you?"

"Merely a student of nature."

"Must have your doctorate by now, I should think."

"Just a bachelor's I'm afraid."

"Is that a complaint," she said, "or a proposal?"

Whoa! "What?"

Slipping me an elbow, she said with a grin, "It's a joke, Bull."

"Well, I, uh—"

"*Well, I, uh?*" she mimicked. "The dreaded prospect of matrimony has you that tongue-tied."

"No, it's just that the last time we discussed this, you seemed opposed to the idea."

"I was," she agreed. "For two reasons. One, I didn't think we were ready at the time, and two, you didn't propose to me."

"I didn't?"

"No," she said firmly. "I would've remembered."

I swallowed through a constricted throat. "Does that mean you'd *like* me to propose?"

"I didn't say that," she objected.

"No, but that is what you're trying to say, isn't it?"

"I don't *try* to say things," she replied stiffly. "I *say* them."

She was saying she wanted me to propose. I knew that much, and it wasn't as though the possibility had never occurred to me. I'd thought about it often with Molly, but the idea still scared me. I'd had two close brushes with marriage, but in each case, when crunch time came, I couldn't go the distance. Part of the problem—a big part—was my parents.

When I was ten, my father punched my mother in the nose. After he stormed out of the house, she reset the cartilage herself, staring into the bathroom mirror, singing something under her breath. I know now how painful it is to have a nose reset, but she did it with no anesthetic and without a whimper. I stood in the bathroom doorway and watched her do it. She didn't get it quite right, and from then on, her nose was always slightly bent and bumpy in the middle. She refused to have the damage professionally repaired, intending it to be a constant reminder to my father. But he countered this ploy by refusing to look at it. From that day on, he came into the house only after my mother went to bed, slept in the downstairs guest room, and was out in the fields before she was up. On those rare occasions when the three of us actually had a meal together—usually on a major Christian holiday—their conversation was limited to "pass the peas" and "hand me the salt." I naturally assumed that they hated each other—what else could I think? But after my mother died and I saw my father mourning her, I realized that he'd loved her all along, and it seemed insane to me that he'd gone twenty years without telling her that. Theirs was the only marriage I ever witnessed at close hand, and it didn't paint a rosy picture of the institution. But I didn't want to lose Molly, and if she was asking for a commitment, I figured it was time to offer one.

I swallowed hard and said, "Okay."

"Okay what?"

"Okay, let's get married."

"No," she said.

"No?"

"No."

"Why not?"

"Two reasons. First, I want it to be your idea, not mine, and second, 'Okay, let's get married' is not a proposal."

"It isn't?"

"No," she said. " 'Molly, will you marry me?' is a proposal."

Dropping to my knees, I pleaded in all sincerity, "Molly, will you marry me?"

She smiled down at me, but said, "No, you idiot, I will not."

"Why not?"

"Reason number one, remember?" she said. "Right now you feel coerced and manipulated, and you're right. I don't want it this way." She grinned. "But before I distracted you, we were discussing pubic hair, I believe."

"Ah. Right. Yes." I tried to recover the mood and found that it wasn't too difficult. "If I remember correctly," I said, "I was about to say that I was especially fond of *your* pubic hair and that I was glad you didn't shave down there."

She moved closer and laid a hand on my chest. "You were?"

I nodded. "I love the way the fine, red-gold hairs grow down your inner thighs. Silk on velvet. Very sexy."

Leaning against me, she asked, "It is?"

I laid her down on Helen's bed, peeled off her jeans, and stroked the object of our discussion. I combed it with my fingers and kissed it, then traced the trail of hair down her inner thighs with my lips and tongue.

When we were both naked, she sat up suddenly and asked, "What time is it?"

"Time?" I asked in confusion.

"We don't want Tim to catch us," she said.

Pulling her back down, I said, "He'll knock. Or we'll hear him coming. And if we don't, so what? If the lecherous sonofabitch catches us in the act, maybe he'll finally get the hint."

She grinned. "You're not *really* jealous of him, are you?"

"Me? No, not at all. I'll probably beat him to a pulp the next time he locks eyes with you, but I don't consider that an unreasonable response, do you?"

She laughed. "Of course not."

"But if you don't mind," I concluded, "I'd rather not talk about Tim Deets right now."

Trailing her fingers down my belly, she said quietly, "Then let's not."

As it happened, we didn't have to worry about Tim. We had restored our presentability in the bathroom and were completing our search by the time he came whistling across the bridge.

We went out to meet him on the porch.

"Evening, Tim," said Molly.

"Tim," said I.

"Evening," Tim replied.

Then Molly and I looked at each other and broke into guffaws. We tried to stop, even briefly succeeded, but as soon as we looked at each other, or at Tim, we'd start up again. He hesitantly joined in our laughter and didn't ask any questions, but I had a hunch he'd divined our dark secret.

11

This was the last night that the Sheriff's Department would provide free guard service at the summerhouse, and Molly had finally talked Helen into contracting a private security company to take over the job.

That evening, some school friends of Molly's took us out for dinner and drinks. I didn't drink much as a rule, marijuana being my drug of choice, but I knew Molly wouldn't appreciate it if I lit up at the table. So I was stuck with wine, and I found that listening to them reminisce was thirsty work.

Alcohol keeps me awake, or limits my sleep to an hour or so between bathroom visits, and by five in the morning, I knew I was up for good. I slid out of bed and pulled on a pair of jeans, grabbed a shirt, a windbreaker, and my running shoes, then went downstairs to make a pot of coffee. While the coffee was perking, I called the summerhouse.

Tim must have been sitting by the phone, because he picked up on the first ring. "Yeah?" he growled.

"Tim, this is Bull Cochran."

Beat. "You're up early, Mister Cochran."

"Couldn't sleep. How about some coffee?"

"Had all the coffee I can hold, but if you wanna come up and keep me awake, that'd be all right."

"Okay," I said, "think I'll do that."

I filled a thermos with black coffee, turned off the alarm, and let myself out through the kitchen door. I cut across the garden, tramping through wet grass and a damp mist, to the gravel road and followed it up the hill. The moon was down, and it was so dark under the trees that I could barely see the road. Dark, but by no means silent. An insect chorus provided a noisy background for rattling limbs and rustling leaves. I jumped when something fell with a thud on the hillside above, and I almost had a stroke when an animal darted across the road in front of me. A moment later, I dropped to my knees as some flying creature (probably a bat) whooshed past my head.

As I'd mentioned to Molly, I didn't like bats. Or to be accurate, I suppose it's the *idea* of bats I didn't like, as I'd never actually had anything to do with the real thing. I'd seen enough photos and documentaries to know what a bat looked like, but because of the rabies thing, what I pictured was a sort of skinny mad dog with leathery wings and very long teeth cruising the airy darkness.

When I reached the brick steps leading up the hill to the summerhouse, I went up carefully, suddenly reluctant to approach an armed man in the darkness. Tim knew I was coming, but what if he conveniently "forgot"? One well-aimed shot, and he'd have a clear field with Molly, wouldn't he?

I considered calling out his name, but that didn't seem appropriate. Instead, I squeaked my running shoes a little more than necessary as I crossed the wooden bridge. Then I stopped in the starlight out in front of the porch and stage-whispered, "Tim?"

"Yeah," he said from close behind me.

I jerked around. "Christ, you scared me!"

"Sorry," he said, and I caught a glimpse of teeth. "Thought I heard something a while ago."

"It was me."

"No, before I heard you. Let's go up on the porch. And keep your voice down." On the porch, he steered me to one of two straight-back chairs. "Rocking chairs make too much noise," he explained.

I took a seat and screwed off the top of the thermos. "Sure you won't have some coffee?"

"I'm sure," he said.

I poured myself a cup and resealed the thermos, then put it on the porch beside my chair and stared out into the darkness, blowing on the coffee until it was cool enough to sip. Now that I was here, I didn't know what to say to him. I wasn't even sure why I'd come.

"Couldn't sleep, huh?" he whispered.

"Had too much to drink last night."

He understood that: man-talk about drunkenness. "Up and down all night?"

"Yep."

He nodded, and we stared into the darkness some more. As my eyes adjusted, I could dimly see the darker mass of woods across the stream and a faint hint of treetops against the star field.

After a moment, Tim asked, "So how long have you known Molly?"

"About five years. How about you?"

"All my life," he said. "We used to play together in these caves here when we were kids."

"Did you, uh . . ."

"Did we date?" He turned to me. "Is that what you're asking?"

"Yeah."

"We went to the movies a couple of times. But she left here when she was twelve, so I missed out on her prime dating years."

Thank God! I thought. *No '62 Ford or Chevy!* Then I realized that Molly had been playing with me all along, and I decided I'd have to get her for that. Smiling to myself, I asked, "You go to UT?"

"Yep."

"Play football?"

The sky was beginning to lighten a little to the east, and I could see him nod. "Second-string quarterback for the

Vols my junior and senior years. Even started a few games when the first stringer went down with a hamstring. Had a decent pass-completion percentage, too, but I couldn't run worth a lick, and when they flushed me out of the pocket, I was dead meat. Course, it didn't help that I was playing behind Johnny Deer."

"Ummm," I said. Deer, a five-time Pro Bowler, was not only a pinpoint passer, he could run like his namesake—the animal, not the tractor—or at least he could until a shattered knee terminated his career the season before.

When Tim turned to me again, I could see a vague schematic of his features. "Hear you played baseball," he said.

Here we go again. "That's right."

"Even pitched a few games in the majors."

"Two starts and three relief appearances," I said, "before I was sent back to the minors."

"Where you killed a man with a high inside fastball."

Slipped that one in, didn't he? "Yeah," I admitted.

"Then, a few years ago, your business partner was murdered in Galveston, and you killed the man who did it."

"Yes."

"A second man was killed, too, wasn't he?"

"That's right," I said. "But *I* didn't kill him, even though he was trying to kill *me*. But then you probably noticed my scars."

"Not much to see, except for the one on your chin." He was referring to the thin slash of pink tissue that ran from the right corner of my mouth to the left corner of my chin. "Then you helped catch the guy who murdered Holy Joe Ahern, and four more people got killed during that investigation."

"That's right," I agreed with a sigh.

"A lot of people die on you, don't they, Mister Cochran?"

"Why don't you call me Bull, Tim?" I told him. "As for this dying thing, I can't explain it. I think of myself as a live-and-let-live kind of guy, but I can't deny that people

85

have been dropping around me like flies."

"Maybe you're a carrier," he suggested, "like Typhoid Mary."

I had to laugh at that, or punch him. "An interesting theory, Tim, but I prefer to think of it as coincidence. Or maybe I just have a knack for being in the right place at the wrong time."

"Or the *right* time," he said. "You got books out of the first two sets of killings, didn't you?"

"Are you implying that I'm responsible for what happened just because I wrote about it?"

"No, I'm not—"

"Because, if you are, I should point out that, as a policeman, you're at least as dependent on death and mayhem for your livelihood as I am."

"That's a good point, Mister Cochran," he said with a grin, his handsome face now fully visible in the gray morning light.

"Call me Bull, please," I insisted.

"All right, Bull," he said. "And I assure you that I meant no disrespect."

"Of course not," I said.

"It's just that, from everything I've heard, you seem to have a real nose for trouble. And I was just wondering if you were up here sniffin' out some more of it."

"I'm not up here sniffin' out anything," I said. "I'm here because Molly asked me to come." I didn't say that she'd wanted me along so I could share her bed, but I hoped the implication was clear.

He nodded and looked away. "Well, I was just curious, Bull."

"And I appreciate your concern, Tim." I figured we might as well keep it friendly as long as we could.

At ten o'clock that morning, Molly and I paid our third visit to Riverside Center.

We gave our names at the reception desk and were strolling through the trees in the atrium when I saw a slender, well-dressed woman approaching us. She said something into a cordless phone, then switched off and strode our way. "Good morning," she said to Molly. "You must be Miz Flanagan and Mister Cochran." She nodded at me.

"That's right," said Molly.

"I'm Doctor Gray," she said, "the assistant administrator. Doctor Fredericks isn't here right now, I'm afraid. He had to give a deposition this morning. I have a few more calls to make, but I'm sure you'd rather see your uncle alone anyway, so why don't you go on up? Just buzz, and someone will let you in."

"How is Dewey?" asked Molly.

"Seemed better this morning," she said. "He was lucid when I spoke to him after breakfast."

Molly thanked her, then Doctor Gray went back to her phone calls, and we headed for the stairs. When we reached the locked double doors on the second floor, Molly put her thumb on a button under a sign that said PUSH FOR ENTRY. After a moment, she pushed it again and glared up at the video camera. She was reaching out for a third time when the door buzzed.

As I followed her through the door, I was hit with the smell of smoke. "You smell that?"

"Yeah," said Molly.

It was strongest near the door and faded as we walked on. The corridor was deserted and so quiet it was spooky, like we'd stepped onto a ghost ward.

I heard a chime, and elevator doors opened ahead to the left. Instead of firemen, two EMTs came out pushing a stretcher and moved briskly down the corridor away from us. Then a burly male attendant emerged from the nurses' station beyond the elevator carrying a fire extinguisher. He was followed by a khaki-uniformed man with a pigtail pushing one of those head-high industrial-strength fans on rollers. The two men hurried past us to a room near the entrance. Smoke puffed out as the door hissed shut behind

87

them, then the corridor was empty and quiet again. The doors to all the rooms were closed, and both the nurses' station and the recreation area were deserted.

I followed Molly into Dewey's room and saw him sitting up, the head of his bed raised, pale eyes staring straight ahead. Molly stopped so suddenly that I almost ran into her, and over her shoulder, I saw the blood. Dewey's wrist—*both* wrists—were cut in raw, ragged gouges. Blood stained the blanket pink, ran down the side of the bed, and seeped into the carpet.

"Oh, Christ," Molly said, and crossed herself.

She moved forward like a sleepwalker and came to a stop almost standing in the blood. She felt for a pulse in his neck, but it was merely a ritual. He was dead, no question about it. No blood was flowing now, or ever would again. She gently closed his eyes, then started to speak a quiet prayer, and I went for help.

12

As I stepped into the corridor, I saw a young woman hurrying by and asked, "Who's in charge?"

She kept going, but said, "See Nurse Layer."

"Where?"

"Try room twelve," she called back.

I said, "Thanks," but she'd already pushed through a room door and vanished.

A nurse in room twelve told me to try room five, and I visited rooms three and nine before finally tracking the person down in a tiny office at the back of the nurses' station. She was the charge nurse in this wing—a stout woman in her late forties—and her name was Lehr.

Nurse Lehr called Doctor Gray, then accompanied me back to the room.

After she satisfied herself that Dewey was beyond help, Molly asked her, "How could this happen?"

The woman had obviously seen a lot in her years as a psychiatric nurse, but she appeared to be as shocked as we were by what Dewey had done to himself. "I assure you," she said, "that we don't allow our patients sharp objects with which to cut themselves."

"Look down," Molly told her, "in front of my left foot."

I stepped in and saw a bloody plastic knife lying half under the bed. The serrated edge didn't look sharp, and using it must have hurt like the devil.

"Do you recognize it?" Molly asked her.

The nurse put her hands on her knees and took a closer look. After a moment, she conceded, "I suppose it could've come from his breakfast tray, but we use plastic utensils to *avoid* this very thing."

Molly didn't point out that it hadn't worked this time. She nodded at Dewey and said, "He's cold, been dead half an hour at least. Don't you people ever watch your monitors?"

Nurse Lehr sighed. "They aren't working today."

"Why not?"

"Maintenance says the console needs a part."

"How often do you physically check the rooms?"

"Depends on the patient's condition," she said. "Because of your uncle's improvement, he was down for hourly checks, but it's been so busy this morning."

"Busy, how?" asked Molly.

"We had a new admission and medical complications with a couple of others. One patient became agitated, and as often happens, he started to infect the rest. Then, on top of all that, we had the fire."

Molly nodded. "We smelled it when we came in. What happened?"

"Nothing serious," Nurse Lehr assured us. "A patient set some newspapers on fire in a waste can."

"You let your patients have matches?" Molly asked.

"Of course not," she replied. "We don't know where he got them."

Molly shook her head. "I don't want this room entered until the police get here."

"No, of course not."

As Nurse Lehr left to call the police, Doctor Gray, the assistant administrator, showed up. She'd been told what to expect, but it was still a blow. In a hushed voice, she said, "I'm so sorry, Ms. Flanagan."

Molly glanced at the door, where two women were peeking in. "This room should be sealed until the body is removed."

"Absolutely," the doctor agreed. To one of the women, she said, "Lawton, close that door, and post yourself outside. Don't let anyone enter." To the other, she added, "Mitchell, I'm sure you have work to do."

As the faces vanished, Molly told her, "I have to call for a priest to administer last rites."

"Yes, of course," said Doctor Gray. "You can call from the nurses' station, and I'll see that he's sent right up."

After making her call, Molly waited by the bed, and I stood at the window staring down the slope of the lawn to the sluggish green water of the Holston River. Sluggish or not, at least it was moving, which was a big improvement over the stillness behind me. My stomach was jittery from lack of sleep and too much coffee, and the metallic smell of blood was making me sick. The smell was so thick that I was amazed I hadn't noticed it as soon as I stepped through the door. You would think I'd recognize the smell of blood by now.

Tim had observed that people did a lot of dying around me, but he didn't know the half of it. It seemed to me that I'd spent my life careening from one corpse to the next. You saw a lot of dying on a farm. Pigs slaughtered, chickens with their heads cut off, horses shot for breaking a leg. My father used to say that dying was the most natural thing in the world, and that I had to learn to take it with a grain of salt. But I could never do that.

I found out about my mother's death in the locker room after throwing a no-hitter against Michigan. I couldn't believe it at first, then I got angry at her for doing this to me. She'd always resented baseball, the time I spent at it, the time it kept me away from the farm, from her. She'd said she relied on me, that she needed me there, that I was all she had. But I had refused to give it up, and she had finally taken her revenge by dying just at the right moment to sabotage my greatest triumph!

It was one of those crazy thoughts that occasionally slip

91

past the mental censors, always at the most inappropriate times. All of us have such thoughts, but I didn't know that, and I was stricken with shame and self-disgust. I couldn't believe that I was capable of such a thing. I thought I must be a moral degenerate, a freak of nature, or some soulless spawn of Satan to harbor such thoughts about my mother. And I knew there was no way to hide a defect like mine, that it had to be obvious to anyone who laid eyes on me—a mark as plain as if it were scrawled in blood across my forehead.

Then, at her funeral, my worst fear became a reality. I couldn't cry. I'd cried buckets since her death, but now that I needed it, now that everybody was watching, I couldn't produce so much as one solitary tear. I knew my secret was out. Even for those few stupid or insensitive enough not to have seen it already, it should now be self-evident. Anybody who couldn't cry at his own mother's funeral had to be a monster.

After a couple of hundred hours of therapy, I'd managed to ditch that particular bugaboo, and I no longer thought of myself as a freak. I knew now that I was merely one of a sick species, a species capable of imagining anything, including limits to the imagination.

Recovering my sanity hadn't stopped the dying. The chain of corpses stretched unbroken into the present, and they seemed to be closing in on me. I was always in the middle of it now. I was there when Juice was shot, as I was for the killings that followed. I didn't see Joe Ahern die, but I sat in a boat for hours with his killer and his killer's killer, the deck awash in their blood. And now, finding Dewey like this . . .

"Bull?"

"Yes."

Molly stood in front of me. "They're here," she said quietly.

"Okay."

92

A patrolman asked us questions, then a detective arrived and asked some more. When a police photographer showed up to shoot the scene, the detective took us out to the nurses' station to finish his questioning.

When the EMTs came to take the body away, Molly told them they'd have to wait till the priest had done his thing.

Fortunately, the priest arrived close on their heels. He was in his early thirties, chubby and out of breath, wearing a black polyester clerical suit. Shifting an overnight case from his right hand to his left, he extended the freed hand to Molly and said, "Hello, I'm Father Paxton." He drew a breath. "And you're Miz Flanagan?"

"Molly," she said absently.

"A pleasure to meet you, Molly," he said, "though I regret the circumstances, of course."

She nodded. "This is Bill Cochran."

"Mister Cochran." He gave me a quick, medium-strong handshake, then turned to business, asking Molly, "Where is he?"

She nodded down the corridor. "The room with the EMT standing in the doorway."

"Ah, yes," he said, then nodded to both of us and headed for the room.

Doctor Gray leaned across the counter and said, "I just spoke to Doctor Fredericks. He asked me to relay his regrets and to tell you he's on his way here now."

"Yes, I'd like to talk to him," Molly told her. "If possible, I'd like to talk to everyone who works in this wing. When does the shift end?"

"At three."

Molly glanced at her watch. "It's not eleven yet, so we should have time when I get back."

"Back?"

"Have to go break the news to my aunt. I don't want her to hear it from a stranger."

"No, of course not," Doctor Gray agreed.

93

"But please don't let any of the staff in this wing leave until I've had a chance to speak to them."

The doctor nodded. "We'll be here."

I wasn't eager to face Helen's grief, and it appeared that Molly wasn't either. She took her time driving back into town, probably trying to figure out what to say. How do you tell a woman that the man she's been married to for fifty years has just killed himself?

St. Mary's Medical Center sat on a rounded hilltop surrounded by parking lots, and we found a space in the big one across from the visitors' entrance. We went inside and took the elevator to Helen's floor, but Molly stopped me outside the door. "Would you mind waiting here, Bull," she asked, "so I can break it to her alone?"

"No problem," I said, trying to hide my relief. "I'll wait right here."

She nodded, then took a moment to prepare herself before pushing through the door. I leaned against the wall, glad that it was her delivering the news and not me. Two middle-aged nuns rustled past, blessing me with their benign expressions, and it occurred to me that living with death and disease every day would either cement your faith or destroy it.

When Molly finally opened the door and let me in, I was relieved to see Helen looking composed. She had cried and would cry again, but her eyes were dry now. She sat erect, as always, but I could see the effort it required.

Reaching out to take my hand, she said, "I lived with him fifty-two years, Mister Cochran. Can you imagine that?" I couldn't, but didn't say so. "He came to Atlanta, showed up at my seventeenth birthday party, and asked me to dance. I was dancing with Briley Hawkins at the time, the young man my father intended me to marry, but Dewey cut in and wouldn't let me dance with anyone else the rest of the evening. The next afternoon he came by and took me riding. At least that's what we told my parents, though, in fact, we made it no further than the barn. He made love like he danced. He just wouldn't stop. I wasn't a virgin," she informed us. "Briley had relieved me of that burden two months before, but it was nothing like it was with Dewey."

She seemed totally unembarrassed about revealing these intimate details, but I had a notion she wasn't really talking to me. "People told me he was wild," she went on. "They said he'd shot a man, that he'd had an affair with an older woman and had gotten a younger woman in trouble, but I didn't care about any of that. I knew I couldn't marry anyone else, and I told my father he needn't try to stop me. One way or another, with or without his blessing, I would be Dewey Flanagan's bride. Daddy warned me that Dewey would cause me grief and heartache, and he was right about that. But we had our share of joy, too, and Dewey could always make me laugh. I admit there were times, over the years, when I actually wished he was dead, but I'm paying for those evil thoughts now. And at this moment"—she shook her head, fighting tears—"I can't imagine going on without him."

13

We made it back to Riverside Center by twelve-thirty. After the receptionist greeted us by name and offered her condolences, she said, "Would you mind waiting here for just a moment, please? The Director wants to speak to you."

As she reached for the phone, I spotted Doctor Fredericks jogging our way and said, "Never mind, ma'am, I think he's seen us."

We went to meet him, and he slowed to a halt in front of us. "I'm so very sorry, Miz Flanagan," he said breathlessly. "I should've been here when it happened, but I was called to give a deposition." Leading us toward the stairs, he continued, "When I saw your uncle this morning, he seemed calm, and I frankly thought we were over the hump with him." As we started up the stairs, he added, "I fully expected to be releasing him in a day or two." He shook his head in disbelief. "At any rate, you have my sincerest sympathy and regret."

Molly said, "I told Doctor Gray I wanted to talk to everyone who was there."

"Yes, she told me," he said. "It was an unusual request, and our lawyers strongly recommended against it, but I've decided to ignore their advice and have instructed the staff to cooperate fully."

Disarmed by his unexpected acquiescence, Molly said nothing.

At the locked door on the second floor, the doctor

swiped his card and punched in his code to open the door. As we approached the nurses' station, he asked, "Do you have any more questions for me now?"

"Not at the moment, no," she said.

"Then I'll leave you in Doctor Gray's charge." He nodded at the doctor, and turned back to Molly. "If you need me, I'll be on my rounds. Something like this affects everyone, and it's time for me to do what I can to help them through it." His tone was matter-of-fact, but his concern seemed genuine.

As he walked away, Doctor Gray asked Molly, "So where would you like to start?"

"Is there someplace quiet where I could speak to your staff individually?" she asked.

The doctor glanced at Nurse Lehr, who said, "Yes, of course, you can use my office."

"Thank you," said Molly.

"I hope you don't mind if I sit in on the interviews," said Doctor Gray, "but I'm afraid the interests of the hospital have to be looked after as well."

"Of course," Molly said, then followed Nurse Lehr into her office.

The doctor started after her, then glanced back at me and said, "Mister Cochran?"

"It's going to be crowded in there," I said, "so if it's okay with you, I'll just wait out here."

She didn't like letting me out of her sight, but Doctor Fredericks had told her to cooperate, and she had no real grounds for objection. "Very well," she said.

Molly winked at me behind the doctor's back. We'd discussed it on the drive back from St. Mary's and had decided that, if possible, I would do some snooping on my own.

As the door closed behind them, I glanced around the nurses' station, noticing that Nurse Lehr kept an eye on me as she took a phone call.

The chest-high counter across the front of the nurses'

97

station was shaped like an elongated capital C. There was a desk-high shelf behind the middle part of it long enough for four people to sit side by side and write reports or talk on the phone. A rack of plastic charts occupied one curved end, and a three-tiered cockpit of five-inch screens, the other. Brushed steel and black plastic gave the monitor console a glossy, high-tech look, but just now, the screens were dark and useless.

As Nurse Lehr hung up the phone, I nodded at the console. "Does it break down often?"

"This is the first time," she said.

"Hmmm," I said.

She nodded. "But isn't that the way with machines? They stop working just when you need them. Like the day I moved into my apartment, the elevator broke down."

I laughed and waved at the console. "Who's fixing it?"

"The maintenance man said he'd get it back on line this afternoon."

"Where is he?"

"Had to go get a part."

Well, if somebody *had* killed Dewey, it was certainly convenient that the monitors happened to be down at the time, but it occurred to me that a diversion would also come in handy. "Could I take a look at the room where you had the fire?"

"I don't know if we should . . ." she began.

"Just a look," I said. "There's no patient in there now, is there?"

"Well, no, but—"

"I know we're in the way here, and I'm sure you'd agree that the sooner we get this over with, the better."

She nodded. "Well, yes—"

"And I can tell you right now that Molly will want to take a look at that room."

"Why?"

I shrugged. "She's a cop, and that's what cops do. They look at things, anything that might be relevant."

"But I don't see how—"

"Neither do I," I said, "but you can take my word for it: She'll want to see it. However, if I look *for* her, we can get this over in half the time." When she still resisted, I added, "I promise not to touch anything."

And she finally gave in, if only to shut me up.

The room was virtually identical to Dewey's, except that both bed and patient were gone. The fan I'd seen being rolled into the room now stood in the middle of the floor blowing the smell of smoke toward the open windows. But the sharp, acrid odor still hung in the air.

"Where's the wastebasket?"

"It was washed and put out back because of the smell."

"Where did the patient get the papers?" I asked.

"Saved them up, I suppose."

"Then your patients are allowed newspapers?"

"Some of them," she said, "depending on the doctor's recommendation."

"How many of them have this privilege?"

"A half dozen on this ward."

"Was this patient one of them?"

"No, but he wasn't confined to his room, and he could have collected somebody else's papers."

I thought about it, but didn't know where to take it from there, so I shifted to another tack. "Does this patient have a history of setting fires?"

"There's no mention of it in his chart."

"Then he wasn't a pyromaniac."

"Well," she said, "patient histories are not always completely accurate. Families often try to hide these sorts of tendencies."

"How did you discover the fire?"

"An alarm sounded at the nurses' station, and Nurse Mitchell ran in here to find the room filled with smoke and the patient on the floor."

"Could I talk with the patient?"

Nurse Lehr smiled, but shook her head. "We certainly

want to help you any way we can, but I'm afraid we can't allow you to talk to our patients. That wouldn't be ethical. Besides, he had to be sedated, so he wouldn't be much help to you anyway."

"All right," I said. "So while Dewey was dying, you were all trying to put out the fire?"

"Not all of us," she replied. "As I said, we had a busy morning. There was the new admission to deal with and a man running up and down the hallway without any clothes on. Another man went into an elderly woman's room and shoved her out of her bed onto the floor, and the poor woman had to be taken to the hospital." I remembered the EMTs pushing the stretcher off the elevator and down the corridor. "A woman threw up all over her room. And a blood test came back on another woman, showing that she had infectious hepatitis, and we had to place her in isolation."

"Is it always like this?"

She smiled. "No, but believe it or not, I've seen it worse."

"What about the patient who pushed the old woman out of bed?"

"He's been unresponsive since the incident."

"Did the victim tell you he pushed her?"

"She didn't say anything. She was barely conscious when they took her away."

"Then you can't be sure he did the pushing."

"He was in the room," she pointed out.

"That doesn't prove he did it," I said. "It's possible, isn't it, that what you called distractions could have been diversions?"

"You mean somebody *else* set the fire and pushed the woman out of bed?"

"It's possible, isn't it?"

"Well, I suppose it's *possible*. But why would anybody want to do those things?"

"So your staff would be too busy to check on Mister Flanagan?"

"You think *he* did all that, then went back to his room and killed himself?"

"Or somebody else did it *for* him."

Again she stared at me. "Then you think it was murder?"

"I think it *could've* been."

She wasn't convinced. "There were no signs of a struggle."

"The killer could have straightened up afterward."

"Why didn't Mister Flanagan scream for help?"

"If he was sufficiently sedated—"

"No," she said, shaking her head, "Prozac and Xanax wouldn't block that kind of pain. The only explanation is that he stifled his own screams, so we wouldn't intervene. You see, most so-called suicide attempts are intended to fail, but I believe that Mister Flanagan was sincere in his effort."

"Why do you say that?"

"Because he took the first available way out, and he kept it simple."

"You call sawing open his arteries with a dull knife 'simple'?"

"I didn't say it was easy," she said. "But he couldn't have gone about his suicide in any more straightforward a manner than by opening his veins and allowing himself to bleed to death."

She had a point there. "How long would it take for him to do that?"

"Not long. With the pain and the rapid blood loss, he might have gone into shock almost immediately, and the vasovagal reaction could have killed him in minutes."

"The what?"

"In cases of intense pain, or abrupt blood loss, the vagus nerve can suddenly shut down the circulatory system. The vessels dilate; blood pressure plunges; heart rate and respiration slows, then stops."

101

"But he could still be saved, couldn't he?"

"If he was found immediately," she said, "he'd have about one chance in ten of surviving, with the help of a crash cart and trained personnel."

"Which you have."

"Which we have," she agreed. "But he *wasn't* found, and his chances would have gone down rapidly after that. Brain death would have been irreversible in minutes."

"Long before we found him."

"I'm afraid so."

She showed me where the old woman had been pushed out of bed. The room was at the other end of the corridor from the fire room, and there wasn't much to see, so I drifted back to the nurses' station.

I had a cup of coffee and chatted up the staff, keeping it casual, not so much asking questions as getting a feel for their reactions. Most wore mournful expressions and seemed honestly disturbed by Dewey's death. Some were scared—probably for their jobs—but they talked as freely as their natures would allow, and none of them appeared to be hiding anything.

On our way home, I reported what I'd learned, telling Molly about the naked man running around the halls, the old lady being pushed out of bed, the patient barfing all over her room, and the hepatitis scare. "With all that and the fire," I concluded, "it's no wonder that a small matter like suicide went unnoticed for half an hour."

"Suicide," she repeated under her breath.

"You don't believe it, do you?"

"I don't *want* to," she admitted. "What about the fire?"

"I suppose it could have been a diversion," I said, "but I wasn't allowed to talk to the patient, and—"

"Did you expect to?" she asked.

"No, I guess not," I agreed. "But, depending on the guy's condition, I guess it's possible that somebody *could* have gone into the room, stuffed papers into the trash can, and set them on fire, then sneaked out again before the patient woke up. But as I say, it wasn't really necessary. That place was already a madhouse."

She didn't even crack a smile. "What about the video monitors?"

"It's the first time they went down."

"Hmmm," she said.

"That's what *I* said. But things do break down, and it could have been a coincidence that it happened today."

"I don't like coincidences," she said.

"Me neither. Learn anything from the interviews?"

She sighed. "I didn't spot any murderers, if that's what you mean."

"You okay?"

"Not really."

"Want me to drive?"

"No," she said, and I left her alone.

Molly might not be a devout Catholic anymore, but she'd been raised to believe that suicide was a mortal sin. There still had to be a stigma attached to the act, and Dewey was her favorite uncle. No wonder she was fighting it.

14

Helen called after we got back to the bighouse. She'd already talked to her older daughter, Rachel, and had left a message for the younger one, Ruth, and she had spoken to several others who were closest to Dewey, but that still left many friends and relatives and business associates to be informed of his death. She asked Molly if she would make the rest of the calls for her, and Molly said she'd be glad to.

I had made the calls after my father had died, and I knew how draining it was, so I stayed with her, providing company and moral support, as she worked the phone. She started with Shamrock—speaking to Mr. Borland, the foreman, and Mrs. Witherspoon, the business manager—moved on to Darrell and Duncan, and slowly made her way through the list. When she got thirsty, I brought her water or tea, and when she showed signs of flagging, I made her a sandwich and persuaded her to stop and eat it. Among the other calls, she spoke to her boss in Galveston, Captain Parkinson, to explain that she didn't know when she'd be able to get away from Knoxville and to say that she'd probably need an extension on her leave of absence. She saved her father for last. When she reached him, I asked her to give him my best, then left them to talk in private.

Wednesday morning, we greeted friends and family. That afternoon, we brought Helen home from the hospital, and *she* greeted friends and family while Molly and I went to the airport to pick up Donald. The Celica wasn't comfortable for more than two people, so she drove Dewey's silver-gray Lincoln Town Car.

As we headed out of town, the day was hot and still, the sky whitewashed with overcast, the trees sporting the last lush green of the season. We took 129, crossing the Tennessee River at the western edge of the University of Tennessee campus. From the bridge, I could see a bend in the river off to the right, where it veered from a northwesterly flow to due south. To the left, the river was turned again, this time back to the east, by towering cliffs that lifted in a great arc along the south side of the river. Molly said they were called Cherokee Bluffs.

On the other side of the bridge, the road rose between a University of Tennessee agricultural research station on the right and the huge UT Medical Research Center & Hospital off to the left.

We were passing a tiny Navy and Marine Corps Reserve Training Center beside a wide, glassy stretch of river when I said, "You never did tell me why your father moved to Texas."

"He wanted to go into business for himself."

"The other brothers did that, and they didn't have to leave Knoxville."

"Daddy saw a market for his engineering talent in the oil fields, but he needed to be on the spot to study the problems. And there was a man in Houston who was eager to manufacture several of his patents."

"Then it was purely a business decision?"

She stared ahead for a moment, then shook her head. "No, something happened between Dewey and Daddy."

"What?"

"I just know they had an argument, and they didn't speak for a long time. Daddy would never discuss it, so I don't know what it was about. But they must've finally settled it, because they sometimes talk on the phone now. Or," she realized, "they *did*."

* * *

105

Molly's dad was delivered to us at the gate in a wheelchair, looking thinner, grayer, and a lot more fragile than I remembered.

The steward pushing his wheelchair smiled at us, then at his charge, and said, "If you'll wait here a moment, Mister Flanagan, a courtesy cart will take you and your party back to the main terminal."

"Thank you, Chris, but that won't be necessary," he said. "I'm still capable of moving under my own power."

"I don't doubt that, sir," said the young man, "but the cart's on its way, and it really is a fair distance back to the terminal."

"I appreciate your concern, Chris," said Donald, "but you can call off the cart. If I get tired of rolling myself, I'm sure I can find some kind soul willing to give me a push."

The young man's smile looked strained for a beat, then he shrugged and cheerfully agreed, "Very well, sir. It was a pleasure to serve you, and I hope you'll be flying with us again."

"Since I have a round-trip ticket, Chris," said Donald, "I think you can count on it."

As Chris took his leave, Donald accepted a kiss from Molly, then stuck out his hand to me and said, "Bill."

I took it and said, "Don." He'd insisted on using first names from the start, explaining that being called "Mister Flanagan" made him feel old.

Right now, he *looked* old, much older than Dewey had looked, even on his deathbed. Donald's color was bad, a bloodless gray, and most of his hair was gone. Only a few stray wisps and odd clumps dotted his skull, radiation treatments having killed the rest. He had worn a wig for a time, but he'd hated it. He had even talked about shaving his head, but he had told me once that he'd had a vision of himself with a shaved head and said he had looked like the vampire in *Nosferatu*. I thought it was just as well that he didn't have a mirror handy at this moment, as the comparison had never been more apt.

Catching me staring, he said sourly, "Not pretty, is it?"

"I've seen you look better, Don."

"I should hope so," he replied dryly. Then he pulled a sporty glen plaid driver's cap out of his jacket pocket, clamped it down on his head, and said, "Let's get out of here."

When Molly made a move toward the back of his chair, I told her, "I'll push. You two talk."

"No, *I'll* push," Donald said, giving his wheels a shove, "and you two talk. I want to hear everything."

Knoxville was a medium-sized town with a medium-sized airport, everything new-looking and very clean. Beyond the first gate, we entered a wide, carpeted, brick-walled passageway that wound at a gentle incline down to the terminal. The problem was no longer pushing Donald's chair along, but slowing it down, and when Molly and I each took a handle to help him, he didn't object.

I didn't know what he thought of me or how he felt about my relationship with his daughter. He had never volunteered an opinion, and I had never asked. We didn't see much of him, as he spent most of his time traveling from hospital to hospital. He had been one of the top mechanical engineers in the world, with more than fifty patents to his credit, and had consulted on projects all over the globe. I knew he must have many fascinating experiences to relate, but he had little time for storytelling these days.

Molly gave him a quick rundown of everything that had happened since our arrival in Knoxville. I assumed he had heard some of it before, but he didn't interrupt, and we were on our way back into town when she finished. He sat up front with Molly, and I had the backseat to myself.

"Poor Dewey," Donald said finally. "Smart as he was, nothing was ever simple for him."

"That's what Tim Deets said about us," said Molly. "That nothing was ever simple when our family was involved."

His laughter turned into a phlegmy cough, and Molly

gave me a worried glance in the mirror.

When Donald got it under control, he said hoarsely, "Tim always was a bright one."

After driving along in silence for a few minutes, Molly looked over at him and asked, "What did you and Dewey fight about?"

"Fight?"

"All those years ago, before we moved to Texas."

He was silent.

"Dad?"

"I'd rather not talk about it," he said.

"Why not?"

He stared out the window. "Because I made a promise."

"To Dewey?"

"That's right." He glanced back at me. "What do you think, Bill? Does the death of the promisee relieve the promisor of his obligation?"

"I'd think it would depend on the terms of the promise."

He said sourly, "You should have been a lawyer, Bill. But in this case, I believe the terms are clear. I promised not to reveal the subject of our argument until he told me I could do so, and he died before he could release me from that promise."

"Does that mean you won't tell me?" Molly asked.

"Not at the moment."

"Later?" she asked.

I caught a fleeting smile at her persistence. "Perhaps later."

As Molly helped Donald out of the car, I got his wheelchair out of the trunk and set it up on the veranda.

When he saw what I was doing, he said, "Thanks, Bill, but I feel like stretching my legs."

"You sure?" Molly asked him.

He patted her hand. "I'm not crippled, Emily, just sick. And I feel strong today."

Still concerned, she said, "Just don't overdo it, okay?"

"That's a promise."

Cyrus opened the front door and broke into a huge grin at the sight of Donald. He took his hand and pumped it, saying, "It's awful good to see you, Mister Don."

Donald grinned back at him. "Good to see you, too, Cyrus. Where's that ornery wife of yours?"

"Layin' out a fancy dinner for you. I sure hope you brought your appetite."

"For Ida's cooking?" he asked. "I'm hungry right now."

"Well, I'll go get your things out of the car." He nodded to the right. "Miz Helen's in the front parlor."

"Thanks, Cyrus. I know the way." He started toward the open doors, and Molly had to jog to keep up. Sick or not, when Donald got up a head of steam, he could move.

He stopped just inside the room, as Helen stood and came to greet us. She was dressed as I'd seen her that first day—in a silk blouse and a gray skirt—but she was on her feet now and moving with new energy. She kissed Molly on the cheek and squeezed my hand, then she took both of Donald's hands, and they stood there looking at each other for a moment.

Eyes brimming, he said finally, "I'm sorry the old bastard's dead, Helen. You know I loved him, too. But now, at last, you're free to marry the right Flanagan brother."

Smiling through her tears, she said, "You're a tease, Donald. You wouldn't want an old woman like me."

"The hell I wouldn't," he declared. "I may be a dried-out husk of my former self, but you're still as fresh and beautiful as the day Dewey brought you home."

Glancing at us, she said, "We mustn't give the young ones the wrong impression."

"They're not that young," he said, "and what do we care about their impressions?"

She shook her head and told us, "Let this be a lesson to you, children. Old flirtations never die."

"And unlike old soldiers," Donald added for our edification, "neither do they fade away."

They continued in this playful, bantering vein, but there was a definite spark there, maybe even a banked fire.

When we were back in our room, I asked Molly, "How much of that was real?"

She shook her head in amazement. "Don't ask me. I couldn't believe what I was hearing."

"Then you didn't know about their . . . feelings for each other?"

"Never had an inkling," she said. "And I'm supposed to be the detective."

"You don't suppose Donald's fight with Dewey was over Helen, do you?"

"Right now, I'd say that sounds like a reasonable hypothesis."

While dressing for dinner, we switched on the news and learned that the Medical Examiner had ruled Dewey's death a suicide. And Doctor Frederick's hunch about a physical basis for Dewey's behavior had proven prophetic, as the M.E. had discovered a previously undiagnosed brain tumor that was believed to be the culprit. It appeared that Dewey had been driven to take his life by a diseased lump of tissue in his brain.

15

Ida outdid herself with dinner. The main course was a golden-crusted Beef Wellington, as mouthwateringly tasty as it was beautiful. We unanimously agreed that it was a triumph, but Molly and I had to eat more than our share, to make up for Helen, who ate little, and Donald, who ate hardly at all.

Helen had heard about the Medical Examiner's ruling, too, and wasn't pleased. "David Cleveland was Dewey's friend," she said stiffly. "How could he say such a thing?"

"I'm sure," Donald said quietly, "that Doctor Cleveland was only giving his frank appraisal of the evidence."

Helen turned on him. "Are you saying Dewey killed himself?"

He raised a hand. "No, Dewey wouldn't do that."

She was confused. "But then—"

"*He* wouldn't," he said, "but the tumor might."

A tear rolled down her cheek. "Then it wasn't Dewey?"

"No, Helen," he said gently, "it was the madness."

After giving her a moment to recover, Molly said, "I, for one, think you have grounds for suing Riverside Center."

But Helen didn't care for the idea. "Lawsuits," she said with an expression of disdain, "are always so messy."

"As well as embarrassing," said Donald. He turned to Molly. "I know that Dewey meant a lot to you, Emily, and I understand your need to find a guilty party in this, some-one to blame. But you need look no further for the culprit than Doctor Cleveland's ruling. It was a tumor that drove

Dewey mad. Now, you might question whether Doctor, uh—"

"Fredericks," she supplied.

"Yes, there might be some question about whether Doctor Fredericks should have found the tumor sooner," he said. "But from what you've told me, he was doing all he could with the equipment he had. He would have needed something more sophisticated than X rays to positively establish the presence of the tumor, and yet he saw a hint of it where others hadn't. It would appear that he was on the verge of locating the problem, but he simply wasn't given time. As you know, juries are extremely unpredictable," he concluded, "but I doubt you'd win a malpractice suit against him."

"What about negligence?" she asked. "Dewey was clearly left unattended for too long. And there's the plastic knife."

He nodded. "As for the knife, you might have more luck suing the supplier, or the manufacturer. But whoever you sue, Dewey's recent behavior will become evidence. Do you think he would have wanted the question of his sanity to be a matter for public discussion?"

"No," said Helen.

Molly started to disagree, but changed her mind and said only, "The decision's yours, of course."

"Yes," Helen quietly agreed, "it is."

When she and Donald began to reminisce about better times, Molly got into the spirit and contributed some memories of her own. Because these were generous people, they even tried to make me part of the discussion, explaining references and relationships whenever possible. But I would have needed a genealogy table to keep track of all the players, and they eventually tabled the reminiscing in favor of more universal matters, such as my writing. Donald had just finished my first mystery, and after hearing his generous comments, I no longer felt left out.

If I was right about Helen having a drinking problem, I

saw no evidence of it that evening. She didn't finish her first glass of wine.

Donald barely touched his. He smiled more than usual, obviously pleased with the company, but his energy was fading fast, and I suspected he was in pain. The signs were subtle, no more than an occasional flinch or tremor, but he'd had lots of practice at concealing it. He struggled to finish the meal, but gave up the fight as dessert was being served.

Shoving his chair back, he said, "This has been one of the most enjoyable evenings I've spent in years. Wonderful food, good conversation, excellent company." He smiled at each of us and ended with a sitting bow to Helen. "But it's been a long day, and I'm feeling tired." As Cyrus helped him into his wheelchair, Donald caught our worried expressions and said, "It's only jet lag. I'll be fine in the morning."

We smiled and nodded, and none of us believed him.

"He's dying," Molly said to me a few minutes later, on our way up the stairs.

"Is that what the doctors say?"

"Oh, I could find one to say almost *anything*," she replied with a sneer. "A month ago, one told me my father was in remission and assured me we had nothing to fear for a few months at least. Three days later, daddy was back in intensive care." She shook her head in frustration. "Now one gives him six weeks; another says six months; and the most honest one in the bunch just shakes his head and throws up his hands."

"What about the one who said he was in remission?"

"He hasn't got back to me yet," she said dryly. "The truth is, they're all just guessing." As we reached the top of the stairs and started down the hallway, she said, "Tell me the truth. How does he look to you?"

"I thought he was a goner when they rolled him off the plane," I admitted, "but he was a new man when he got here. And when he saw Helen . . ."

"I know," she said, "he seemed years younger. But to-night he was so weak, and I knew he was hurting." She threw open the door to our rooms, and I followed her in. I closed the door as she hurled open the French doors to the veranda and cried out to the distant Smokies, "It just makes me mad! I see him like this, and I know there's not a damn thing I can do about it. And I feel so useless."

"I know," I said.

"I know you know. That's why I can talk to you about it. Because you've been there, with your father, and you know what it's like to watch it happen. But you've only seen Daddy when he was sick. I remember him as tall and strong and always on the move. That this should happen to such a man—" She shook her head. "I was going to say it isn't fair, but everyone knows that fairness has nothing to do with it. But I'll say this much," she said. "If I *believed* in God, he'd have a lot to answer for."

"That's the problem with God," I agreed. "If he's responsible, he's a homicidal maniac. If he isn't, what good is he?"

She laughed bitterly. "It just *hurts* to watch, that's all."

"I know." What else could I say? I wanted to go to her and hold her, but I knew it wasn't time. She was back to pacing now, and she'd have to kill some of her momentum before I could touch her.

"I just don't know how much fight he has left in him," she said.

"You have to hope, right?"

"And pray," she said. "I may not believe, but I still pray." She shrugged. "It's just a habit, I guess. But some-times it helps to talk things out, even if it's only with your-self."

"Well, if talking to yourself counts," I said, "then I pray all the time."

She laughed. "Maybe that's it: Maybe prayer was in-vented by somebody who didn't want to look like an idiot when he got caught talking to himself."

"You might have something there," I said.

As promised, Donald was much improved the next morning. He ran out of energy again in the afternoon and had to retire to his rooms for a few hours. But he seemed restored by his nap, and he was able to go with us to pay our respects to Dewey's remains. Helen had originally wanted Dewey laid in state in the bighouse, but Molly had persuaded her that it wasn't a good idea.

The funeral home was a big white Victorian house on a hillside below St. Mary's Medical Center. The porch boards boomed hollowly underfoot, but inside, it was all lush carpeting and hushed silence.

A dapper older gentleman in a dark suit greeted us inside, solemnly asked the name of the deceased, and with a conjurer's wave, directed us through open doors to the right. I caught a glimpse of another viewing taking place in the room across the hall, and judging from the traffic in the corridor ahead, there was at least one other dead person being showcased here tonight. It would appear to be a recession-proof business. People might give up a lot of things in hard times, but they were bound to keep on dying.

The viewing room occupied the northwest corner of the house, running about forty feet by twenty, with a high ceiling and tall windows along the long wall to the right and the shorter one straight ahead. The room was pleasantly homey with comfortable furniture arranged around the fireplaces at opposite ends, and the casket sat between them against the left-hand wall. It had been transformed by a jungle of floral tributes into a parade float, and the smell was thick and sweet enough to make you gag.

As was typical of such viewings, the appearance of the corpse was the hot topic of conversation. But as common as it was, it always struck me as weird to hear people talk about how good the deceased looked. It was true that

Dewey's corpse was the veritable picture of ruddy good health, but who was that meant to fool? Nobody wanted to see his or her loved one go out on a bad hair day, or with a sloppy makeup job, but no matter how good he looked, Dewey was still as dead as chivalry.

I suffered through an endless series of introductions, promptly forgetting most of the names before their owners turned away. I made a feeble stab at memorizing all the Flanagans, but I'm no good at names, and there were just too many of them, most with the requisite red hair and ruddy cheeks, green eyes and freckles, and that quietly well-groomed look of the well-to-do. Molly had explained that the family's interlocking commercial interests kept the majority of them gainfully employed.

Dewey and Helen's daughters, Ruth and Rachel, were there. Ruth was my age, forty-five, Rachel a couple of years older, both married with children. Ruth made her home in Louisville, Kentucky, Rachel in D.C. Ruth was a housewife and Junior Leaguer. Rachel ran a political consulting firm. Ruth looked matronly in her Laura Ashley. Rachel remained slender and attractive in her Donna Karan. Ruth made a show of kissing her father and was led away sobbing by a stout man I took for her husband. Rachel looked down at Dewey for a moment, kissed a finger and pressed it to his cold lips, then walked away with tears in her eyes. I couldn't say which was the more heartfelt demonstration, but as a matter of taste, I preferred restraint.

Rachel, who seemed to be alone, came straight from the casket to give her mother a hug, then sat with her and Donald on the couch, where Helen was receiving condolences. Meanwhile, Ruth took up a position on the other side of the room with her stout hubby and a chubby teenage boy and stared at her mother with tight-lipped disapproval. I was going to ask Molly what that was about when I was distracted by an older woman in outlandish mourning attire, who swept up to us on the arm of a well-dressed young man.

The woman wore a black silk dress, a black feather boa

around her shoulders, and a tall, black-feathered hat. The dark veil had been thrown upward to expose her face and hung from the feathers of her hat like a misplaced badminton net. The woman looked considerably older than Helen, but her true age was difficult to determine under the troweled-on layers of makeup that she wore to conceal it.

"Oh, Helen, my dear, my dear," she moaned in a hoarse whiskey voice, bending to touch her cheek to Helen's and leaving a faint smudge of color behind. "I know how desolated you must be by this calamity. Such a shock!" she cried. "I just couldn't believe it. I accused the scoundrels of lying to me at first. It sounded so preposterous! And"—she dropped into a stage whisper—"as for this silly business of suicide, I don't believe it for a moment, do you? Well, of course you don't," she went on without pause. "How could you? Not our Dewey. I defy anyone to say such a thing in my presence!" Casting a haughty eye to all sides in search of challengers, she continued, "Such a good man, good father, and good brother. And," she quickly added, "good husband, I'm sure. What a tragic irony that he should be taken from us at this time, when his last great fight was yet to be fought. A misguided fight, I believe, as you know my feelings about Shamrock. But it was to be Dewey's sad fate to defend her to the bitter end. Perhaps," she solemnly concluded, "this was God's way of relieving him of such a tiresome burden."

At the end of this bewildering ramble, Helen said simply, "It's good to see you, too, Beatrice."

"Well, of course it is, my dear," said Beatrice. "Always a pleasure. And if there's anything, absolutely *anything*, I can do for you, you know you have only to call."

"You can count on it," Helen assured her.

"Anything," the woman repeated.

"Anything," Helen agreed.

With that, the woman made kissy motions with her lips, then fluttered her fingers in farewell and sailed away on the arm of her youthful escort.

"Who was that?" I asked in a whisper.

"Aunt Beatrice," Molly whispered back, "Darrell's wife's sister."

"Haven't seen a getup like that since Gloria Swanson in *Sunset Boulevard*."

"Beatrice is eccentric."

"Seemed a tad incoherent," I said.

"That, too," Molly agreed. "She may be certifiably insane, but who's going to tell her? She owns a small township up near the Kentucky line, and anyone who doesn't approve of her behavior is simply asked to leave."

"Is the young man her son?"

She laughed.

"Ah."

There were more black people in attendance than I would have expected. Several worked for Shamrock, but I also met a prominent dentist, a city councilman, and Reverend and Mrs. Nehemiah Waters of the Five-Point Baptist Tabernacle Church. Molly explained that the Reverend's church had a terrific gospel choir, and that Dewey had been one of their biggest fans.

Darrell and Duncan arrived late, but they worked the room hard to make up for their tardiness, shaking hands and speaking quietly to everyone in sight.

They were conferring with Beatrice when Darrell spotted somebody and left the group. He intercepted a young black man just inside the door and spoke to him quietly. The young man didn't look pleased with what Darrell had to say, but he finally nodded and left. Curious, I thought.

After speaking to Ruth and her husband, Darrell and Duncan went to say their farewells to Dewey. They took a respectful moment at the casket, then turned toward us. At which point Helen smiled at her last mourner, then unhurriedly got to her feet and made a dignified exit, leaving Darrell and Duncan with sad faces ready and nobody to condole.

16

The funeral mass was held at one o'clock on Friday afternoon at Holy Ghost Catholic Church, located on North Central across from a defunct Sears. It wasn't a big church, but it was handsome, especially on the inside, with its Norman Gothic arches and vaulted ceiling, intricately carved altar and splendid stained-glass windows.

Molly and I sat on the right front pew with Helen and Donald and Helen's older daughter, Rachel, plus Helen's brother and sister and their spouses, who had driven up from Atlanta. There were a handful from Dewey's side of the family seated behind us, scattered among rows of Shamrock employees and their families. But the majority of Flanagans, including Helen's younger daughter, Ruth, sat on the other side of the central aisle, where Darrell and Duncan and their respective broods occupied the places of honor down front. I caught the brothers looking at Helen several times during the service, but she never so much as glanced their way.

It appeared that Dewey knew everybody who was anybody in Tennessee. The VIP list included the Lieutenant Governor, the Mayor, one Senator, two members of Congress, and the whole City Council, as well as a famous country singer, whose first job had been at Shamrock, and a Pulitzer Prize-winning novelist, who based a recurring character in a series of books on Dewey. Also present was Knoxville's first Bishop, Reverend Anthony J. O'Connell, ordained and installed in 1988. The funeral mass was performed by the pastor of Holy Ghost Church, Reverend Andrew C. Lanahan.

Music was provided in foot-stompin' black gospel fashion by the Five-Point Baptist Tabernacle Choir, wearing shiny gold robes bought for them by Dewey. They were led by Reverend Nehemiah Waters, whom we'd seen at the viewing the evening before. The choir loft was located over the main entrance at the back of the sanctuary, and there was a good deal of neck craning and head bobbing every time they broke into song.

The novelist spoke for the deceased from the lectern. "Dewey George Flanagan was bigger than life, which made him perfect for fiction." To polite chuckles, he added, "He was a man of curious contradictions. A hard-hearted businessman, who actually cared about his workers." There were amens from behind us. "A tight-fisted SOB, who'd give his last farthing to a friend. And a bad poker player, who took more unemployment checks off me than I'd care to remember." More laughter, heartier this time. "He was no saint, but he was a man of his word." More amens and a general murmuring of agreement. "Even his enemies would tell you that." It could have been a coincidence that he glanced toward the other side of the aisle on the word "enemies," but I had to wonder how much he knew.

"I owe the man a debt of gratitude that he sadly didn't live to collect," he went on, "but I'll continue to do what I can to repay him. He'll live on in my stories, if only because I can't afford to let him die, and if I can ever manage to make my readers see the man I knew, then maybe we can finally call it even." Looking down at us on the front row, he said, "To his wife, Helen, I can only say that you won't be alone in missing him, sweetheart." She smiled and gave him a nod, then he bowed to her and left the podium.

The singer was up next. He'd made himself a real southern success story by transforming a brief stay at the county work farm as a teenager into a lifetime as The Outlaw Troubadour. He always wore black, so his present attire didn't necessarily denote mourning, but he seemed sincerely broken up about Dewey. With tears in his eyes, he said in that familiar, gravelly voice, "If it wudn't for Dewey Flanagan, I'd be dead now, or in prison. He give me a job when I needed one bad and good advice when I didn't wanna hear it. He saw I had talent long before I did, and he forced me to do something with it. He even bought me my first tour bus. I grew to hate that bus," he concluded with a grin, "but I never felt anything but friendship for the man who give it to me."

Short and stirring. I was impressed.

As the altar was prepared for the Eucharist, he joined the singers in the choir loft to sing his rendition of the Lord's Prayer. His voice was pretty rough these days, but he could always caress a lyric, and he didn't miss with this one.

Calvary Cemetery was small, reflecting the relative scarcity of Catholics in the area. Granite and marble tombstones were jammed into a tight little fenced-in square of hillside on Martin Luther King Boulevard. It was located near 5-Points—generally considered to be the most dangerous part of town—on the eastern edge of the downtown area, not far from Shamrock Coffee, situated between the two largest low-income housing projects, Austin Homes to the west and the Walter P. Taylor Homes to the east.

A crowd of the country singer's fans had watched us leave the church, then had apparently hopped into their cars and had driven ahead to wait for us at the cemetery. Older, fatter, and for the most part, considerably better-behaved than most groupies in my experience, they politely lined up to catch a glimpse of their idol from behind crowd barriers and a cordon of police. Leaning down to stare into the limo as it slowed down, their chubby pink faces squinting in the sunlight, they wore expressions of painful anticipation.

I was watching a policeman escort an overexuberant female fan back behind the barriers when I spotted a face I knew. As the car rolled on, I lost the face for a moment, then caught a final glimpse before it was swallowed by the crowd. Hard and masculine, with strong vertical lines on either side of the mouth and long dark hair tied back in a ponytail: more the face of a roadie than a groupie. I couldn't think where I'd seen him before, and he was out of sight before I could show him to Molly.

The old concrete driveway that led through the cemetery was so narrow and the turns so tight that only the hearse was allowed to enter. The rest of the cars in the procession were parked along Martin Luther King, and the mourners had to get out and walk into the cemetery.

There was a reception for friends and family at the big-house after the graveside service.

There was food and drink, sadness and tears, loud talk and intermittent laughter, singing and people taking turns on the grand piano. It was a curious mix of mourning and celebration, a party with a quiet corner—the one where Helen sat on a couch.

Rachel sat to her left and Donald to her right, and Molly and I stood behind them. I was wondering if I could sneak out for a joint when I saw Darrell approaching with Duncan at his side.

Duncan spoke first. "I'm so sorry, Helen."

Carefully matching his brother's tone, Darrell added, "What a tragedy."

Helen stared up at Darrell coldly and said in a clear, strong voice, "Yes, it *is* a tragedy, Darrell, and I hold you responsible."

The people around us suddenly grew quiet.

Darrell drew back, stuttering, "B-But I-I-I—"

"By insisting that he be locked up," Helen went on, "you killed him as surely as if you'd put a bullet in his brain. So I'll ask you to leave now. You're no longer welcome in our house."

Darrell's mouth moved, but nothing audible emerged.

Only Duncan came to his defense, saying quietly, "I think you're being unfair, Helen."

"Then you can go with him, Duncan," she said flatly. "As his ally, I consider you equally responsible, and I'll ask you to leave my house as well."

Darrell angrily gathered up his family and left, but Duncan stopped to speak to several people on his way out, making it clear that he would leave, yes, but at his own pace. The people he spoke to looked uncomfortable, but Duncan didn't seem to notice. If his wife or children were present, I didn't see them.

After an hour or so, the party spilled out of the house into the garden, and soon there were drunken revelers in the pool. Some wore swimsuits borrowed from the pool house, and one audacious young couple wore nothing at all.

Molly and I decided that was going too far, and we were trying to get them out of the water and back into their clothes when the boss of the security detail came to tell us that the summerhouse had been ransacked.

We left the couple to their nudity and stepped aside with the security man to discuss the matter.

"You call the cops?" Molly asked him.

"Thought I'd better tell you first," he said.

She nodded approvingly. "When did it happen?"

"Hard to say," he said. "We get up there every half hour or so, give it a walk-around, and check the padlock on the screen door. But the lock was still in place this time, so he either picked it, then put it back, or he got in some other way. I was about to head for the car when I saw that a door to one of the rooms was open a crack, and I decided we'd better go in and take a look."

"I want to see it," she said.

"What about the cops?" he asked.

"Call them," she said, "and leave somebody on the gate to let them in. We'll be up at the summerhouse."

* * *

The place was torn up: every drawer pulled out; every mattress stripped; every closet emptied; the contents of every kitchen container dumped onto the counters or the floor.

"Damn thorough," said Molly.

"Looks malicious to me," I said.

"Probably in a hurry, too," she said, "having to do it in half-hour rushes between visits from the security guards."

"Who has a grudge against your family?"

"I don't know," she said. "I'm out of touch. Haven't spent any time here in thirty years."

"Maybe it's an old grudge," he said, "something from the past."

She shrugged. "I was only a kid when I left, and I can't think of anybody."

"Looks like we already searched everything *he* searched."

"Yeah," she agreed.

"So chances are he didn't find anything."

"Probably not."

"Then he might come back."

"That's right."

"Maybe we should station one of the guards up here."

"Good idea," she said. "I'll tell them."

It was dark when I finally got a chance to sneak away down to the grape arbor to smoke a joint. Clouds were moving in from the west, and the wind was kicking up. It looked like rain, and I figured we'd soon have to move the party back inside.

I found a couple of other guys down there for the same purpose, and they greeted me in the manner of pot smokers everywhere, treating me like an old friend and generously sharing their joint, pipe, and bottle of cold Chablis. When I had a good buzz on, I headed back to the party before Molly missed me. She tolerated my smoking, but she was a cop, after all, and I preferred to keep it to myself as much as possible.

As I stepped out of the grape arbor, somebody collided with me from the left and knocked me onto my backside.

Then a shadow bent over me, and a raspy voice asked, "You okay, buddy?"

"Think so."

He laughed. "Feelin' no pain, huh?"

"Not much," I agreed.

"Does Molly know you're a pothead?"

"What?"

"You heard me," he snarled, suddenly getting nasty. "Does she know?"

"Who the hell are you?" I snapped back.

"You don't want to know," he replied coldly.

"Yeah, I do," I said, talking tough, but feeling vulnerable with him hanging over me like that.

"Take my word for it," he said, putting menace into a voice that didn't need it. "You don't want to know anything about me."

"That's a threat, right?" I said, scooting backward.

"No, but this is."

I heard the distinct double click of a gun being cocked. Then there were voices behind me, and I turned to yell, "Hey!"

A voice asked, "What?"

When I turned back, the shadow was gone. I heard him running off to the right, but he was already out of sight.

I was back on my feet when the two men stepped out of the arbor.

"Was that you that yelled?" one asked.

"Nope."

"That's weird," he said.

"Yeah."

But the other one was oblivious. "Good weed, huh?"

"Kick-ass," I agreed, and we went back to the party together.

Several times that evening, I started to tell Molly what had happened, but the incident didn't seem quite real. And

what could I tell her? That I'd been knocked down, threatened by a shadow, and had heard what sounded like a gun
being cocked? It sounded foolish, even to me, and when
you tossed in the fact that I was stoned at the time, well
. . . In the end, I said nothing about it.

17

Saturday morning, during breakfast on the veranda, Molly said, "It's time we checked out Darrell's mobster."

I wasn't quite awake yet. "His what?"

"The bookie Helen mentioned? The one Darrell owes money?"

"But we don't even know his name, do we?"

"I know somebody who might be able to tell us his name."

She called another old school chum, now a reporter for the *News-Sentinel*. He was at his desk on a Saturday morning finishing something for the Sunday edition, and Molly made a date to meet him for lunch at Regas Restaurant, the same restaurant where Dewey was supposed to have met Duncan the previous Friday.

As she hung up, she said, "I'd like to talk to Lester Prine, but I'm not sure where to find him."

"Prine is the developer with the twenty-three and a half mil?"

"Right on the first try," she said proudly. "We need to talk to everybody who might profit from Dewey's death."

"But what would Prine be looking for in the summer-house?"

"The same as Darrell or Duncan," she said.

"Which is?"

"I don't know," she admitted. "If he only wanted Dewey

127

out of the way, he already had that. Still, it wouldn't hurt to find out if he's in town."

She called his offices in Atlanta and learned from an assistant that Mister Prine was in Miami, but that he would be flying up to Knoxville sometime the following week. Molly explained who she was and said she'd like to speak to him while he was in town, and the assistant promised to mention it to her boss.

On our way to the meeting with Molly's journalist friend, I got my first real taste of Big Orange Country. I'd noticed the hand-painted GO VOL signs on shop windows all over town, but today the orange was out in force, glaring in the sunlight: orange flags and pennants, pom-poms and sport jackets, cowboy hats and boots, ties and vests, fake-fur chaps (I especially liked those) and handbags, hair and complete suits of clothing, even orange-painted vehicles.

We got caught in game traffic—a line of cars creeping along, bumper to bumper, stretching out of sight in front of us. Most were presumably on their way to Neyland Stadium on the University of Tennessee campus to see their powerful, high-scoring, and much-beloved Tennessee Volunteers beat the bejeezus out of some much-despised opponent.

"This is ridiculous," I said. "Is there another route?"

"I doubt any of them will be much better," she said. "I forgot about the game today."

"We better try something."

"Okay," she said with a sigh, "take a left at the next cross street."

"If we ever get that far."

We worked our way via backstreets, dodging traffic where we could, and made it to our appointment only about ten minutes late.

Regas Restaurant was on the northern edge of downtown, almost underneath an elevated stretch of I-40, on the corner of Gay and Magnolia. Yes, Knoxville had a Gay

Street. Outside, the restaurant was a two-story building of freshly painted brown and beige brick. Inside, it was a quietly elegant place, smelling of good food and coffee, after-dinner mints, and the hostess's musky perfume.

Molly's friend was at a table in the back corner of the lounge—a tall, skinny guy in black horn-rims and a wrinkled summerweight suit. He was probably a few years younger than me, around Molly's age, but I was secretly relieved to see that he was nearly bald on top.

He stood, almost overturning the table in the process, and narrowly averted knocking over his water glass by righting it with one hand as he reached for Molly's with the other. "Good to see you, Molly," he said in an unexpectedly high and twangy voice that made me even happier.

"You, too, Ollie. This is Bull Cochran. Bull, this is Oliver Fryman."

We shook hands and agreed that it was a pleasure to meet each other, then he said to Molly, "We'll have to order now. I need to be back at the paper in an hour."

As the waitress left with our orders, Oliver said, "I was awfully sorry to hear about Dewey. He was one of my favorite people, and Knoxville won't be the same without him."

"No, it won't," Molly agreed, "and thanks."

"You said you wanted to pick my brain. 'Bout what?"

"Organized crime."

He grinned. "In K-town?"

"That's right."

"Well, I can tell you right off that it's more criminal than organized."

"No big-time mobsters around?"

"They wouldn't be *here* if they were," he said. "Which isn't to say that we have no crooks. There're lots of small-timers around and one or two medium-size money men, who provide the capital for the drug traffic and sports gambling."

"Who?"

He frowned. "You know, these aren't the kind of people you walk up to and say, 'How's tricks?' "

"I *know* that," she said. "I'm a cop, remember."

"Not around here, you're not. And the local cops might not appreciate your interfering in their bailiwick, or appreciate my helping you do it. Why do you need this information?"

The waitress appeared with our iced teas. After she left, Molly confided, "Somebody I know has a gambling problem, and I'm afraid he's in deep to one of your money people."

Oliver smiled. "This somebody wouldn't be your uncle Darrell, would it?"

She said, "How'd you—?"

He chuckled. "I'm a reporter, remember? And this is my beat."

"How much do you know?"

"I've heard that he likes long odds and high stakes, and he had a rep as a good loser."

"Meaning what?" I asked.

"Meaning he paid off his losses on time. But rumor has it that his bets are getting bigger and his payoffs slower, and he's starting to run up tabs with guys who don't offer credit."

"Do you know who?" Molly asked.

"I might have some idea," he said. "But you have to understand that I have a kind of relationship with these people, and they expect me to abide by certain rules in my dealings with them. One rule is that I don't hand out names and addresses to just anybody. But," he concluded, as the waitress brought our salads, "give me a few days, and I'll see if he's willing to talk to you. How does that sound?"

"Sounds fine," she said.

"Good," he said. "Then let's eat."

* * *

That afternoon, Molly decided she wanted to take another look at the summerhouse.

We concentrated on the floors this time, forcing us to move some of the debris out of the way and do a little straightening up as we went along. Molly even had me going around wiping off traces of fingerprint powder left on doors and doorjambs and doorknobs and dresser drawers. We started with the storeroom on the west end and worked our way east, mostly on our knees, looking for loose boards or a trapdoor. We worked at it off and on for a couple of hours, taking a break now and then so I could rest the knee I'd twisted in the minors. I'd hurt it tripping over a base—yes, I was a demon on the base paths—and it had recently started to throb, especially in wet weather. We searched the backs of drawers and the undersides of mattresses and cushions, checking to see if they'd been resewn, and we looked in the wood stove and the stovepipe. But we didn't find anything.

Sunday morning we went back up to the summerhouse to finish our search. At noon, Cyrus brought us a thermos of iced tea and a picnic lunch of roasted chicken, coleslaw, and potato salad. It was a pleasant day, and we ate under a tree by the stream.

After lunch, we searched the attic. It was hot and stuffy and dusty, and judging from the unbroken cobwebs, the burglar hadn't made it up there, but we gave it a good look anyway. I swapped a fair amount of sweat for a thick layer of dirt, but our most interesting discovery was an abandoned squirrel's nest.

Afterward, I washed off in one of the bathrooms and chugged a tumbler of spring water, then poured myself another and joined Molly on the porch. Halfway through the second glass of water, I felt restored enough to ask, "What's left to search?"

"Just the caves."

"Oh, right."

She laughed and said, "Don't panic. You won't have to face them until Tuesday at the earliest. Tomorrow's the reading of the will."

The reading took place Monday afternoon at the posh art deco offices of Ayers, Cross, and Murdoch. They were located on an upper floor of the Plaza Tower, built by ex-con, ex-banker, Jake Butcher.

The affair was a tense one, with warring parties encamped on opposite sides of a long, mahogany conference table. I sat with Molly, Helen, Rachel, Donald, Ida, and Cyrus on one side, while the younger daughter, Ruth, sat with Darrell and Duncan on the other. And again I couldn't help wondering why Ruth bore such a grudge against her mother.

The Murdoch of Ayers, Cross, and Murdoch—a dignified older gentleman with a baggy face and steel-gray hair—sat at the head of the table in front of a curtained window. After attesting to the will's legitimacy, he read it to us in his resonant baritone. The document was brief.

Helen got Dewey's stocks, bonds, and money market accounts, plus the bighouse and most of his other lands and properties. The house on Douglas Lake went to Cyrus and Ida as a retirement home, along with a generous monthly stipend to cover their living expenses, taxes, and the upkeep of the property. Ruth and Rachel each got two hundred thousand dollars, and trusts had been established for each of their children. In addition, there were numerous smaller gifts of money and property, including a house and something called "Mitch's Market" to a Ms. Sybil Deets.

Molly answered my questioning look by mouthing, "Tim's mother."

There was something for almost everyone at the table. Donald received editions of Kipling and Dickens, Molly a first-edition set of C. S. Lewis's *Chronicles of Narnia*. Darrell got a book called *Beating the Odds: How to Kick the*

Gambling Habit, Duncan the collected epigrams of Oscar Wilde, and Aunt Beatrice, who wasn't present, a copy of *Witchcraft Through the Ages*.

There were covered smiles on our side of the table, but none of our opposites seemed to find it even faintly amusing.

18

Rachel was booked into the Hyatt Regency—a curious, Aztec-like lean-to of reinforced concrete east of downtown. It sat on a hilltop overlooking the river, across Hill Avenue from the Civic Auditorium and Coliseum. All of us from Helen's side of the table went there for drinks after the reading and sat in the lobby bar gazing up at seven stories of balconies, watching the tinted-glass elevators ferry guests to the upper floors.

We all had beer or wine, except the Wesners: Ida because she didn't cotton to strong drink, and Cyrus, who cast an occasional longing glance at my beer, because he was driving. The reading had left us a quiet group, and nobody had much to say until Helen talked Rachel into giving us the lowdown on current Washington gossip. That kept us entertained until Donald began to weave in his chair, then Helen asked Cyrus to drive them home. But Molly and I stayed to have dinner with Rachel.

We went to her suite after we ate and talked until midnight. We told her what we knew about her father's death, and she answered some of our questions.

She remembered Dewey's fight with Donald. "Started one evening after dinner not long before you went to Texas," she said to Molly. "But you know that; you were there."

"For some of it," said Molly. "I remember them going into the study. But as soon as they started to raise their voices, Ida hustled me out of there and up to my room, so I didn't hear what it was about."

"It was about Mother, of course," said Rachel.

"You *know* that?"

"Well, I didn't actually hear them shout her name," she said. "Just as I was starting to catch a few words, they went out into the garden."

"Was it a real fight?" asked Molly. "Were punches thrown?"

"Oh, yes, and they wrestled on the ground a little. But mostly they stalked around in circles yelling at each other."

"Could you hear what they were saying?"

"No, though Ruth and I tried. Ida wouldn't let us open the French doors, but she couldn't keep us away from the windows."

"Then you don't know what they were arguing about?"

"I didn't hear it, no," she said, "but I didn't have to. I knew what it was about."

"How old were you?"

"I was eighteen," she said. "It was the summer after my freshman year at UT."

"And Ruth?"

"She would have been fifteen at the time."

"How did you know what it was about?"

"It was no secret to anyone in the house."

"It was to *me*," Molly objected.

Rachel gave her a sisterly pat. "I guess you were too young. But for the rest of us, it was pretty obvious. I don't mean that Mother and Donald were indiscreet, because they weren't. They never touched in our presence, but your father ate dinner with us most evenings, and the looks they gave each other spoke paragraphs."

"Then you never actually saw them touch?" asked Molly.

Rachel blushed. "I . . . well, yes, I did, actually. I'm ashamed to admit that I spied on them one evening. It wasn't premeditated, but when my chance came, I didn't look away. It was after midnight, and I'm sure they thought we were all in bed, but I was on my way to the kitchen for a snack when I spotted them in the back parlor. The door was open only a few inches, but I could see them well enough. They stood still in the middle of the room, a couple of feet apart, holding hands and staring at each other. They looked . . . I don't know . . . I guess 'contented' is the word. I don't mean in a sexual sense, I mean with each other, with just standing there holding hands and gazing at each other." She laughed quietly. "It was, without a doubt, the most romantic moment I've ever witnessed."

"How serious was their relationship, do you think?" asked Molly.

"Did they consummate it, you mean? I didn't think so at the time, but now, I don't know. Daddy was having one of his flings and was away a lot. He was frequently out all night, and he vanished for whole weekends a couple of times, so Mother and Donald certainly had their chances. She was alone, and your father had lost your mother the year before." Again she shrugged and gave us a crooked smile. "How physical it became, I couldn't say, but I couldn't find it in my heart to begrudge them whatever pleasure they found."

Molly smiled. "That sounds like an awfully adult attitude for an eighteen-year-old."

"You grow up fast in this family," said Rachel, "or you don't grow up at all. But you know that. All you have to do is look at Darrell."

"Why is your sister so angry at your mother?" I asked.

"Ruth *did* begrudge them their pleasure," said Rachel. "She never forgave Mother for what she thought of as a betrayal of her father."

"Did Ruth know about your father's infidelity?"

"I don't know," Rachel said, "but I'm not sure it would have made any difference. Daddy had stopped coming home, and Ruth blamed Mother for that."

"Did Ruth always side with her father?" I asked.

"Usually."

"Just as you sided with your mother?"

"I didn't *want* to take sides," she objected. "I loved them both. I knew Daddy wasn't as happy-go-lucky as he liked to pretend, and I could see how much Mother was suffering. I would've helped them if I could, but there was nothing I could do, and at that point, more than anything, I just wanted out. Out of Knoxville, out of the house, and away from the family. I had it all planned: I'd get my bachelor's in three years, go to Georgetown for graduate work, then make a career in politics."

"All of which you did," said Molly.

"Well, the job isn't quite what I envisioned," she admitted. "I'd hoped to be the first woman Senator from Tennessee."

"I think you've done damn well," said Molly, "and I admire you for it."

Rachel smiled. "Thanks, but *you* were the real surprise in the family." She laughed in delight. "A Flanagan girl with a badge? Impossible!"

"How did people react to it?"

"As you'd expect. Most were surprised, me included. Some were shocked, or pretended to be. Some made jokes. Others said they admired your courage. But there were a few who just didn't like the idea of a woman being a cop."

"Probably more than a few," said Molly.

"Maybe fewer than you think," Rachel replied. "Don't sell people short."

"You're right," Molly said contritely. "What about Dewey and Helen?"

"Mother was worried about your going into a such a dangerous profession, but she also told me that she was proud of you, and I knew she meant it. As for Daddy, he thought it was a hoot," she said with a laugh. "He cackled about it for weeks, bragging that he was the one who'd taught you how to shoot and declaring to anybody who would listen that the bad guys might as well pack up and head for Dallas, because they no longer stood a chance in Houston."

Molly grinned. "Sounds like Dewey."

"*I* was proud of you, too," said Rachel.

"I know you were," said Molly. "I still have the letter you wrote me after I made detective."

"And you did it not just once," Rachel said in frank admiration, "but *twice!*"

When Molly was with the Houston Police, she filed a sexual harassment suit against her Captain. She won the suit, but felt ostracized by her fellow cops. She kept getting passed over for good assignments and found herself condemned to endless desk duty. But she worked a joint investigation with the Galveston police, and a Lieutenant Parkinson (now *Captain* Parkinson) told her to give him a holler if she ever needed a job. And she eventually hollered. She took a cut in pay and had to start over as a patrolman, but with Parkinson's help, she made it back to detective in record time.

Rachel said, "I know a little something about trying to prove yourself in a man's profession. Women are still a minority in my field as well. But the *police?* What made you do it?"

"I suppose Pat Lowry, my mother's younger brother, had a lot to do with it," said Molly. "He was a detective in Dallas, and I met him and his family not long after we moved to Texas. He had a girl about my age, who I was expected to play with, but I was more interested in riding around in Pat's police car, his radio crackling with static and strange messages. I decided right then that I wanted to be a cop, but I outgrew the idea, or so I thought.

"Seven years later, when I was a sophomore at Rice, Pat was killed saving a woman's life. He and his partner were off duty, standing in line at the bank, when four guys with shotguns and automatic weapons came in and told everybody to hit the floor. The place was too crowded for any cowboy stuff, so Pat and his partner went along, and even with the silent alarm, the perps should have been in and out before the cops arrived. But a patrol car just happened to cruise past, and the patrolmen saw the robbery going down through the front windows. They pulled over and called for backup, but the first perp out spotted them, did a quick about-face, and was back inside before they could get a bead on him.

"One of the gang started firing his automatic weapon into the ceiling and shouting that he was going to shoot his way out. Then another one grabbed the woman next to my uncle, and Pat went for his piece. He took out the guy holding the woman, but a shotgun drew down on him from ten feet away and caught him with a load straight in the chest, killing him instantly."

She shook her head. "When I heard what had happened, I could see it all so clearly. I even knew what Pat was thinking. I figured he *had* to see it coming when the perps failed to make their escape. And when the man grabbed the woman, that was it. Pat couldn't let him use her as a shield and probably get her killed. He was paid to stop it, so he did. It was as simple as that, and I wanted to be just like him.

"My forensic psych prof introduced me to a Houston detective named Denise James, and Denise talked to me about being a cop. She told me about the frustrations of the job. She said the hours were lousy and the pay only adequate. She explained that it was hell on a home life, that divorce rates among cops were ridiculously high, and that alcoholism and/or drug abuse were occupational hazards. It sounded perfect," she said with a grin, "and I signed up immediately."

Rachel smiled, then asked seriously, "Don't you ever get scared?"

"Of course I do."

"But you keep on doing it?"

Molly nodded. "They'll have to fire me, or retire me."

"Or you could get hurt," said Rachel.

"I was stabbed once in Houston when I was a rookie. Got peritonitis and spent a month in the hospital, so I know what that's like, too."

"And yet you went back," said Rachel.

"Yeah," she said. "The rough stuff is only a small part of it. Most of my work has nothing to do with that. Usually I just talk to people. I look at the scene of a crime and search for evidence. I sit in a car six, eight hours at a time, drinking bad coffee and watching a certain house, or car, or boat, or alley. Once in a very long while I get into a high-speed chase, but only three times have I had to shoot anybody."

"And one of those times," I said to Rachel, "was to save my life. She stopped a man from cutting me to pieces."

Molly grinned. "Seemed like a good idea at the time."

Rachel turned to me and touched her chin. "That's where you got this?" she asked.

"Yeah," I said. "Molly says it gives me character, but I noticed she shot the perp quick, before he could give me any more of it."

Rachel laughed, but Molly was tired of talking about herself. "So what happened after we moved to Texas?"

"Things didn't turn around overnight," said Rachel, "but they got better. Daddy was home more. He'd come close to losing Mother, and I think it scared him. He started going to AA and gave up drinking, or *tried* to. He fell off the wagon now and then, and Mother had her own drinking problem, though it was never as serious as his. They still fought, and I doubt that Daddy remained completely celibate outside the marriage bed, but at least he was more discreet about it.

"During the last ten or fifteen years, they've grown very close, and they've hardly been apart in all that time." She shook her head. "But that's what worries me. Mom's a tough lady, and she knows this is going to be hard, but I don't think she has any idea *how* hard."

That implied that Rachel *did* know, which sounded

equally unlikely to me. I had a notion that Helen was even tougher than her daughter realized, but I knew Rachel was only concerned for her mother's welfare, so I just nodded in agreement.

19

It was pouring rain, so I left Molly under the covered entrance, pulled my jacket over my head, and ran to get the Celica. I jogged down the sidewalk to the parking lot at the west end of the building and cut straight across to the car. The lot was nearly empty after midnight on a Monday evening, and I got halfway across before having to hold up for a minivan. Then I put my head down and loped the last fifty feet.

The Celica was just ahead, and I was reaching for the keys when I heard brakes screech to my left and turned to see a pickup truck bearing down on me. I froze for an instant, pinned by the headlights, then leapt out of the way— or tried to—but the truck kept veering in my direction.

I sprinted toward the Celica, but the truck was coming fast. It was close enough for me to see every dent in its battered grill when I threw myself into the air. I stretched out my arms toward the hood of the Celica and almost made it, but the truck's antenna barely ticked the toe on my trailing foot. Though it was just a touch, it nearly tore the antenna off, and it spun me completely around. I landed awkwardly, knocking the breath out of me. But I was facing the truck as it flashed past, and I caught a brief glimpse of the driver—a pale face and long dark hair pulled back into a ponytail.

Something clicked, and I saw another face: the one I'd spotted among the country singer's fans at the cemetery. And I suddenly remembered where I'd seen the face before.

*   *   *

"Riverside Center?" asked Molly.

"The maintenance man," I said, as I pulled the Celica away from the entrance, "the one we saw pushing the fan into the room where they had the fire."

She shook her head. "I remember the fan."

"It was *him*," I said. "And he was at the cemetery, too."

"The man you recognized in the crowd?"

"Right."

"So where is he now?"

"He drove away."

"Out of the lot?"

"Yeah . . . well, I think so."

"You didn't actually see him leave the lot?"

"No, I didn't," I admitted.

She glanced over her shoulder. "Then he could be behind us." Looking back at me, she asked, "You're sure it was the same man?"

"I'm sure the man at the cemetery and the maintenance man are the same."

"And the driver of the pickup?"

"Well, I—"

"Did you see his face?" She sounded tired and a little drunk.

"Just a glimpse," I admitted.

"And?"

I shrugged. "The ponytail looked the same."

"The ponytail," she repeated.

"Why would he try to run me down, if it wasn't the same guy?"

"*If* he was trying to run you down," she said.

"He came damn close to doing it!" I declared, irritated by her attitude.

She sighed. "You said you only saw the ponytail."

"And a white face."

"Well, that narrows it down," she said. "Half the good ole boys in this state sport ponytails. They're *all* white, and

143

they all love to get drunk and drive their pickups too fast."

"Why did he keep veering toward me?" I asked.

"The truck could've been out of control," she said, "and if he was drunk enough, he might not've even seen you."

"You think I'm jumping at shadows?"

"It's possible," she said. "Nearly getting killed is bound to make you nervous."

That was true, and I wondered if maybe I was letting my imagination run away with me. I hadn't actually seen the driver's face, and I couldn't imagine why the man would want to kill me anyway, but I decided to keep an eye out for him, just to be safe.

As we got onto I-275, I said, "We should go back to Riverside Center and check out the maintenance man."

"If he's still there," she said, covering a yawn.

"Even if he isn't, they should be able to tell us who he is."

"If he used his real name," she said, "which I doubt. But it gives us a place to start."

I watched for the pickup, but I couldn't see much in the rain. The wipers were barely coping with the deluge, and we were completely blinded every time a semi blew past, so I soon gave it up as a lost cause. By the time we reached 640, Molly was having trouble keeping her eyes open, and as I pulled onto Tazewell Pike, I saw that she'd dozed off.

Like most roads in East Tennessee, the pike never ran flat and straight for long. It rose and fell, veered and swerved, so I had to keep a constant eye out for the next kink in the road.

I was creeping along at twenty miles an hour, hunched over the steering wheel peering ahead, when a vehicle appeared behind me, headlights on bright. It was higher off the ground than the Celica, and the headlights were aimed straight into my rearview mirror.

"Molly," I whispered.

Nothing.

"Molly!"

144

"Wha?" she asked, still half-asleep.

"I think he's back."

The truck surged forward and hit us.

She sat up straight. "Wha'wazzat?"

"Sonofabitch rammed us!"

She looked back, suddenly wide-awake and sober. "Guess you were right," she said.

"Wish I'd been wrong."

"Better speed up."

"I can't see anything!"

As he hit us again, she turned to looked ahead, frowning at what she saw. "Where are we?"

"On Tazewell Pike."

"*Where?*"

"I don't know," I said. "A mile or two from the place where it turns east."

Glancing back, she said, "Here he comes again!"

"I see him!"

The impact was harder this time and accompanied by a bright crunching sound.

"The bastard's wrecking my new car!" Molly cried, and leaned forward to peer through the rain. "I see clear road ahead! Floor it!"

I did, and the pickup's headlights dwindled behind us.

"There's a veer to the left coming up," she said. "See it?"

"No."

"There!"

"Yeah!"

Accelerating out of the veer, I asked, "How well do you know this road?"

"I used to know it very well," she said. "Went down it every day when I was a kid. And I came back when I was sixteen and learned to drive here."

"That could be handy," I said.

"Depends on how much I can remember." Glancing over her shoulder, she added, "He's back."

"Uh huh."

"There're curves ahead. You'll have to slow down."

"Not yet," I said.

There were three curves, not sharp, but closely spaced, and the pickup fell back a little at each one. I got cocky on the last one and came out of it too fast, and I felt the rear end slip on the wet pavement. As I steered into the skid, I caught a flash of headlights ahead, and they were almost on top of me by the time I had it under control. I slipped back into my lane as the car roared past, its horn angrily Dopplering down the scale.

Trembling from our narrow escape, I saw in the mirror that we'd lost our lead on the pickup. It was closing fast again, so I floored the accelerator, and we shot up a hill.

Then Molly cried, "Dip ahead!" and we were airborne, hanging over a steep descent.

We hit hard on the downslope, and I looked back to see the pickup topping the crest behind us.

"I think there's a curve coming up," said Molly.

"You *think?*"

"I'm pretty sure."

"When will you *know?*"

"Now! There!"

I made the cut late, and the rear end slipped again as I came out of it. Again there were headlights in front of us, and again I swerved back just in time to avoid a collision. But the car began to fishtail as we came out of it.

I was fighting to regain control when the truck hit us again. The impact shoved us toward the right edge of the pavement, and I wrestled the wheel frantically to keep us on the road. I straightened the car out just before he slammed us again.

Molly yelled, "Curve ahead! To the left!" but it was too late.

I knew I couldn't make it, so I didn't even try. I steered straight for a low place in the approaching bank. The front wheels jumped the ditch easily, and the car had enough speed to pull the back ones through as well. Then we ran up a low bank and ripped through a barbed wire fence. I spotted a tree dead ahead and pulled hard to the left. The rear end swung around and missed the tree by inches. Then we jolted up another hill and slowed to a halt, the tires spinning freely in the mud. I killed the engine and jerked on the emergency brake, and we slid back a few feet before finally coming to a stop.

I slumped down out of sight, shaking with adrenaline, as Molly pulled her Glock and asked, "Do you see him?"

I peeked over the windowsill, looking back toward the torn fence. "Can't see much, but there're no headlights."

"If he meant to kill us, he'll be back."

"*If* he meant to kill us?" I asked in disbelief. "You think there's some question about that?"

"I think running somebody off the road is an awfully unreliable method of murder."

"Came damn close to working," I pointed out.

"But it *didn't*." She looked over at me and said quietly, "You can let go of it now."

I followed her glance and saw that my left hand was still locked to the wheel.

"Go ahead," she said gently. "Let it go."

It wasn't easy. I had to peel my fingers off the wheel one by one, and the hand remained flexed into a claw for minutes afterward, aching and trembling from the strain.

Molly said, "You did good, Bull."

"I thought it was a little rough there at the end."

"As the old barnstormers used to say: Any landing you walk away from is a good one."

"Sorry about the car."

"Don't suppose you got the bastard's plate number, did you?"

"No, sorry."

"Oh, well."

"Can I ask you a question?"

"Sure."

"What's going on here?"

She sighed. "I'd say somebody's mad at us."

"That much is clear," I said. "But why?"

"Beats me," she said, "but I don't think we should wait here any longer."

"No." I reached for the ignition key. "Now, the trick is to see if this heap'll get us out of here."

"Be gentle," she added.

"Of course," I said.

20

I had to manhandle her car out of the pasture, and I wasn't able to be as gentle as I'd promised. When we were finally back on the pike, I found a place to pull over and climbed out in the rain to bend out a piece of body panel that was rubbing against a tire. Molly found an umbrella in the trunk and used it to shield me from the worst of the downpour.

"Want to walk the rest of the way?" I asked. "We might find a place open where we could call a wrecker."

She sighed. "No, we'll go on. I doubt we can make it much worse."

"We might be safer on foot," I said.

She thought about it. "I'm not sure about that, and I don't think I'm up for a long hike in the rain tonight."

"If he tries to run us off the road again, we'll never outrun him in this thing."

"No, but at least we won't leave the road very fast."

"There's that," I agreed.

We made it back to the bighouse without further incident, and Molly called the wrecker service, but only *after* she'd called the Sheriff's Department. A patrolman arrived before the wrecker, and he had barely finished taking our statements when Tim's partner showed up.

He nodded at me and said to Molly, "We were introduced the other morning, Detective."

"I remember," she said. "You're Detective Rooker."

"That's right," he said. "I know you've had a rough eve-

149

nin', and that you've already told the patrolman what happened, but I'd appreciate it if you'd go over it again for me."

"I'd be happy to tell you anything, Detective," she said, "but it didn't start this evening, and to get the whole story, you need to talk to Mister Cochran here."

So, he turned to me. "Mister Cochran?"

I told him about seeing the man with the pigtail at Riverside Center and at the cemetery, then I moved on to what had happened this evening. But I didn't mention being knocked down outside the grape arbor the night of the wake. He might ask what I was doing down there, and I didn't know how he felt about pot. Also, I hadn't seen my attacker's face that night. He was the right size and shape, and I had a strong hunch it was the same man, but as I said, I didn't mention it.

"The pickup," he said, "what make was it?"

"A Chevy. I saw the emblem on the grill."

"And the color?" he asked.

"Looked wine-colored to me," I said, "dark red or burgundy. But the fog lights in the parking lot at the Hyatt do weird things to colors."

"I thought the truck that ran us off the road was dark green," said Molly.

"Also possible," I said.

Rooker made a face. "Did you see the license plate?"

I shook my head. "You don't have plates on the front, and I didn't look at the one on the back. I should have, but I didn't."

He nodded. "Can you positively identify the pickup that ran you off the road as the one you saw in the Hyatt Regency parking lot?"

"Not positively," I said. "I was too busy trying to stay on the road, and all I could see was the lights. But I'd lay odds it was the same pickup."

Molly said, "It was a Chevy pickup with a bashed-in grill, just like Bull described the one at the Hyatt."

"Did you notice the model?" he asked her.

"Twenty years old, or older."

"Sounds about right," I said.

He made a note, closed the pad, and slipped it into a sagging jacket pocket. "Guess that's all for now. I'll speak to the security people on the way out and ask them to keep their eyes open."

"You think he'll be back?" I asked.

"Possibly," he said. "But he has to know were lookin' for his pickup, so my guess is he'll get it off the road."

"Thank you," said Molly.

"My pleasure." He nodded at me and said, "Mister Cochran," then turned and headed for his car.

We didn't get to bed until three, and we both had trouble getting to sleep, so we didn't make it to Riverside Center until eleven Tuesday morning.

Doctor Gray saw us in her office. It was spare and modern with blond Scandinavian woods, creamy leather, and Monet prints on the pale green walls. "Oh, yes," she said, "I know the man you're talking about. Lyle Baird is his name. He's the one who disappeared."

"He is?" I asked. "I mean, he did? I mean, when did he do this?"

"It's been a week now," she said, "and it took two days to find a replacement."

"How long did he work for you?"

"Only a week," she said. "We hired him on a Saturday, and he was a real lifesaver. Our regular day-shift maintenance man didn't show up that day, didn't call, and didn't answer when we tried to call him. And we were desperate because somebody had turned on the heat, and we couldn't turn it off. It was over ninety degrees in some of the rooms before Baird showed up and took care of the problem, and I thought he was a godsend. Then, a week later, he just vanished."

"When was that exactly?" I asked.

"A week ago Friday."

I nodded. "He went out to buy a part for the monitor board, didn't he?"

"That's right. But he never came back."

"That was the day Mister Flanagan died?"

Suddenly seeing where this was going, she said hesitantly, "Well, yes, that afternoon."

"Do you have a photo of Baird?" I asked.

She slipped a sheet of paper out of a Manila file folder and slid it across the desk. "Just that."

It was a bad photocopy of a Tennessee driver's license. The photo was a vaguely facelike collection of dark smudges that could have been virtually anybody, any race, and either sex. But I could make out the license number, so I wrote it down. Above the license was a photocopy of a Social Security card, and I scribbled that number down, too.

Molly asked, "Did Baird make any friends while he was here?"

"Not that I know of," she said, "but then I don't have much contact with the maintenance people."

"What about his references and resume?" she asked.

"We asked for them, of course," she said, "but it appears that he never supplied them."

I had a thought. "Wasn't it a maintenance man that Dewey bashed with his breakfast tray?"

"That's right."

"Was it Baird?"

She realized, "It had to be."

Molly asked her, "You don't have the tape of the attack, do you?"

"I'm sure we do. Doctor Fredericks is on his rounds—let me page him." She tapped a key on her intercom. "We watched the tape together, as we always do whenever an incident might lead to a lawsuit. He probably has it." The phone chirped, and she picked up the cordless receiver. "Robert? Yes—yes, they're here now. Of course I will. The reason I called: I was wondering about the tape of Mister Flanagan's attack on the maintenance man. I remember you said—oh, you do?" She smiled and nodded at us. "All right—yes, of course." She hung up and said, "He has it in his office, and he'll be right down."

Doctor Fredericks went in for darker woods and leathers and theatrical posters on the walls. He was seated at his desk watching a Sony monitor, on which images flickered at high speed. Glancing away from the screen, he said, "Sit down, please. I'll have it cued up in a jiffy." Looking back at the monitor, he went on, "It's an eight-millimeter tape. Better visual resolution than VHS and a lot more portable." He held up his finger and thumb about three inches apart. "Little thing like that, about the size of an audiotape. This is a copy, of course," he added. "The original was sent to our lawyers for safekeeping." He leaned forward to stop the tape and backed it up a bit. "Here we go."

The image was black-and-white and silent, and the scene was severely underlit. The camera was aimed at the closed door from the corner of the room behind the bed, and because I knew Dewey was there, I could just pick him out of the shadows at the far left edge of the frame.

What happened then happened fast. The door opened, and Baird stepped in, closing the door behind him. I caught a quick glimpse of his face, not quite straight on, then he turned as Dewey stepped out of the shadows raising the tray. Baird couldn't get his hands up to block it, and the tray glanced off his head, sending him staggering farther into the room. The second blow drove him to one knee, but he blocked the third and latched on to the tray as Dewey pulled back. Baird scrambled to his feet, still holding on to the tray, and tore it out of Dewey's hands. Dewey fell back, then went for the door, and Baird took a step after him. As Dewey threw the door open and ran out, Baird stopped. He stood unmoving for a moment with his back to the camera, as he'd remained since that one, brief, not-quite-straight-on glimpse of his face. After a moment, Nurse Lehr appeared in the open doorway and said something. Baird held up the tray, and she gestured for him to follow. As the door closed behind them, Doctor Fredericks switched off the tape.

Molly said to me, "It could be the man who shot at us the day we arrived. He's the right size and build." She asked the doctor, "Why was he in the room?"

"He went there to fix the plug on the bed. Said there was an exposed wire."

"Was there?"

"Yes, there was," he said.

"Then you checked?"

"That's right."

"Did you doubt his word?"

"No, I merely wanted to get the facts straight."

"Why do you think Dewey attacked him?"

"Wanted to get out of here, I suppose."

"But why attack the maintenance man?" I asked.

"I doubt it was anything personal," he said. "I imagine he would have attacked anybody who came through that door."

"Why?"

"Perhaps he meant to strip him and use his work clothes as a disguise for his escape."

"But they weren't the same size," I said. "Dewey was half a head taller and couldn't have worn Baird's clothes."

"Irrational behavior is often illogical as well."

I couldn't argue with that. "Who reported the exposed wire?"

"I don't know. Let me check." He spoke on the phone to a few people and said finally, "We're not sure who reported it, but it was down in the maintenance log."

"Any previous encounters between Dewey and Baird?" I asked.

"Not to my knowledge," he said.

154

"You know that Baird disappeared from the hospital shortly after Dewey's death?"

He nodded. "Doctor Gray informed me about it, but I had no reason to connect it with Mister Flanagan's death."

"And now?"

"I'm afraid I still don't see any connection." To Molly he added, "Your uncle's death was a suicide, after all."

"Was it?"

"*Wasn't* it?" He sounded surprised.

"There's some question about that," she said, "especially now that we know this man, Baird, was on the scene."

He stared at her. "Then you think he might have killed your uncle?"

"Or drove him to suicide," she said.

"How?"

"I don't know," she admitted.

"Neither do I," he said. "Driving someone to suicide would be difficult under any circumstances, and I would think it impossible to accomplish in a few days."

"Wouldn't that depend on who was doing the driving?" I asked.

"A good point," he concurred. "But who was this Baird to Mister Flanagan?"

"Nobody, as far as we know," said Molly. "But then we don't know much. There's only one thing we can be fairly sure of."

"What's that?" the doctor asked.

"That his name isn't Lyle Baird," she said.

Nurse Lehr said, "I never liked that Baird. Knew he was trouble from the start."

We'd gone up to see her after talking to Doctor Fredericks, and she'd invited us into her tiny office.

"What bothered you about him?" asked Molly.

"He reminded me of a boy I went to school with," she

said. "One of those boys that even the bigger kids stayed away from. One who'd grin and stare at you as though he'd as soon kill you as look at you. Baird was like that, only grown-up."

I said, "You spoke to him after Mister Flanagan attacked him."

"Yes, I asked him what he thought he was doing, going into that room alone."

"Then he wasn't supposed to do that?"

"He certainly was not," she declared, "not after what happened before."

"What do you mean?"

"The first day Baird was here, I heard voices raised as I passed the room. When I went in, they were standing close together, neither of them saying anything. I asked what was the problem, but Mister Flanagan said there wasn't one."

"Did he seem scared?" I asked.

"Not particularly," she said. "When I saw he was all right, I told Baird to come with me, and I took him into my office and told him I didn't want him upsetting the patients. I ordered him to stay away from Mister Flanagan and said that, if he needed to go into his room again, he was to get one of us to accompany him."

"And what did he say to that?" I asked.

"I don't believe he said anything. He never had much to say. He'd just give you that grin of his and go on his way."

"But he didn't listen, did he?"

"No, he surely didn't," she concurred. "It was only the next morning that Mister Flanagan attacked him. And I gave Baird a good piece of my mind about it, too, let me tell you. I told him, if he ever did it again, I'd see that he was fired."

"If you don't mind my asking," I said, "why didn't you mention this about Baird before?"

"Well," she said hesitantly, "it didn't seem to have any-thing to do with Mister Flanagan's suicide."

Molly said gently, "And you were afraid that mentioning

it might make the hospital look bad, weren't you?"

"I suppose I was," she confessed, a little embarrassed.

"Well, thank you," I said.

Nurse Lehr nodded and told us, "I'd watch out for that Baird, if I was you."

We agreed that that sounded like good advice.

21

The failure of the original maintenance man to show up
for work on the day that Baird came looking for a job
was entirely too much of a coincidence, so we decided to
pay him a visit. Doctor Gray told us his name was Carl
Horton and that he lived in a trailer park in South Knoxville.

"South Knoxville" meant south of the Tennessee River,
and we crossed on the Henley Street Bridge—a five-lane,
reinforced concrete structure with black wrought-iron
lampposts. To the left, a couple of hundred yards away,
was the more utilitarian-looking, green-painted steel of the
Gay Street Bridge. The river cut deep here, and the water
was a hundred feet below us, creating a vine-covered cliff
on the south bank. On top of the cliff, stretching to fill the
area between the two bridges, was the sprawling, beige-
brick East Tennessee Baptist Hospital. There seemed to be
more than enough hospitals in this town, and all of them
big.

Once across the bridge, we turned right and dipped
down through a one-lane railroad underpass into a mixed
industrial/residential area. We passed the Knoxville Glove
Company, Blessed Hope Baptist Church, and a scattering
of shotgun houses on scrubby, junk-littered lots, then
we turned onto Maryville Pike at Mary Vestal Park and
headed out of town. Just past a sign marking the Knoxville
city limits, we turned right at a trucking company and saw
the trailer park off to our left.

As trailer parks went, this one wasn't bad. There were trees and bushes and patches of grass, even a neat little picnic area. But with trucks pulling in and out of the gravel lot across the road all day, everything in the trailer park was covered in a layer of chalk-white rock dust.

A sign on the first trailer to the left said MANAGER, so we pulled in beside it. The trailer was white with blue trim and had a screened-in carport, probably to keep out some of the dust.

As we got out of the car, a scrawny middle-aged man pushed open the screen door and said in a bored whiskey drawl, "C'n I help you?"

Molly said, "Yes, you can. We were wondering which trailer belongs to Carl Horton."

"None of 'em," he replied.

"I beg your pardon."

"He ain't here no more." The man didn't move from the doorway, or invite us in, but he seemed willing to talk.

"When did he leave?" I asked.

He stroked his stubbled face. "Woulda been a week ago last Friday. Paid me what he owed, hooked up his Airstream, and took off."

It was the day Dewey entered Riverside Center.

"Did he seem scared?" Molly asked.

"Damn right he was scared," he said. "Man was white as a sheet."

"Did you ask him why?"

"Nope," he said.

"Weren't you curious?"

"I look, and I listen," he said, "but I don't ask."

I figured we'd just heard a summary of the man's philosophy of life.

"Did he have any visitors before he left?"

"Nope," he said.

"Could you have missed one?" Molly asked.

"Nope." He jerked a thumb over his shoulder. "I sit right here on this porch ever' day from sunup to sundown.

If I don't see 'em, I hear 'em. Whatever it was happened to him happened somewheres else."

"How do you know something happened to him?" I asked.

" 'Cause he come skiddin' in here in his station wagon kickin' up dust, already whipped into a lather."

"Did he look beat up?" I asked.

He thought about it. "Well, he wudn't marked on his face or nuthin', but I thought he was walkin' kinda careful." He nodded to himself. "Mighta takin' a beatin' at that."

"Was there anybody here he talked to," I asked, "anybody who might know where he was going?"

"Not that I know of," he said. "He mostly kept to hisself. But his trailer was next to the Snider woman's, and if anybody dug out where he was headed, she'd be the one."

Molly thanked him, and we tried the Snider woman. She could have been either side of sixty, a chubby woman with a pouf of teased-up strawberry-blond hair and a chubby, unlined face. She was more than eager to bear witness to all her neighbors' foibles, but about Mister Horton, she regretfully had nothing bad to say. She related almost apologetically that he was a quiet man, always polite, who didn't drink and went to bed with the chickens. Unfortunately, she didn't know where he was headed, or how we might be able to contact him.

I pulled over at the first pay phone on our way back into town, so Molly could call the Sheriff's Department. She spoke to Tim, telling him about the tape of Dewey attacking Baird, and he asked us to drop it by the squad room.

The City-County Building was downtown, beside the old, redbrick courthouse, half a block from the Twin Towers. It was a modern, multilevel brick and glass structure built on a steep hillside that plunged from Main Street down to the Tennessee River. We found a parking meter on Main, went inside, and took an elevator down one level to L1, where Major Crimes was located.

Tim and Rooker were on their way out of the squad room when we arrived, but they promised to look at the tape the first chance they got. We also gave them Baird's driver's license number and Social Security number.

On our way out of the building, Molly stopped at a pay phone to try to reach Ruth Flanagan. Rachel had said that Ruth was staying with Duncan, so Molly called his house, but Duncan's wife said that Ruth and her family had started back to Louisville this morning. Molly tried calling Sybil Deets at home, but got no answer, and the girl who picked up at Mitch's Market said she hadn't seen Ms. Deets all day.

On our way back to the car, Molly said, "Guess it's time for the caves."

"Great," I said, and she laughed.

Molly had attempted to relieve my anxiety by talking about caves and by trying to pass on some of her passion for exploring them. The effort had met with limited success, but at least it was educational.

I already knew that a person who made a hobby of exploring caves was called a "spelunker," but I hadn't realized that East Tennessee was such a paradise for these people. It turned out that there were caves all over the region, only a small percentage of which had been explored, and Beaver Ridge, on whose southern flank the summerhouse stood, was honeycomed with tunnels and caverns.

We stopped at the bighouse, and Molly led me back to the kitchen area, then down a steep flight of stone steps to the wine cellar. Long racks of dusty bottles occupied a tennis-court-size area off to our left, but she went to the right, down a short hallway, into a room filled with tents and packs and lanterns and sleeping bags. On shelves at the back, she found a couple of miner's helmets—hard hats with chin straps and carbide lamps on the front. After testing several of the lamps for brightness, she handed me a helmet, along with a coil of rope and a canteen. Then she picked up a small backpack, tossed in a canteen and helmet of her own, and took me back up to the kitchen.

We filled our canteens, and Ida made sandwiches.

"Where's Cyrus?" Molly asked her.

"Gone to town."

"We need the key to the summerhouse."

"The copy's on a board in his workroom."

"How will I know which—?"

"They're labeled."

"Thanks."

"Uh huh." Never a wasted word with Ida.

Molly stepped through a door and was back in a moment with the key.

The summerhouse had been cleaned up and closed for the winter: wooden shutters bolted over the porch screens and the windows and the screen door.

We undid some butterfly nuts and took off the shutter over the screen door, then unlocked the padlock. It was dark inside, so Molly switched on the lights in the entry hall.

I hung the canteen on my belt and strapped on my helmet, then picked up the rope and followed Molly through the archway at the rear of the entry hall. The hallway ran at a shallow angle off to the left, so you couldn't see the entrance to the cave from the entry hall. The flagstone floor and the pine paneling continued for about twenty feet, up to a steel-mesh screen that was stretched over a framework of two-by-fours.

"To keep out bats?" I asked.

"And anything else that might come out of the caves," she said.

"Such as?"

"Well, when it was first put up, there might have been a few bears around."

"But not now?"

"These days, you only see bears up in the Smokies."

"I wouldn't think these screens would stop a bear, anyway."

"No," she agreed, as she unlatched the screen door, "but it might slow one down a little."

I followed her through, moving from flagstone to packed dirt.

As I flicked on my helmet lamp, she said, "You won't need that here." She walked to a gray metal junction box attached to the rock to our left, threw the switch, and lights sprang on along the walls of the tunnel.

Then she slipped on the pack containing our lunch and started walking. I shouldered the coil of rope, hitched my canteen into a more comfortable position, and followed. She'd said we probably wouldn't need all this gear, but that it always paid to be prepared when you went into the caves. I didn't find that tremendously encouraging, but I didn't tell her so.

22

The caves were cool and dry and smelled of dust and rock and something metallic—maybe a taint of iron. The tunnel appeared to be mostly natural, following a seam in the rock created by some ancient shifting of the tectonic plates, but there were stretches where the passage had obviously been widened. The ceiling sometimes rose far over our heads and sometimes dropped low enough to make me duck, and in places, wooden or metal frameworks had been erected to support presumably unstable masses of earth and rock.

"Ever have cave-ins?" I asked.

"Nothing major."

"Then you have *minor* cave-ins?"

"An occasional small-scale mud or rock slide, that's all."

"Still sounds dangerous."

"They're very rare," she assured me.

"Well, I'm glad to hear that."

The tunnel twisted and turned like a snake back into the ridge, intersecting occasional tributaries along the way, and I would have been lost in minutes without Molly and the string of lights to guide me. But I also noticed faded chalk arrows and numbers, always on the left, the arrows always pointing behind us, always located just before a fork in the tunnel.

"They point the way out," Molly explained, "and the numbers tell you how close you are to the summerhouse."

"Who made them?"

"The white ones were made by my great-grandfather, Sean Michael."

"They're always on the left."

She nodded. "So you know where to look for them and don't get turned around."

I caught a whiff of something foul. "Whew! What's that?"

"What it smelled like," she said. "Sewage is piped from the summerhouse into a natural septic tank in the caves, but you only smell it from that one spot. Don't know why, since the tank is back behind us someplace." She waved off to the left.

"Where are we going?" I asked.

"Want to show you something," she said.

The floor was mostly clay, but there were stretches of bare rock and a few places where sheets of plywood had been laid across narrow cracks or holes. One crack was twenty feet wide and had to be crossed on a suspension bridge.

The bridge creaked and swayed, and the wood felt dangerously spongy underfoot. The air was damp, and when I glanced over the side of the bridge, my helmet lamp glistened off water far below.

Just past the bridge, Molly led me through an opening in the left wall of the tunnel and flicked on some lights to reveal a room-sized chamber. There was a square wooden table at the center, a half dozen hardback chairs, and shelves of rough wooden boards against one wall, containing dusty canteens, packs, and helmets.

"This was our clubhouse," said Molly, "and we set out on our expeditions from here—me and Darrell's daughter, Sarah, and Tim and his brother, Lonnie."

"Your gang?"

"Not mine," she said. "If we had a leader, it was Lonnie. He was the oldest."

After a look around, she doused the lights, and we moved on. But we didn't go far, as the tunnel lights soon ran out.

We turned a corner into darkness, and Molly stopped me with a touch, saying, "Don't move. You're on a ledge."

"I'm not moving."

She stepped to the left. I heard a click, and spotlights revealed a large cavern. A couple of feet in front of me, the floor dropped away at a forty-five-degree slope to a narrow stream running along the bottom. Somewhere in the shadows high above was the roof, but the main attraction was on the opposite wall of the cavern, a hundred feet away. Moisture leeching through mineral deposits had created a frozen cascade a hundred feet tall and maybe three times that in width, white as a movie star's teeth and shimmering with rainbow highlights like mother-of-pearl.

"Sean Michael called it the 'Milkfall,'" said Molly.

"It's magnificent," I said. "I'm surprised this place isn't a tourist attraction."

"The family wouldn't hear of it," she said. "This is Flanagan property and intended exclusively for our personal enjoyment and that of our friends."

"Sounds a tad selfish," I said.

"You got it," she replied.

"You don't always sound entirely approving of your family."

"Of course not," she said. "Are you of yours?"

"No," I admitted, and glanced around. "How can we search all this?"

"We can't." She flicked off the spotlights, extinguishing the Milkfall. "What we're looking for is behind us."

"And what are we looking for?"

She grinned. "Would you believe a secret room?"

"Oh, good. They're even better than secret panels. So where is it?"

"I don't know," she said. "That's what makes it secret. But it was supposed to be Sean Michael's lair, the place where he kept his chest of gold."

"You sure it exists?"

"I don't know about the gold, but I believe in the secret room," she said. "When I was eight years old, I followed Dewey in here, but I let him get too far ahead. He disappeared around a curve in the tunnel, and when I caught up, he was gone."

"Did you look for him?"

"Not then," she said. "His vanishing act scared me, and I hurried back to the summerhouse as fast as my legs would carry me. Later, I looked for the room many times, but I never found it."

I grinned. "Then we're searching for Sean Michael's gold?"

"As I say, I'm not sure about the gold, but I hope to find whatever the burglar was looking for. If you had a secret room and something to hide, where would *you* put it?"

Made sense.

We headed back over the suspension bridge and retraced our steps, until I knew we had to be fairly close to the summerhouse. We passed through a junction of three tunnels, then went around a sharp bend to the right and walked on for about thirty feet.

As the passage started curving to the left, Molly stopped and turned back. "This is what I saw when I was eight," she said. "I was coming around this curve when Dewey stepped around the bend."

Ahead to the left, just before the faded white arrow and the number five, there was a shallow, chest-high niche in the wall. Directly beneath the arrow and the number was a knee-high shelf of rock about three feet deep.

"I didn't like being alone in here," she continued, "so I hurried on."

She led me past the niche and around the shelf, through the ninety-degree bend to the left, to the three-way junction. The main tunnel—the lighted one—continued straight ahead. One branch cut sharply to the right, quickly curving out of sight, and the other veered to the left, back in the general direction of the house. Or so Molly told me, and I had to take her word for it, since I was lost.

On the theory that she would have spotted Dewey if he'd gone down the main tunnel, we concentrated on the branches. And since he could have vanished faster down the one on the right, we started there.

This branching tunnel was unlighted, so I finally got to use my helmet lamp. After the tunnel curved to the right, we spotted a vertical crack in the left-hand wall. It was about a yard wide, and we could see maybe fifteen feet into it, but we couldn't tell if the crack stopped after that, or just curved out of sight, so we checked it out.

We went in sideways, facing to the left, with Molly in the lead, and the going was easy at first. The crack widened as it curved, then narrowed again and began to tilt me onto my back. The angle steepened gradually and never went past twenty degrees, but that was enough. I'd been okay as long as the crack was vertical, but with the tilt, I began to sense the massive weight above me.

"You don't have earthquakes around here, do you?"

"Not often," she said.

"What does that mean?"

"I only remember one the whole time I lived here, and it wasn't much."

"Wouldn't take much," I said. "One tremor, and we'd both be mashed into a gooey paste."

"This crack's probably been open for thousands of years," she said. "It's not likely to close up this afternoon."

"But it could happen, couldn't it?"

She stopped and turned her head. "Want to go back?"

"No, I just had a few questions, that's all."

"So ask them."

"I just did."

"That's it?"

"For now."

"Then we can go on?"

"Sure."

She nodded and moved ahead.

I followed, and after a moment, the crack began to tilt upward again.

It was nearly back to vertical and curving slightly to the left when Molly said, "I see something."

"What?"

"It's shining. See it?"

"No, I . . ."

Still moving, she said, "It looks like, uh—oh-waaaaaah!"

As she fell away from me, I reached out and caught her hand.

She cut off her cry and clawed up my arm until she was pressed against me.

"You okay?" I asked.

She nodded and swallowed. "Lean past and take a look."

I did as she said, looking around the slight curve, and saw something white and gleaming in my helmet light. The Milkfall! I kept leaning until I stuck my head out of the crack into the cavern and stared straight down a hundred-foot vertical fall. Looking to the left, I saw a dimly lighted opening in the cavern wall about three hundred feet away. The same opening, I realized, from which I'd first seen the Milkfall. All that walking, and we'd moved only three hundred feet.

Molly pulled me back, gave me a kiss, and said, "Thanks, partner. Now you know why you never go spelunking alone."

"No danger of that," I said.

We worked our way back out of the crack, then proceeded on down the branch tunnel. As we approached a fork in the tunnel, I saw a faded arrow and a number one chalked on the rock to the left. Below it, in yellow chalk like the piece Molly carried, was a carefully drawn capital M.

"That's my mark," she said, "so I was here once."

Starting down the left fork, I said, "I'm surprised you don't know this tunnel well, it's so close to the house."

"Guess I took a look at it and passed it by after that," she said. "We usually concentrated on the deeper caverns and tunnels further away from the house, always trying to extend the mapped areas."

"You have maps of all this?"

"Much of it," she said. "They're in a cabinet in the living room."

The left fork wound ahead for fifty feet or so, then narrowed and quickly became impassable. We backtracked, shining our lamps into any cracks and crevices we passed. When we got back to the chalk marks, we tried the other fork.

This one ran straight and level for thirty feet, then began to descend. The slope was shallow at first, but grew steeper, and we were soon clambering down a set of giant steps created by flat-topped boulders. The steps ran out at a vertical rock face rising out of a wide crack in the floor. Molly held on to my arm and leaned out to look down into the crack, but she couldn't see the bottom.

When we made it back to the lighted tunnel, we ate our lunch sitting on the knee-high shelf around the bend. After a short rest period, Molly led me into the left branch.

There was a gray metal junction box just inside the tunnel on the left, and Molly threw a switch to light the first thirty feet of the tunnel. The walls here were deeply scarred and highly irregular, seamed and folded to create a series of odd little nooks and crannies. This peculiarity continued into the darkened portion of the tunnel, but the string of lights turned left into one of the seams, and Molly turned with them.

"A slight detour," she said. "I want to show you something."

The seam ran straight and level for twenty feet or more, growing so narrow in places that I had to move sideways. As it curved to the right, the air became noticeably cooler. Then it started to descend, and I smelled moisture in the air.

After another fifteen feet or so, the floor leveled out, and the curving passage opened into a roughly circular chamber. The ceiling was lost in the shadows above, and a dark pool of water bubbled up at the center. The pool was about six feet across and almost perfectly circular, draining its overflow down a narrow channel to the right and out through a hole in the wall. A gas-powered pump squatted to the left, with a plastic hose stuck into the pool and another leading into a crack in the wall behind it.

"It's an artesian well," said Molly, "tested as one of the purest in the region. We get our water for the summer-house from here, and every week or so during the season, somebody has to come back here to start the pump and top off the cistern."

I knelt and scooped up a palmful of water that tasted sweet and clean and icy cold. Then I followed Molly back out through the seam to the branch tunnel and turned left.

As the lights fell behind us, I flicked on my helmet lamp. Then I heard something and said, "Wait up."

Molly stopped. "What is it?"

"Shhh."

After standing quiet and still for a moment, we heard a voice faintly calling for Molly, so we headed back to the main tunnel and around the bend toward the house.

When the voice again called, "Molly!" it was much closer, just beyond the curve ahead.

She called back, "Tim," as he stepped into sight.

He froze when he saw her and said with obvious relief, "Good. Cyrus said I might find you in here."

"What's the matter?" she asked.

"Ida took a header down the steps to the wine cellar."

"My God," said Molly. "Is she all right?"

"Broke her hip, looks like, and she's on her way to St. Mary's now."

As we started back to the summerhouse, Molly asked, "Did you pick up the call for the ambulance?"

"No, Cyrus called us," he said. "He found her when he got back from town."

"But why did he call *you?*"

" 'Cause Ida said she didn't fall. She says she was *pushed.*"

23

Ida had broken a hip and a wrist, while accumulating some nasty bruises and abrasions. She didn't tell us this, of course; we had to get it from the doctor. Ida didn't want to talk about it, or about much of anything else, for that matter. She was immobilized for her broken hip, wore a cast on her wrist, and was wrapped with elastic bandages for her bruised ribs. She looked uncomfortable and generally disgusted by the whole experience. Not a happy camper.

By the time we got in to see her, she had repeated her story to the paramedics, the cops, the nurses, and the doctors, and she had pared it down to the bare essentials. "Heard him come up behind me as I opened the door to the cellar," she said. "But 'fore I could turn to see who it was, he give me a shove, and down I went."

"Then you didn't see anything?" Molly asked.

"Nope."

"You said you heard him behind you," Molly said. "What did you hear?"

"A footstep."

"What did it sound like?"

Nearing the end of her patience, Ida said, "Like a foot steppin'."

Molly smiled. "I mean, was there a squeak, like you might get with an athletic shoe, or did it sound like a hard-sole shoe?"

"No squeak," she said.

That was all the detail she could, or would, provide. Somebody had pushed her. She didn't see who, and she didn't hear a squeak. End of story.

After Tim and Rooker talked with her, they came out to speak with the rest of us in the waiting room—me, Molly, Cyrus, Helen, and Donald.

"Okay," Rooker summarized, after we'd had our say, "you think it's all related: the attack on Missus Flanagan and Mister Wesner; the break-ins; the car bein' run off the road; and Mrs. Wesner gettin' pushed down the stairs?"

"And Dewey's death," Molly added.

"Yeah." Rooker glanced at Tim, not happy about that one.

"Baird was at the hospital," she said.

"He worked there," he pointed out.

"For one week," I said. "From the day after Dewey checked into Riverside Center until just after he died. Then Baird went out to get a part for the monitors—which he'd probably sabotaged to begin with—and he never came back. Doesn't that sound suspicious to you?"

"Yeah, it does," he agreed, "especially now that we know his name isn't Lyle Baird."

"You ran him through DMV?" Molly asked.

"Yep," he said, "and we got a different face. The age is about right, but the real Lyle Baird is a scrawny little weasel-faced fellow, standing about five-four and weighing a hundred and twenty pounds, nothin' like the man you described."

"You play the tape yet?" I asked.

"No, we had to run down a lead on another case, but we'll get to it."

Tim added, "We may have found the pickup that ran you off the road."

I asked, "Where?" as Molly asked, "When?"

"Today," Tim said, "in an abandoned quarry out off Asheville Highway. Kids go swimmin' there, and one of 'em spotted a truck on a ledge about fifteen feet down. We haven't pulled it out yet, but a diver went down and said it fit the description. No license plate, though, and there was no body inside."

"Well, that's something," I said.

"Yeah," he agreed, "but it may not help much, 'cause the truck also fits the description of one reported stolen last week. My hunch is it won't be registered to the suspect, and I'd be surprised if he left anything incriminating behind."

"Me, too," Molly agreed.

"So," said Rooker, "who do you think this guy's workin' for?"

"Too many possibilities," she said. "An impatient bookie, Lester Prine, Darrell."

I shook my head. "But why would any of those people want to push Ida down the stairs?"

Molly shrugged. "Maybe it was a message for Helen, or for us." She looked back at Rooker. "It could've been somebody's way of letting us know we aren't safe anywhere, even in the house in broad daylight."

Rooker frowned. "Why would they want to send such a message?"

"To stop us?" Molly suggested.

"From doing what?"

"From looking around," she said, "and asking questions."

Rooker asked, "Have you learned anything that might threaten somebody?"

She shrugged. "All we know is what we've told you."

"Not much there," he said flatly. "Nothin' worth pushin' an old lady down the stairs, or runnin' a car off the road, or killin' a man over." He shook his head. "It just doesn't add up. Unless it's personal."

"I think it *is* personal," she agreed.

Rooker examined her. "And you think your uncle might be involved?"

"I don't like the idea," she said, "but four million dollars makes a good motive."

He nodded. "And you still don't know what the burglar was looking for?"

"No."

"But you don't think he found it?"

"He's still around," she said, "so my guess is no. I just hope we find it first."

"Maybe that's what he's waitin' for," said Rooker. "For you to find it *for* him."

"Then why would he try to scare us off?" I asked.

"Maybe that's not what he was doin'," he said.

"So what *was* he doing?"

He shrugged and looked at Molly. "Maybe he was tryin' to goad you on."

She stared back at him for a moment and finally nodded. "Could be, if he knew me well enough."

"Whatever his reasons," he said, "you might wanta think about layin' on a few more guards."

She agreed that that was a good idea.

"What about the videotape?" I asked.

"We'll take a look at it first thing in the morning," Rooker promised. "Then we'll work up a sketch."

Tim smiled and said, "Don't worry about it. With the new CPF software, we'll show you this guy's face in no time."

Molly called the security company from a hospital pay phone, and they promised to have another car and two more guards on patrol in a couple of hours.

It was five o'clock by the time we made it back to the summerhouse. Molly wanted to continue our search for the secret room, but she carried her Glock and insisted that I carry the .38.

I got out of the car and attached the holster to my belt in front, where I could reach it quickly. If she was worried, so was I. With that in mind, I said, "We have only about three hours left of daylight, and I don't like the idea of being up here after dark."

"Me, neither," she agreed, "so we'll be out before then."

The guard stepped out of the woods at the top of the brick steps: a wiry, stern-faced man in his late fifties or early sixties, with snow-white hair and bright, sky-blue eyes—probably a retired cop. He worked his chaw of tobacco as he eyed our weapons, then shifted the wad to the side, spat, and drawled, "Can I help you folks?"

"I'm Molly Flanagan," she said, "and this is my friend, Bull Cochran. We're going into the summerhouse."

He nodded and said flatly, "You got some ID?"

I had mine out first.

He held it at arm's length, squinting to bring it into focus, and said with faint disapproval, "Texas."

"Yep."

He glanced back and forth between my face and the photo several times, then leaned in to check the color of my eyes and back to take a guess at my height. Reluctantly deciding it was me, he handed back my license, then held out his hand for Molly's and treated her to the same intense scrutiny.

I had an idea he might be playing with us, but he kept a hand on the butt of his gun throughout, and I didn't want to test him on it.

When he finally returned Molly's license, she said politely, "Thank you, sir."

And he muttered, "You're welcome, miss."

"How long have you been on duty?" I asked.

He tilted his head back to give me a gander and said, "Been here since eight."

"Had any visitors?"

"Nope, you're the first." Then he spat out another stream of tobacco juice and concluded, "Well, I have to finish my rounds. Good day to you." With that, he stepped back into the trees and moved away.

177

* * *

Molly held her weapon at the ready as she opened the screen door, but I left mine in the holster, figuring the longer I could put off drawing it, the healthier it would be for everyone concerned.

She took a quick look to both sides along the length of the porch, then tried the front door. "Still locked," she said.

She waved me against the wall to the right of the door and waited for me to get into position before she unlocked it. Then she flattened herself against the wall on the other side and shoved it open. She listened for a couple of beats, then darted through the opening. Thirty seconds later, the lights went on inside. But another minute passed before she invited me in and locked the door behind me. The door wouldn't stop Baird, any more than the screens over the cave entrance would stop a bear, but as with the bear, it might at least slow him down.

We found our equipment where we'd left it, and I was soon rearmed with my trusty helmet, the coil of rope, and the canteen—freshly refilled with cold, sweet artesian well water from a tap in the kitchen. Then Molly slipped on her pack, and I followed her back into the caves.

We took up where we had left off when Tim had come to find us, continuing down the branch tunnel that led past the turnoff to the well. But I was spooked by then and couldn't stop looking over my shoulder. And it only got worse beyond the lights, where it was just our helmet lamps against the blackness.

The tunnel wound down and around, up and over, widening and narrowing, as the ceiling rose and fell.

I was shuffling along in a crouch through a stretch of tunnel with an exceptionally low ceiling when I heard something behind us and froze. "You hear that?" I whispered.

"What?"

"Listen."

178

She listened, but said finally, "I don't hear anything."

"No," I agreed with disappointment. "It sounded like the scrape of a shoe, but I don't hear it now, either."

"You're probably just hearing our echos," she said. "Caves do weird things with sound."

I nodded and conceded, "You might be right."

We hadn't gone another ten feet when I heard it again, but when we stopped, there was nothing but silence.

"If we *are* being followed," I said, "maybe we should turn back. We don't want to lead him to the secret room."

"*If* we were being followed, I'd have to agree with you."

"It wouldn't be hard to do, you know. With all the twists and turns, we can rarely see more than ten feet in either direction."

"That's true, too, Bull, but I still haven't heard anything."

I couldn't argue with that, so we moved on.

Around the next bend, we emerged into a wide straight tunnel that sloped gently downhill for fifty feet or so. The passage leveled out just before it forked, and Sean Michael's white chalk arrow was visible on the left-hand wall, pointing back the way we'd come. I imagined that he was warning us to get out while we could, but in retrospect, it was more likely that he was just telling us not to bother. The left fork ran out after only thirty feet or so at an ancient rockfall. We searched for a way around it, or through it, but it was hopeless. The passage was blocked by an impenetrable mass of boulders, earth, and gravel.

So we backtracked and tried the right fork, which led us into a marvelous limestone grotto. Water had eaten the limestone away over the centuries, creating a glittering fairyland maze of white stone walls and archways and chambers, and somebody had marked a path through it in green chalk.

"Seamus," said Molly. "He was the only one who used green."

"Seamus?"

"My grandfather's brother, the one who was thrown from his horse on his wedding day."

"Oh, right."

The chalk marks led us through the maze into another tunnel, which wound around a bit before terminating in a fifty-foot drop at the edge of a large cavern. There was a collection of sharp-looking boulders at the base of the drop and some stalagmite formations farther out on the floor, but the light from our helmet lamps couldn't reach the other side.

When we got back to the main tunnel, we took a break, while Molly tried to figure out what to do next. We still had a couple of hours left before dark, and she wasn't ready to give up. She sat on the same shelf of rock where we'd eaten lunch, and I stood beside her, leaning against the chest-high ledge.

"Too many pieces," she said in frustration. "Too many players."

"Yeah," I said, to keep her talking.

"And the crimes just don't make sense."

"No, they don't."

"If they wanted something from Dewey, why would they kill him before they had it, or at least knew where to find it?"

Turning to shift the weight off my bum knee, I said, "Good question."

She went on like that, talking all around the problem, as she zeroed in on a train of thought. "Even if we identify Baird," she said, "we still have to *find* him. And that isn't going to be easy."

"Couldn't we leave that to the police?"

"Can we?" she asked. "I know they'll do what they can, but they have limited manpower and resources, and they don't have our motivation."

"What happens if we find him?"

"Then we tell Tim and Rooker where to look," she said.

"Right." I leaned on the ledge, tracing the line of an old impression in the clay with my finger.

"But there are just too many gaps in what we know," she said. "Ruth's gone, and we haven't talked to Sybil Deets or the bookie or Lester Prine. We don't know how any of them are involved, or even *if* they're involved."

"No." I pulled back to examine the impression in the clay.

"I feel like we've been running in place the whole time."

"Or in circles," I said, realizing the impression was a footprint.

"That's it," she agreed. "Running in circles in the dark."

What was a footprint doing up there? You'd need a stepladder to reach it. The ledge formed an uneven niche in the wall ranging between two and three feet deep and maybe six from side to side, with darkness showing at either end, like the wings of a stage.

"I have a feeling," she said, "that this Baird, or whatever we call him, is laughing at us."

"I wonder . . ." I began.

"You don't think so?"

"No, it's . . ." I stepped past her.

"What's the matter?" she asked.

"I have to see something."

"Where are you going?"

"Come on."

I went around the bend and started back down the tunnel we'd just searched, examining the left-hand wall.

"What did you see?" she asked.

"A footprint."

"Huh?"

"Hang on."

I worked my way from crack to nook to seam, and finally, just short of the turnoff to the spring room, I found what I was looking for. I'd noticed it on the first trip down the tunnel, but hadn't thought anything of it at the time. It didn't look like much—a gaping seam maybe five feet deep, barely wide enough for a man to squeeze into. But why would anybody bother, since it obviously didn't lead anywhere? I squeezed in anyway, facing to the left, and found what I expected to find near the back. The side of the seam I was facing didn't quite reach the back, though you couldn't see that from the front. The gap was wide enough for me to edge through.

The crack beyond was dark and narrow, so I flicked on my helmet lamp and moved sideways. I went about five feet before Molly slithered in behind me. The way soon opened up a little, and we could move forward, though still in single file. The passage veered right, then came to a short flight of steps cut into a steep bank of clay, and I could see light ahead as we reached the top.

We came out on the rock ledge I'd been leaning against, and I showed Molly the patch of clay. "Footprint," I said.

She grinned and punched me on the arm. "A regular Sherlock Holmes."

"With a much better-looking Watson."

"And smarter, too," she said. "But lead on, Holmes. The game is a footprint!"

On that groaner, we proceeded. At the other side of the shelf, the opening led back into the darkness, the passage angling slightly off to the right. It ran straight for a stretch, then curved sharply to the right. The passage straightened out again as it widened, and I saw a sheet of khaki canvas blocking the way ten feet ahead.

I rushed forward, brushed the canvas aside, and swept my helmet light around. Three roughly chiseled stone steps led down into a rock-walled chamber rigged like an office. A secret room if ever I saw one.

24

I was looking around for another switch box when Molly lit a Coleman lantern she found on the desk.

"Probably couldn't risk running electricity in here," she said, "afraid somebody would follow the wires."

She held the lantern out and looked up. The ceiling rose near the center into a circular chimney that led upward into darkness, while the rest of it was hung with slender stalactite formations like petrified icicles. Any corresponding stalagmites had apparently been chipped away, and the uneven surface of the floor had been covered with layers of rugs in the Victorian fashion.

The desk was a thick slab of dark wood laid across two squat wooden kegs. Behind it was a tall, crudely built, and mostly empty bookcase. A four-drawer wooden filing cabinet stood to the right of the bookcase, and a map on an easel to the left. The map was of Knoxville and its environs with shaded areas that Molly identified as Flanagan real estate holdings. Judging from the prevalence of shaded areas, the family owned a fair portion of the town. A couch sat against the wall to the left, and there was what looked like a throne in a natural alcove in the far left corner—an ornately carved high-backed chair in gilt-painted wood with red velvet upholstery and a matching footstool. The third wall was an irregular expanse of rock, near the middle of which stood a rosy stalagmite-stalactite column. The fourth wall began with the three chiseled-out steps leading up to the canvas-covered opening. Beside it, on a waist-high shelf of rock, sat an ancient wooden chest strapped with tarnished brass.

"The treasure chest?" I asked.

Molly didn't answer, just walked to the chest and lifted the lid. It was full of goodies, including a stash of expensive Cuban cigars and half a dozen dust-encrusted bottles of Napolean brandy, but no gold or anything else that might help unravel our mystery.

After that, Molly searched the filing cabinet, and I walked around the room, looking for hiding places. I inspected the ottomanlike footstool that sat in front of the throne, thinking it might conceal some sort of chest. But the top wouldn't budge; the padding was just padding; and neither the footstool nor the throne were heavy enough to be cast from gold. The couch was just cushions laid on a wooden framework, and when I tugged it away from the wall, I saw no hiding place behind it. One shelf of the bookcase served as a bar, with a drinks tray holding a couple of highball glasses, a pair of snifters, a bottle of Scotch, and one of Napoleon brandy. The Scotch was sealed, but the brandy had been opened, and a small amount was gone. Keeping liquor on hand seemed like a dangerous game for a recovering alcoholic, but Helen had said that Dewey thrived on stress. There were only a handful of books in the bookcase: a King James Bible, a dictionary, a couple of law texts, and the first of my two nonfiction books, the one about Juice Hanzlik's killing. On one of the lower shelves, there was a half-empty gallon can of fuel for the Coleman lantern.

Meanwhile, Molly had found what appeared to be the ledgers for her grandfather's bootlegging operation during Prohibition in the bottom drawer of the filing cabinet. The heavy paper was yellowed with age and crumbling around the edges, and Molly handled the pages with care. The ones she showed me were covered with faded, but still readable rows of numbers.

"What makes you think it has to do with bootlegging?" I asked.

"The dates," she said. "The earliest are in the twenties, and the latest is nineteen thirty-three."

"The year Prohibition was rescinded," I said.

"Exactly," she said. "I knew Grandaddy made money at it, but we're talking millions here. He must've had stills running night and day all over the valley."

She returned the ledgers to the drawer, and I took a look at the desk. There wasn't much on top. Some advertising circulars and a pen set with a black marble base, a silver-framed photograph of Helen and a fancy wooden cigar box. Inside the box I found, of all things, cigars. Big fat, expensive ones with Havana labels, like those we'd found in the chest. I checked one out, sniffing it, squeezing it, listening to it crinkle, and judged that it smelled, felt, and sounded fresh. That meant Dewey had been here fairly recently. *Like the day he took the potshots at Darrell?* Was this where he was headed when he came tearing up the hill, almost running Cyrus down? I hoped so, because we were rapidly running out of ideas.

There were no drawers to search in the desk, as it was just a thick slab of wood propped on barrels. Molly helped me to shift the top aside far enough to see that the barrels were empty, then we slid it back into place.

The desk chair was something out of the fifties: a contraption of brown vinyl and chrome-plated steel, the chrome finely speckled with rust, the cracks in the vinyl repaired with black electrician's tape. It stood on a worn rectangle of linoleum glued to a slab of plywood, giving the casters something flat and solid on which to roll.

The chair creaked and *pinged!* as I took a seat, and a castor squealed as I pulled it up to the desk. I went through the circulars and found that all were postmarked about two weeks before, offering further evidence that Dewey had been here at least that recently.

I sat back and looked around the room, thinking that everything in here had to have been moved here by one man. *No, not necessarily.* News of the existence of the place had to pass down somehow. Did the other brothers know about it? I tended to doubt it. Did it pass only from father to eldest son? If so, where did that leave Dewey, since he had no son? Had he left sealed instructions somewhere for Darrell or Duncan, telling them where to find it? Or had he intended to take the secret with him?

There didn't appear to be any other way in or out of the room except the way we'd come, so the furniture must have been brought in by the same route. No problem with the carpets, the chest, or the footstool, and the desk chair probably came apart into several pieces. I wasn't sure about the filing cabinet, but the couch was definitely too big to fit around some of the tighter corners in the passage, so the framework must have been dismantled and reassembled in here. The bookcase was at least eight feet tall and six feet across and had to have been built on the spot, and I doubted that the throne could have made it down the passage, either. Apparently it, too, had arrived in pieces.

As for the desktop, it was only five feet long and a little over three feet across and would probably have made it in one piece. When we'd moved it to check the barrels, I'd noticed it wasn't as heavy as expected. Not nearly heavy enough for a solid slab of wood four inches thick, I realized. When I knocked on the top, it sounded hollow, so I slid out of the chair and looked underneath.

I examined the underside closely and made out faint seams outlining a square panel. I pushed on it and probed the edges with my fingers, but it wouldn't budge. So I got back in the chair and pulled it up to the desk. I felt along under the edge, figuring that any release mechanism should logically be accessible to somebody sitting there. I went inch by inch and finally detected a thin lip off to my right, about a foot from the end. I pressed on it and around it with no apparent effect. In disgust, I pulled on the lip, and a piece about four inches across hinged up and away from the front. As it did, I heard a click, and a false bottom dropped down. I rocked forward in the chair, and a heavy, ledger-type book slid into my lap.

The ledger was old and falling apart, the faded green cloth cover coming loose from the cardboard stiffeners. A thick Manila envelope was stuck between the pages.

I pulled out the envelope, and Molly stood beside me as I slid out the contents: a letter typed on a bad manual typewriter and a thick stack of black-and-white eight-by-ten glossies. Candid shots, all different, with proof sheets at the back. Duncan was in most of the photos, and the order told a simple story:

Duncan at the wheel of his silver Mercedes.
A young black man standing beside the car
    talking to Duncan.
The black man climbing onto a motorcycle.
The motorcycle parked in front of a motel room.
The Mercedes driving under a tall neon sign that
    shouted SUNSET MOTEL.
The Mercedes parked next to the motorcycle.
Duncan climbing out.
Duncan entering the motel room.

The photos that followed were all taken from a viewpoint inside the motel room:

Duncan kissing the young man.
Duncan sitting on the bed, the young man
    before him.
Duncan unzipping the young man's pants.
Duncan sucking the young man's cock.
The two of them naked, embracing on the bed.
Several shots of the young man sodomizing Duncan.

"I saw this man at the funeral home," I said. "He came by himself, and Darrell spoke to him. He didn't look happy

187

about what Darrell had to say, but he finally turned and left.''

''So, he came to see Duncan,'' she said, ''and Darrell wouldn't let him.''

''That's what it looked like.''

''Well,'' she said, ''now we know what the burglar was looking for.''

''Yeah, but it's kind of disappointing, isn't it?'' I said. ''I mean, Duncan's gay. So what? Nothing worth killing over. Did you know?''

She shook her head. ''I had no idea. But I can tell you it would be a huge embarrassment for Duncan if it came out.''

''Why huge?''

''Because he's a big shot in local conservative circles, and all his buddies claim to despise homosexuals.'' She added with a grin, ''Plus, his wife, Ann Marie, is a spokeswoman for the local Traditional Values campaign.''

''Ooops,'' I said.

''Right.''

Molly glanced through the letter that came with the photos and said, ''It's addressed to Dewey from a private investigator named Lucas Halsey.'' She read on. ''The black man's name is Michael Nixon . . . He was Duncan's lover . . . but he agreed to invite Duncan to the motel for a thousand dollars.''

''So Dewey was blackmailing Duncan?'' I said.

''That's the way it looks,'' she agreed unhappily.

''Trying to get Duncan to vote against selling Shamrock?''

''Probably,'' she said.

''And with Duncan's vote, Dewey could defeat the motion.''

''You got it.''

I shook my head. ''What a family.''

25

On our way to the City-County Building Wednesday morning, we decided not to mention the photos. We both knew it was a crime to conceal evidence, but we had no reason to believe the photos were related to Dewey's death. Molly wanted to talk to Duncan about them first, and I agreed because I wanted to hear what he had to say, too. Also, the photos were my discovery, and I wasn't ready to hand them over to the police just yet.

The sign on the open squad room door said MAJOR CRIMES. We entered at the corner of the room, with the door to the lieutenant's office in the perpendicular wall to the right and the squad room stretching off to the left. It was a white-walled room about twenty by thirty, containing six mismatched metal desks, each equipped with a typewriter, a phone, and one of those old-fashioned brass desk lamps with green glass shades. Each detective had his own filing cabinet and a bulletin board attached to the wall over his desk.

A pudgy detective in his late thirties stood behind a desk to the left, arms crossed over his red suspenders and a long-suffering look on his face. In front of him, a fat, tattooed Hell's Angels wannabe in a dirty tee shirt and low-riding jeans held a smaller and considerably skinnier biker type in a headlock.

"Make him let go a me!" the skinny one kept repeating, as the pudgy cop said wearily, "Let Billy Ray go, Leon. Then we can all sit down and talk about it, get it out in the open, and see if we cain't clear this thing up. How does that sound?''

Sounded sensible to me, but Leon didn't seem to be listening. He was turned away from us, bending over as he held Billy Ray in the headlock, giving us an unsolicited view of the crack between his buttocks.

Detective Rooker sat at a desk to our right, phone receiver pressed to one ear, hand cupped over the other, trying to hear what his caller was saying over Billy Ray's complaining. Finally he said something and hung up, then got to his feet and pulled out a Glock 9-millimeter, like Molly's. He took three tired steps and laid the barrel behind Leon's ear. "If you don't let him go, Leon," he said in a quiet voice, "I'll have to shoot you."

Leon froze, and Billy Ray shut up.

"You wouldn't do that," Leon said in a gravelly voice.

"I don't want to," Rooker explained solemnly, "but I can't take any more of Billy Ray's whining. I'd shoot *him*, but that doesn't seem right, you being the aggressor and all."

Leon's hunched back looked thoughtful. "You cain't get away with it," he decided.

"Who would object?" asked Rooker. "Detective Bradley, could you live with yourself if I had to shoot Leon here?"

"Well, Rook," Bradley said seriously, rubbing his chubby face, "I reckon I could muddle through, if I had to."

"And I know Billy Ray wouldn't mind, now would you, Billy Ray?"

"Make him let go a me!" Billy Ray began.

Rooker said calmly, "Shut up, Billy Ray," and Billy Ray shut up. Turning to us, Rooker added, "We have visitors to the squad room, Leon. Turn and say hello to the nice people."

Prodded by the gun, Leon turned to us, causing Billy Ray some discomfort in the process. Leon didn't look much better from this side—stringy hair, straggly beard, and a pale, lumpy, mean-looking face—but at least we were spared the sight of his ass. He glowered at us, but didn't deign to speak. Billy Ray blinked and started to say something, then glanced at Rooker and changed his mind.

Rooker said to us, "I'm afraid we don't have time for proper introductions, but do you folks have any objections to me shooting this man?"

Molly and I looked at each other. We were just tourists here, and we had to assume that Rooker wasn't actually going to shoot Leon, even if he sounded completely serious about it. In the end, we decided to play along.

"Not me," said Molly.

"Nope," I said, "no objections."

"There, you see, Leon? Nobody wants to hear any more of Billy Ray's moaning." Billy Ray cut off in midmoan. "And it just doesn't look good for you to be holding him in a headlock in the middle of the squad room like this. It doesn't look professional, and we pride ourselves on our professionalism around here. So if you don't let him go by the time I count to five, then I'll have to shoot you."

"You wouldn't—" Leon began.

"One," said Rooker.

"You can't—"

"Two," he continued.

"You're bluf—"

"Three."

"—ing."

"Four."

"I don't—"

Rooker said, "Five," and cocked his gun.

And Leon threw Billy Ray away from him, saying, "Okay!"

The gun didn't waver. "Good," said Rooker. "Now, you tell him you're sorry."

"I—"

"You what, Leon?"

The big man swallowed and spat out, "I'm sorry!"

Billy Ray opened his mouth, but Rooker stopped him with a look. "That's good, Leon. Now, you sit down—both of you—and behave yourselves." When they were seated, Rooker uncocked his gun, holstered it, and turned to us with a pleasant expression. "You just missed Tim," he said, walking over. "He was called out on a case. Which is too bad really, since he's the wiz with the CPF."

"He mentioned CPF last night," I said. "What does it stand for?"

"Comphotofit," said Molly.

"You have it in Galveston?" asked Rooker.

"Not yet," she said, "but I've heard about it, and I know it's supposed to be good."

"It is," he said, leading us to a computer terminal that sat on a table against the wall beside the door to the lieutenant's office. "We just finished the training course, and I don't pick up this stuff as fast as Tim does, but even I can see how much better it is than the old ways."

There were three photocopies tacked to the wall next to the terminal, demonstrating the methods of producing ID sketches. The first and, until CPF came along, the most reliable method was to have a witness or victim work with an artist to produce a pen or pencil sketch of the culprit. The sketch was good, but as Rooker explained, even the best was just lines and shading, and it was often difficult for a witness to relate it to a real human face. That's why the Smith & Wesson system was developed. In this system, the witness picked through a box of transparent plastic overlays onto which fragments of photographs had been transferred—hairlines, jawlines, noses, mouths, etc.—then mixed and matched the overlays to create a face. The result was certainly more three-dimensional than the pencil sketch, but the range of overlays was limited; the hairstyles outdated; and there was no effective method for blending the features. The third photocopy showed the work of

192

CPF-Plus, the latest version of the Comphotofit software, and its superiority was obvious at a glance. The CPF sketch looked remarkably like a photograph.

Rooker sat down at the terminal and booted up the computer, then nodded at the chair to his left. "Sit down, and I'll show you how it works."

"Before you get started," Molly said to Rooker, "do you have a fax machine I could use? I'd like to send a note to my captain."

He waved at the open door to the lieutenant's office. "Step in and see the boss. He'll let you use his fax."

"You sure he won't mind my barging in?"

"I'm positive," he said. "He's heard about the beautiful Galveston detective in town, and he keeps hinting that he'd like to be introduced."

"Has a thing for policewomen?" she asked.

"Just women in general," he said. "But he's harmless. All the property's in his wife's name."

She laughed and told him, "Thanks." Then she knocked on the open door and said, "Hi," as she stepped in.

There were three thick black plastic spiral ring notebooks on the desk in front of me. "One for white males," Rooker explained, "one for black males, and one for women."

"No Hispanics?" I asked.

"It's on order now," he agreed, "and we've asked for the Asian book, too. But I don't know if we'll get it."

He opened one of the notebooks in front of me. For this one, hundreds of white men had been photographed and their faces dissected into their component parts. Each page was like a proof sheet of small black-and-white photos, and the notebook was divided into sections, each devoted to a different portion of the human face.

"You start with the forehead and hairstyle," he said. "Look them over carefully, and take your time."

As I scanned down the page, I suddenly wasn't sure I

could do this. I'd caught a couple of brief glimpses of this guy, and now I was expected to pick out his forehead? *Who looks at foreheads?*

Recognizing my problem, Rooker asked, "Was it a high forehead, or a low one?"

"High," I said, without hesitation. And knew it was true. Maybe I *had* looked at the forehead, after all.

He pointed at a photo in the top row. "Like this one?"

"Higher." I pointed at one halfway down the page. "More like that, except the hair's wrong." I kept going, turning to the next page, moving quicker now that I knew what I was looking for. "That's close," I said, pointing to one near the bottom, "but the hair still isn't right."

"I might be able to fix it," he said, "but keep going."

I turned to the next page and started to scan across the top row, then stopped. I reached out a finger and laid it on the page. "That's it," I said in disbelief, "right down to the curl of hair dangling on his forehead."

Rooker turned to the monitor, on which he had the program displayed. A square blue window took up more than a third of the screen—maybe closer to half—leaving an L-shaped band about three inches wide running down the left border and across the bottom. Tools and menu options were displayed on this band and were accessed by moving the cursor to the proper icon and clicking the mouse.

He called up the feature and clicked an icon to display it, and a broad, high forehead, with tight black hair and that Johnny Depp curl, appeared in black and white against the blue background.

The hair/forehead combo took up more space than the rest, and the other photos were smaller, leaving room for more of them on the page. I selected a chin and jawline, then moved on to the eyes, nose, and mouth. The eyes were especially difficult, but I finally found them: the ridge of brow, eyebrows slightly turned up on the ends, and that cold, flat, shadowed stare. Seeing it clearly for the first time, it gave me a shiver.

I read off the number to Rooker. He typed it on the keyboard and clicked the mouse, and it appeared on the screen.

When all the pieces had been selected, Rooker asked, "Is he pale like the forehead, or darker like the chin?"

"Pale," I said.

He moved the cursor to the forehead to pick up the shading, then "pulled" it down to the chin. When the shading was consistent throughout the face, he used the program's "smooth" and "autoblend" functions to eliminate seams and meld the components together, then applied an "enhancement" function to sharpen the image. When that was done, he split the blue window into two parts with a thin black line separating them and displayed the same image on both sides.

"The right side will be the keeper," he said, "and we'll work on the left. This way we don't lose what we want to keep."

"Good idea," I said.

"Now we can paint in features, add character lines and other distinguishing marks, scars and such. But," he added, "you'll have to bear with me on this. Like I said, Tim's the wiz on this stuff, not me."

He applied his "strokes" with the mouse, and I knew from experience that handling one with precision took lots of practice. He employed various-sized "paintbrushes," some as small as a single pixel, to "pull" shading from elsewhere on the face, or from the gray-scale pallet that stretched across the bottom of the screen, then used that shading to add identifying features, such as a stubble of beard, a mustache, or the pockmarks of acne.

This was the challenging part, of course, the part that called for artistry, and to me, it seemed unfair to expect that somebody who was good at detecting would just happen to possess this particular skill as well. But it appeared that, whatever was needed, Rooker had. The process wasn't quick, or easy. It required painstaking effort along with many erasures and corrections, especially in drawing those vertical lines on either side of his mouth. But after another hour of work, "Baird" looked out at me from the screen.

A square jaw and a dimpled chin, a thin-lipped mouth and stark vertical lines on either side of the mouth, a straight nose and hollow cheeks, a high forehead and tight dark hair, the stray curl and that hooded stare.

I felt somebody behind me and glanced back to see Molly standing there.

"Looks a little like Tim, doesn't it?" I asked. "The face is thinner, and the eyes are different, but he has a similar chin, and . . ." Seeing her expression, I said, "Are you okay?"

"It's Lonnie Deets," she said.

"Tim's brother?" I asked.

She nodded. "Yes."

"You sure of that?" asked Rooker.

"Yes, I'm sure," she said. "I haven't seen him in fifteen years, but it's him."

Rooker sat back in his chair and stared at the screen.

"When did you say Tim left?" I asked him.

He sat there for a moment without moving, then turned his tired eyes on me. "We went to forensics to see the tape and ran through it a few times. We decided it wouldn't be worthwhile to take a Polaroid of the face. You only saw it for a moment, and the picture wasn't clear, and when you froze it, you couldn't pick out the features at all. When we finished, Tim came back here, and I stayed to talk to one of the techs about a hair and fiber analysis he was doin'. When I got back, Bradley told me Tim had taken a call on another case and left."

Molly said, "I saw the tape, too, and I didn't recognize Lonnie."

He ran a hand over his thinning hair. "But you'd think he'd know his own brother."

"If he *did* recognize him," she said, "it must've been a

shock. Maybe he just needs time to think it out.''

"Could be,'' he agreed.

"You'll hear from him,'' she assured him.

"Sure I will,'' he said.

$$\boxed{\textbf{26}}$$

M olly stopped at a pay phone on the way out of the building to call Darrell and Duncan. She caught them at their separate places of business and told them we had something they should see, and they agreed to meet us at Darrell's office at two this afternoon.

Walking out to the car, I said, "You really think Tim didn't know Lonnie was in town."

"I think he deserves the benefit of the doubt," she said.

"Okay, I'll buy that." When she shook her head, I asked, "What is it?"

"It's Lonnie," she said. "I know he's a hard case, but we were close once, and I wouldn't have thought he'd try to hurt me."

"Maybe he didn't know you were in the car."

Again she shook her head. "I have a hunch he knew."

Climbing behind the wheel of the Lincoln, I asked, "But why would he do it? All of it. Any of it."

She shrugged. "For money, maybe. He was turning to the violent stuff last I heard. Got busted for armed robbery in Florida a few years back, but it didn't stick. The witness changed her mind, and he walked."

"Think he got to her?" I asked, as I started the engine and looked for an opening in traffic.

"That's a strong possibility."

Pulling out, I said, "Was he always in trouble?"

"No," she said with a sigh. "When he was about twelve, he changed. He was angry all the time after that and started

198

getting into fights, which got him into trouble with his teachers. Then he turned to shoplifting, which got the police involved. He graduated from shoplifting to grand theft auto, and on his second conviction, he got ten years at Brushy Mountain. Of which he served eighteen months."

"That's a hell of a reduction."

"But typical," she said. "Tennessee prisons are so overcrowded that a nonviolent, non-drug-related offender gets an automatic one-third reduction of sentence. In Lonnie's case, good behavior combined with an early work release cut it to a year and a half."

I looked over at her. "And you were friends?"

"Yeah." She glanced away.

"What is it?"

"Nothing." She stared out at the scenery.

I was a firm believer in the old adage that what you don't know can't hurt you, but I had to ask, "Were you more than just friends?"

She sighed again. "I told you I came back here when I was sixteen. I expected to see Tim, but he was away at some jock camp. And Lonnie—" She shrugged. "I knew him, but I didn't *know* him. He went to a school for delinquents, grew his hair long, and wore jackets with the collars turned up. I never knew what he was going to do from one moment to the next, and I guess that was part of the attraction."

I drove for a moment in silence, and she finally went on, "But the attraction died late that summer, when he got into a fight with Darrell at a family picnic. Lonnie was only eighteen, and Darrell was a grown man, but it was no contest. Lonnie might have killed him if Dewey hadn't pulled him off. Then Lonnie tried to turn on Dewey, but Dewey knocked him cold with a croquet mallet and went to get his gun—the same Colt forty-five he used on Darrell. When Lonnie came around, Dewey ordered him off his land and told him to never come back."

"And did he?"

"I don't know."

I drove through another long stretch of silence, seeing the first faint tinges of autumn in the trees—a few stray leaves here and there beginning to turn. Molly had told me it was spectacular here in the fall.

As we were coming up on the gates to the bighouse, she said, "Drive on by."

"Where are we going?"

"To find Tim."

Half a mile past the house, she said, "See that store on the left?"

"Yeah." It was a convenience store with gas pumps out front.

"Pull into the driveway just this side of it."

"Okay." I slowed for the turn. "Tim lives here?"

"No, his mother does."

The store was concrete block with peeling white paint and a faded sign that said MITCH'S MARKET. A sloppy hand-painted sign on the gas pumps announced, NO GAS! but a beer sign flashed off and on in the window. The place appeared open for business, but there was only one car in the rutted gravel lot.

"Their daddy's name was Mitch?" I asked.

"Mitch Leary was Sybil Deets' common-law husband," she said. "He was shot to death in a holdup at the store last year."

The ruts were even deeper in the driveway, and the gravel had washed out in places. It led down a steep grade past the store and over a stream on a clattering wooden bridge to a small white aluminum-sided cottage under a willow tree.

The front porch was propped on stacks of concrete blocks and canted slightly to the right. I spotted a dog in the shadows under the porch and thought it was dead until it lifted its tail to wave off the flies. The front door was open, and from the porch I could see through the screen door into a darkened living room.

Tapping on the screen door, Molly called out, "Miz Deets!"

"What do you want?" came from inside, making us both jump.

"It's me, Molly Flanagan."

A short, rounded figure waddled into view. "Molly?" she said. "Well, I'll be. C'mon in!" I had to dodge out of the way as she shoved the screen open. "C'mon in," she repeated, and I followed Molly inside.

The linoleum-covered floor was level, but springy under-foot, as though the supports had rotted away. The room looked clean, but the scent of wood polish couldn't hide the smells of dust and mildew. Ms. Deets flicked on the lights to reveal a couch and chairs upholstered in bright red tartan plaid, covered in heavy, yellowing plastic.

"My Lord," the woman said to Molly, "I haven't seen you since I don't know when. And this"—she darted a co-quettish glance at me—"must be your husband."

"No," Molly said with a smile, "this is my friend Bill Cochran." She usually introduced me as Bull, but Bill seemed more appropriate with this dainty butterball of a woman.

Ms. Deets dropped her eyes and said, "It's a sincere plea-sure to make your acquaintance, Mister Cochran." She talked like that, in a stilted, old-style manner of speech. She gestured at the couch, and Molly and I sat with unison squeaks.

"Would you care for some lemonade?" she asked.

"We don't want to put you to any trouble," said Molly.

"Why, it's no trouble at all," Ms. Deets assured us, as she waddled out of the room.

The walls were covered with an eclectic collection of art-work: landscapes and still lifes that might have been cut from calendars; pictures of animals, especially dogs; and one of those paintings of children with the huge eyes. There were lots of ceramic animals, and directly across from the couch, between the two front windows, there was a floor-to-ceiling bookcase jammed with Reader's Digest Condensed Books.

Then Ms. Deets was back with our lemonade. It was sweeter than I liked it, but I didn't complain. When we were taken care of, she seated herself with several polite squeaks on the chair across from us. Before she could pull her flowered duster down over her plump white thighs and happy-face knees, I saw that she wasn't wearing anything underneath.

"You heard about Dewey's death?" Molly asked her.

"Yes," Ms. Deets said, her cheerful mask slipping for an instant.

"I didn't see you at the funeral," said Molly.

"I don't go in much for funerals," she explained.

"No," Molly agreed, "I don't care for them myself."

Ms. Deets nodded.

"Did you get word that Dewey left you this house and the store in his will?" Molly asked.

"Yes," she said, "a nice young man came by to tell me about it yesterday."

"I'm happy for you," Molly said sincerely.

"Thank you," she said, eyes shiny with tears. "Mister Flanagan was always so generous with us."

Suddenly I wondered if Sybil could have been more than just a grateful tenant to Dewey.

"Do you see Tim and Lonnie often?" asked Molly.

The smile stayed, but two vertical lines appeared between her eyes. "I see Timmie every week."

"And Lonnie?"

The lines deepened, and the smile began to look strained around the edges. "He doesn't come around much anymore."

"Do you know where he is now?"

"No, I don't."

"Is he in town, I mean?"

She stared at a point between us.

"Miz Deets?" asked Molly.

202

"I'm sorry?"

"Are you all right?"

"Well, of course I am," she said unconvincingly.

"I was asking if Lonnie was in town."

"You know, I believe he is," she said.

"Have you seen him?"

"No, as I say, he doesn't come around much anymore." That might be true, but I had a feeling she'd seen him, or knew where he was, or knew something else that she wasn't happy about knowing. A difficult child, Lonnie.

"I haven't seen Lonnie in a long time," said Molly. "Do you know where I can find him?"

"No, I'm afraid not."

"What about Tim?" Molly asked. "Where's he living these days?"

Ms. Deets rubbed her eyes. "Just down the road a piece."

"On the pike?"

"Just off it," she said, still rubbing with one hand, as she waved the other across the room. "Look in the book over there on the desk."

Molly went to her. "What's the matter, Miz Deets?"

She waved Molly off, eyes clenched. "I get these headaches."

"Would you like some aspirin?" Molly asked her.

"No, thank you," she said. "That's very kind of you, but nothing helps except sitting in the dark for a while. Would you mind turning the lights off on your way out?"

It was clearly a polite dismissal, and Molly said, "Of course not." She wrote down Tim's address, then flicked off the lights as we left.

Tim lived in a half-finished subdivision half a mile away. The houses were built on large lots, and trees had been left in place wherever possible, but there was still too much bare red earth and too little grass.

Tim had grass, however, lush and green and freshly cut,

along with a recently trimmed ornamental hedge running across the front. He lived in a brick ranch house that sat on a rise, providing room underneath for a two-car garage. It was a lot of house for a single man, but maybe he didn't intend to stay that way much longer.

Nobody answered the doorbell, and there was no car in the garage, but there was also no mail in the mailbox, so we figured that somebody had been there today.

27

In the elevator on the way up to Darrell's office, I said to Molly, "Would you mind letting me take the lead on this?" When she looked my way, I added, "They'll be expecting something from you, but not me, and I might catch them off guard."

"You might," she agreed.

"Feel free to jump in at any time," I added. "I just have a few questions I want to ask."

"Okay," she said with a grin, "it's yours."

Darrell's receptionist, Ms. Markham, smiled at Molly. "Miz Flanagan, good to see you again. You can go right on in. They're waiting for you."

"Just a moment," I said, as she reached for the intercom. "Would you mind taking a look at something for me?"

"Well, of course not," she purred. "Mister Cochran, isn't it?"

"That's right." I pulled a copy of the Comphoto out of one of the two Manila envelopes I was carrying. The face had been blown up to near life size and reproduced on a color laser printer, showing in black and white against a blue background. "Have you ever seen this man?"

She needed only a glance. "Sure I have," she said. "He was in here a couple of weeks ago."

"And before that?"

"I only saw him that once."

"I'm surprised you'd remember a man you saw only once two weeks ago."

"Well, he was kinda creepy, you know?" She shivered for us. "Sorta scary?"

"I know what you mean," I said with a nod. "And he went in to see Mister Flanagan?"

"Uh huh," she said. "I guess they're old friends or something."

"Did he seem like the type to be Mister Flanagan's friend?"

"Well, no, he didn't, as a matter of fact," she said. "He was a rough sort."

"Do you remember his name?"

"I don't believe he gave me his name," she said.

"If he made an appointment, you'd have it written down, wouldn't you?"

"He didn't have an appointment," she said.

"If he didn't give his name and didn't have an appointment, how did he get in to see your boss?"

"Mister Flanagan came back from lunch right after the man arrived."

"Did Mister Flanagan look happy to see him?"

"Well, I . . ." She shook her head and said apologetically, "It was two weeks ago, and to be honest, I don't really remember how he looked."

"Did he call the man by name?"

She shook her head. "I don't believe so."

"Then what happened?"

"He took him into his office."

"How long were they in there?" I asked.

"I, uh . . ." She stopped and stared at me for a moment, then said, "I'm not sure I should be talking about this—I mean about my boss's business and all."

"You wouldn't want Mister Flanagan to get into trouble, would you?"

"No, of course not," she assured me.

"Well, you were right about this man," I said. "He *is* scary, and we're trying to make sure your boss doesn't get

206

any more deeply involved with him than he already has. Do you understand?"

She frowned and gave it some thought and said finally, "The man was in there for half an hour at least, maybe longer, and Mister Flanagan told me to hold his calls. After the man left, he came out and told me to cancel the rest of his appointments, and he left for the day."

"What was his mood?"

"He was in a hurry to get out of here, I can tell you that."

"Well, thanks," I said, "you've been very helpful."

"And you're very welcome," she said, her smile back at full wattage.

Ms. Markham called in to tell her boss that we were there, and both Darrell and Duncan greeted us at the door.

When we were all comfortably seated in green leather armchairs—Molly and I across from the two Ds—Duncan smiled and said to her, "So you have something to show us? You certainly made it sound sufficiently mysterious and hush-hush."

I said, "We have *several* things to show you, Mister Flanagan." As Duncan transferred his focus to me, I pulled out the copy of the Comphoto and held it out to his brother. "Do you recognize this man?"

Darrell took one glance and passed the sketch to Duncan, saying, "No, I don't think I—"

But Duncan cut him off. "Of course you do, Darrell. It's Lonnie Deets. Not a perfect likeness, but close enough." He held it out to his brother. "Take another look. You recognize him, don't you?"

Darrell looked from Duncan to the face and said, "Oh, yeah."

I asked Darrell, "When did you see him last?"

"Oh, I don't know. A long time."

"Your secretary said he was here two weeks ago."

"That's right, Darrell," said Duncan. "You told me Lonnie had dropped by."

Darrell nodded. "Oh, yes, that's right. I forgot about that." To me he said, "Lonnie came here a couple of weeks ago."

"And what did you talk about?"

"Oh, I don't really—"

Duncan said, "He asked to borrow money, didn't he?"

"Yes, that's right," said Darrell. "He wanted money."

"Did you give him any?" I asked.

"I think I gave him something."

"Why?"

"What?"

"Why did you give him money?"

He shrugged. "Lonnie's an old friend of the family."

Molly interjected, "I didn't even know you two were on speaking terms. Since the beating, I mean."

Darrell reddened. "That was a long time ago."

"Did you hire him?" I asked.

"Hire him?" Darrell echoed. And I realized that the constant repetition was meant to give him extra time to think, not that it was doing him much good.

Rephrasing the question, I asked, "Did you give Lonnie a job?"

"No, I, uh . . . Lonnie doesn't have the, uh . . . proper skills to work for me."

"And you, Duncan?" I asked. "When did you last see Lonnie?"

"The same day," he replied with a smile. "He came to ask me for money, too."

"And did you give him any?"

"I believe I slipped him a fifty. Lonnie's had a hard life. While it's true that much of his trouble has been of his own making, he also didn't have the opportunities we had, and I can't help feeling sorry for him. We no longer move in the same circles, of course, but you don't turn your back on old friends."

"Did you give him a job?" I asked.

"No," he said with that same smile, "I'm afraid I had no place for him, either."

I nodded and glanced down at the envelopes in my lap, then pulled out the bottom one and laid it on top. "I'd like you to look at some photographs," I said to Duncan. "But I warn you that the content is extremely personal, and you might prefer to examine them in private."

"I'm sure I have nothing to hide," he said, reaching out his hand.

I passed him the envelope, and Duncan took out the stack of photos. He knew about them—that much was clear—and he smiled through the first few. But the smile soon began to look strained, then vanished altogether. Two thirds of the way through the stack, he shuffled the photos back together and returned them to the envelope. Obviously they were worse than he'd expected.

Darrell had been looking over Duncan's shoulder, eyes growing progressively wider with each shot. Now staring at the envelope in his brother's lap, they threatened to pop clean out of his skull.

Duncan forced his eyes up to mine and said quietly, "It appears I had something to hide after all."

Feeling a twinge of guilt, I plunged on, asking, "Did you know about the photos?"

Duncan pursed his mouth. "No."

"Dewey didn't mention them to you?"

"No."

"Then he wasn't using them to blackmail you?"

"Of course not."

"Do you know, then, why they were taken?"

Duncan looked me straight in the eye, squared his shoulders, and said, "I have no idea."

"Could it have had something to do with the sale of Shamrock?"

"That's possible, I suppose."

I nodded. "Do either of you know where we might find Lonnie Deets?"

Darrell shook his head, and Duncan said stiffly, "He wasn't taking out a loan, Mister Cochran, just asking for a handout, and he didn't give me an address."

"What about a phone number where he could be reached?"

"No," said Duncan.

Darrell kept shaking his head.

"What has Lonnie done?" asked Duncan.

I ignored the question. "Do you know where we can find Michael Nixon?"

"Why do you need to find him?" he asked.

"Somebody took those photographs," I said. "You say you don't know who or why, and I thought Mister Nixon might have some idea."

Duncan reluctantly gave me an address and phone number.

After taking them down, I held out a hand and said, "I'm afraid we need the photos back."

Duncan's knuckles showed white as they gripped the envelope. "Why?"

"They're evidence," I said.

"Of what?" he asked.

"Of extortion," I said.

After a moment, he gave in with a sigh and handed the envelope over.

I felt sorry for him. I firmly believe that a person's sex life is entirely a private matter, as long as it doesn't involve unwanted pain or injury to another person. If he'd had anything to do with Dewey's death, he should pay whatever the law demanded, but all we knew so far was that he'd been caught in a lie. No big surprise there. A homosexual who publicly damns homosexuals is obviously a hypocrite, but lying and hypocrisy aren't criminal. Which is probably just as well. Like it or not, if all the liars and hypocrites were thrown into jail, civilization wouldn't last out the day.

28

At three-thirty we met with the private detective, Lucas Halsey, in his office on the third floor of a half-empty building downtown on Gay Street.

When I knocked, he bellowed, "Come in!"

The office was deep, but narrow, with Halsey's desk at the opposite end.

Without stirring from his chair, he growled, "You Flanagan?"

"I'm Cochran; she's Flanagan."

"Well, I'm Halsey. Cop a seat." He waved his cigarette at the wooden chairs across the desk.

The area around the desk was crowded and cluttered, but the rest of the room was empty. The middle of the ceiling was blackened with soot, and under the smell of cigarette smoke, I detected a sharper, more acrid scent of burning.

Halsey was a heavyset man with skimpy gray hair, a reddened pockmarked face, and eyes that looked even wearier than Rooker's. Smoke from his Pall Mall drifted in a slanting column of sunlight from the window behind him. Flakes of ash littered the front of his suit jacket and spilled across the desk from a heaping tray of butts.

As I took a seat, I slid a copy of the letter he'd enclosed with the photos across the desk.

He glanced at it and sat back in his chair without a word.

"That's your signature, isn't it?" I asked.

He gave me his poker face. "What if it is?"

211

"We know it's yours," I said mildly. "These are what we call test questions, to see if you're willing to cooperate."

"Why should I do that?" he asked.

I shrugged. "Because, if you don't, we go to see Detective Rooker at Major Crimes, and *he* comes to talk to you."

He shrugged. "It's my signature."

"Those were some hot photos you took."

"Thanks."

"Out of curiosity, where were you when you shot the ones inside the room?"

"I was in the closet."

"How'd you get in there?" I asked. "One minute, you're outside, shooting them entering the motel room. Then the next, you're inside the closet? How'd you manage that?"

"I got a piece-a-shit friend a mine to shoot the outside stuff, while I waited in the closet, all camped out with my thermos and everything."

I shook my head. "What if Duncan decided to hang up his jacket?"

"The black boy was s'posed to take care a that."

"Weren't you taking a chance Duncan might spot you or hear you?"

"I used one of those spy cameras," he said. "Little skinny thing that slips into a shirt pocket. It don't make much noise to begin with, and I told Nixon to put on some music to cover what there was."

"Why didn't Duncan see you?"

"He had eyes only for his queer lover," he said. "Plus, I was all in black, and the closet door was open just wide enough to give me a clear shot."

"Sounds like you've done this before."

"Once or twice," he said dryly.

"Do you know why Dewey Flanagan wanted the pictures taken?"

"He didn't say, and I didn't ask."

"It didn't occur to you that they might be used for blackmail?"

"How a client uses 'em is none a my concern," said Halsey.

"Wonder if a jury would see it that way." When he just shrugged, I asked, "You develop the pics yourself, or farm them out?"

"I do 'em."

"Then I'd like to see the negatives."

"And I'd be happy to show 'em to you," he said, "except this place was broken into two weeks ago tomorrow, and—"

"The day Dewey came by for the pictures?"

"Later that night," he said. "And anyway, all my negatives were burned up or stolen. That's why it stinks in here, and it's how I got that." He jutted his chin at the soot-stained ceiling.

Lonnie had been busy. "You report the break-in?" I asked.

"Oh, yeah," he said.

"And?"

"The cops looked around and dusted the doorknobs. They said they'd get back to me if they found out anything, but that's the last I heard."

"So you're saying that all the negatives from the Flanagan shoot are gone?" I asked.

"Tha's right," he said.

"You know," I said mildly, "we could still go to the cops with this, if we had to."

"Uh huh." Halsey hoisted himself out of the chair. "Why don't I just show you what I got and save you all that bother?"

"We'd appreciate it."

In the corner of the office to his right was a recent addition about the size of a bathroom or walk-in closet, walled with unpainted Sheetrock.

Halsey pulled the door open and said, "Have a look."

The room was maybe five feet deep and ten from side to side, the interior walls a naked framework of two-by-fours

213

backed by the Sheetrock panels. Several eight-by-tens were drying on a clothesline that crossed at eye level from left to right, and cameras hung from hooks on a Peg-Board behind them. There was a counter for developing trays on the left, with a shelf for chemicals above and filing cabinets below. On the right, another counter supported a professional enlarger, with shelves of photographic paper below.

Halsey picked up a metal bucket wrapped in a plastic bag and handed it to me. The bucket was maybe a third full of ashes and melted goop, and even through the plastic, it reeked of burnt cellulose.

"You can search all you want," he said, "but there it is. Every negative, proof sheet, and photo I had was set on fire and left burnin' in the middle of the office floor. Woulda set off the sprinkler system, if the friggin' thing worked, and it's a wonder the whole place didn't go up." Halsey added with the beginning of a smile, "If the lab boys look real hard, they might find something from the Flanagan job in there."

I held up the bucket and asked, "Why'd you keep this?"

"My client got thrown into the nuthouse, then killed himself. And I had a hunch that, sooner or later, somebody was gonna come askin' about those pics."

"You could have saved everybody a lot of time and trouble by going to the police with this back at the beginning," I said.

"The sign says confidential investigations," he replied, "which means I don't kiss and tell."

Disgusted with him, I handed the bucket back. "And you're sure that's the lot?"

"That's it."

I pulled out a copy of the Comphoto and handed it to him. "You recognize this man?"

He examined it carefully and said, "This is that CPF stuff, idn't it?" He nodded appreciatively. "Not bad."

"Ever seen him before?"

"Might have," he said.

"The name Lonnie Deets mean anything to you?"

He looked back at the picture and nodded. "That's him, all right."

"How do you know him?"

"I was with the County when he was comin' up. Busted him once on a B 'n E."

I took the picture, wrote the phone number and address at the bighouse down on it, and gave it back to him. Helen had an answering machine we could use for taking calls on this. "If you stumble over any more pictures or negatives from the Flanagan shoot, we'd appreciate it if you'd send them to us. We wouldn't want to hear that they got into circulation."

"I'll keep an eye out," Halsey promised.

"That'll be all for now," I said, as I got to my feet. "But we may want to talk to you again later."

"I'll be here," he said, plopping back down in his desk chair. "Ain't goin' nowhere."

"What a relief," I said, and we showed ourselves out.

Michael Nixon met us at a small, dark café in the Old City, near his apartment. He was a good-looking, light-skinned black about five-ten. Slender, but tightly muscled, and not at all effeminate. His unlined face put him somewhere in his mid-twenties, but his hairline was receding prematurely. I wondered if that bothered him and assumed it must. I felt for him and knew I was lucky. I might have to battle the bulge, but at least I'd kept my hair.

We sat in a high-walled booth in a back corner of the bar, separated from the other booths by the doors to the kitchen. It wasn't happy hour yet, and there were only two other patrons, both seated at the bar and seemingly engrossed in their drinks. As long as we talked quietly, there wasn't much danger of them hearing us over the Miles Davis playing on the sound system.

215

After we introduced ourselves and shook hands across the table, I said, "Thanks for agreeing to see us, Mister Nixon."

"I didn't seem to have much choice," he said, looking at Molly. She'd called him after we left Halsey's office, catching him as he got home from work. Impatient to get on with it, he said, "You wanted to talk about the pictures."

"That's right," I said. "But first I'd like to establish a few facts, such as where you live and work."

He nodded. "I have an apartment in a building around the corner, and I teach at the Red Shoes Dance Academy, out on Kingston Pike."

"Are you from Knoxville?"

"Yes, sir," he said, putting a subtly derisive emphasis on the "sir." "Born at Fort Sanders Hospital and raised in the Walter P. Taylor Homes."

"How long have you known Duncan Flanagan?"

"A year or so."

"And how long have you been his lover?"

He looked at Molly. "Do I have to answer that?"

"No," she said, "you don't, Mister Nixon. But Duncan's in trouble, and if you help us, we may be able to see that his troubles remain private."

He looked from her to me and said with a doubtful smile, "And that's why you're here? To help Duncan?"

I stared back at him for a moment and finally admitted, "No, it isn't. But it happens that we share a common enemy in this and a mutual desire for privacy." I glanced at Molly, and she nodded.

"What kind of trouble is Duncan in?" he asked.

I took out a folded copy of the Comphoto and slid it across the table. "Do you recognize this man?"

He smoothed it out and took a look. "No, I don't think so. Who is he?"

"Did Duncan ever mention the name Lonnie Deets?"

"Not that I recall. What's he done?"

"The police think he's a murderer."

He was saved from having to respond to that by the bartender, who arrived with our drinks. When we were alone again, he took a sip of beer and asked quietly, "How is Duncan involved with this man?"

"He hired him to recover the photos."

Michael picked up his beer mug and held it for a moment, staring at nothing, then quietly put it back on the table. "So it's my fault that Duncan's in trouble."

"You're part of it," I agreed, "but the police don't know about the photos, and it may be possible to keep your names out of it."

"I don't believe you," he said flatly. "If murder's involved, it'll all come out."

"I didn't say it would be easy," I said, "but it might be possible."

"*How?*"

"Help us make sure that Deets is caught."

"But if he's caught, he'll tell them that Duncan hired him."

"This is an extremely dangerous man," I said, "and I don't think he intends to be taken alive."

He stared at me. "Then I'm supposed to hope they kill him?"

"That would be convenient," I agreed.

"Jesus!" He looked away. After a moment, he said, "Duncan and I have been lovers for over a year."

"Where did you meet?"

"At a bar."

"Duncan goes to gay bars?"

"Sometimes," he said. "When his wife is out of town on one of her trips."

"Does she go on many trips?"

"She's a travelin' fool," he said.

I laughed, and Michael smiled. "Does Duncan pay your rent?"

The smile faded. "Yes, he does."

"Would you describe him as generous?"

"Yes."

"And you consider him a friend?"

"Yes."

"A close friend?"

"Yes."

"And he feels the same way about you?"

He answered impatiently, "Well, he *did!*"

"Did you know you were going to be photographed when you invited him to the Sunset Motel?"

He squirmed. "Yes."

"Why did you do it, Michael?"

More squirming. "I needed money, and the private detective offered me a thousand dollars."

"You said Duncan was generous. Didn't you stand to gain more from the relationship than a quick thousand?"

"I suppose so." He didn't want to look at us.

"Then why did you do it?"

"For the money," he said impatiently.

"The thousand dollars."

"That's right."

"You needed it so desperately that you were willing to betray a friend?"

"Yes."

"Why?"

"I just needed it," he repeated.

"No other reason?"

"No."

"That doesn't make sense, Michael."

"I was stupid," he said.

"You don't seem stupid."

"Thanks."

"The private detective didn't make any threats, did he?"

Beat.

"He did, didn't he?"

Michael stared off for a moment, then reluctantly admitted, "He threatened to ruin me."

"How?"

He glanced at Molly, then at me, then down at his hands—both of which were clamped around his beer mug. "He said he'd tell my boss I had sex with children." He looked back at me. "It's not *true*, but that wouldn't have made any difference to Missus Galloway, the woman who runs the academy."

"You mean she'd just accept an unsupported accusation like that?"

He sighed with force and came out with it. "I have a juvenile record, a charge of rape and sodomy. The boy was fourteen, and I was sixteen, and the cops caught us doing it in the backseat of a Chevy Caprice in a Kroger parking lot. The charges were dropped, and the whole thing was hushed up because the boy's family had money, and that was the way they wanted it. Juvenile records are supposed to be sealed, anyway, but somehow this detective found out about it and threatened to tell Missus Galloway." He shook his head. "I have ten classes of children every week, and if the rumor of something like that got out, I'd never work again."

"What Halsey did was extortion," I said. "You know that, don't you?"

"No kidding," said Michael. "Of course I know it's extortion, but who am I going to tell?"

Molly said, "You tell the cops."

He asked in disbelief. "And you think they'd do something?"

"I think they could probably get Halsey's license suspended," she said.

He considered it. "Would I have to testify?"

"Probably."

"But if I do, the whole thing will come out, won't it?"

"It might," she said.

"If it did, I'd lose my job, and Duncan would be ruined."

"It could happen that way," she agreed.

"Then, if you don't mind," he said, "I'll leave well enough alone."

She said, "It's because nobody wants to testify that Halsey gets away with this."

"I'm sure you're right," he said, "but I'll let the next guy be the hero."

"When did you last see Duncan?" I asked.

"That night at the motel."

"When the pictures were taken?"

He nodded. "Since then, he won't talk to me."

"Then he knows you were involved?"

He nodded. "He called and said I'd betrayed him, and I couldn't deny it. I tried to explain, but he wouldn't listen."

"You came to Dewey's viewing, didn't you?"

"How do you—?"

"I saw you talking to Darrell."

"Yes," he said. "He promised that Duncan would get in touch with me, but he hasn't." He sighed and shook his head. "And I understand how he feels. How could he ever trust me again?"

Not knowing what to say to that, I thanked him again for talking to us, and we left.

29

That evening, Donald told us that he would be admitted to Fort Sanders Medical Center the following morning and would spend the next ten weeks undergoing an experimental cancer treatment at the Thompson Cancer Survival Center, which was adjacent to and associated with Fort Sanders. He had been on the Survival Center's waiting list for six months and had phoned them the day he arrived in Knoxville to ask if they could find a bed for him, and the Center had finally called this afternoon to say that an opening had been found. Molly offered to drive him to the Center in the morning, but Donald explained that Helen had volunteered to take him.

Thursday morning, Molly and I were awakened by a call from her reporter friend, Oliver Fryman, who informed us that we had an appointment with Darrell's bookie at one o'clock that afternoon. Then, during breakfast with Donald and Helen, we received a call from Lester Prine's personal assistant, Simon Truscott, who said that his boss would be pleased to see us on his boat at ten this morning, if that would be convenient.

If *I'd* owned Lester's boat, I would have called it a yacht. All white except for the many-colored flags and pennants flying from the radio mast, it stretched sixty feet in length and looked like it could comfortably sleep a couple of dozen. It was docked in the Tennessee River at the marina on Neyland Drive, in sight of the great brick and steel edifice of Neyland Stadium, the home of the Tennessee Volunteers and the spiritual center of Big Orange Country.

We were met at the gangplank by a muscular young man in tennis whites. I took him for a bodyguard, but he turned out to be the personal assistant, Simon Truscott, the one who'd called us about the appointment.

His boss was mixing Bloody Marys under a sun awning on the boat's afterdeck. Lester was a bear of a man in his seventies with a meaty, but still handsome face, no hair on top, and a close-cut fringe of silver-gray. He wiped his hands on a towel as we approached and reached out to shake Molly's hand, saying with a hint of an East Tennessee twang, "I'm Lester Prine, Miz Flanagan."

"A pleasure to meet you, Mister Prine."

"Call me Lester, please."

"All right, Lester. Call me Molly. And this is my friend, Bull Cochran."

He took my hand and gave it a firm squeeze. "Glad to meet you, Bull."

"You, too, Mister Prine."

"Lester."

"Lester."

He glanced at his assistant. "That'll be all for now, Simon, but would you check on the luncheon preparations?"

"Certainly, Mister Prine." Simon nodded at us, then did an about-face and marched off to the galley.

Turning back to the bar, Lester said, "Sorry I can't invite you for lunch, but I'm afraid it's strictly business today. I'm having a couple of city councilmen down for a little strokin'."

"That's all right, Lester," said Molly. "We don't want to take up too much of your time."

"It's my pleasure," he assured her, pouring Bloody Marys into heavy crystal goblets and thrusting them our way. We took them, and he waved at a couple of padded chaise lounges, saying, "Make yourselves comfortable."

I sat and sipped my drink, finding it deliciously tart and spicy, a real eye-opener.

As he poured one for himself, he said solemnly, "I was sorry to hear about Dewey."

Molly nodded. "A great loss to the family."

"To anyone who knew him," he assured her.

Molly watched him over her drink as he lowered himself onto the chaise lounge across from us. He accomplished this with slow, grunting effort, carefully settling his rump onto the padding and stretching out his legs with a grateful sigh.

When he was seated, she said, "I'd always understood that you and Dewey were famous enemies."

He laughed. "Don't know about famous," he said, "and there was a time when we were friends. In fact, he was the best friend I had, and he might have stayed that way if not for Helen."

"What happened?" asked Molly. "All I know is that she went out with you."

"Once," he said.

"Just once?"

"That's right," he agreed. "It was a deal with her father. She was supposed to marry Dewey in a month, but her father promised to release half of her dowry to her if she went out with me. And if she chose to marry me instead of Dewey, she would not only get the rest of the dowry, but he would pay for a round-the-world trip for our honeymoon."

"Why was he so hot for her to marry *you?*" Molly asked.

"Oh, it wasn't me in particular," he said. "As far as her old man was concerned, *anybody* would've been better than Dewey."

"Why?"

"It was a conflict of personalities," he said. "Dewey rubbed him the wrong way. But it was also a class thing. Helen's people were old Atlanta money, like mine were old Knoxville money, and our families had known each other for generations. But Dewey's people had been here less than fifty years, and Helen's father didn't think this newcomer was good enough for his daughter."

"Then you and Helen knew each other before your date?"

"Oh, yeah," he said. "I played with her as a kid on trips down to Atlanta, and she came up with her family to visit me a few times. But I hadn't seen her in ten years when Dewey brought her to meet everybody." He added with a grin, "I was there with the rest of the gang to meet his train, and Dewey introduced us without realizing we knew each other."

"Then you and Dewey really *were* friends," she said.

He laughed. "Hell, yes! We got into a lot of trouble together. Even spent our first night in the drunk tank together, and that's something you don't forget."

"So why did you agree to go out with his fiancée?"

"Well, Helen was a real beauty," he said, "and I thought I deserved a crack at her, same as Dewey. Plus, I figured I had dibs, since I'd seen her first. And it was also part of the game we played. Always competing at cards and snooker and women, always trying to see who could drink the most, spit the furthest, or fart the loudest." He laughed some more. "But I didn't realize until it was too late that Helen wasn't just another girl for Dewey. He was in love with this one."

"So you just asked her out?"

"No, as I said, it was all set up by her father. He wrote mine a letter, couching the whole thing in business terms. He offered me an impressive sum for just asking her out and a very handsome settlement indeed should I persuade her to be my wife. Then he wrote Helen a letter, explaining the terms as they applied to her."

"And she accepted?"

He smiled. "Helen was always a practical woman at heart."

"So what happened?"

"We spent the day together and had a picnic down at the river. We went for a ride in my Packard, and that evening we had dinner and a party at my parents' house. But Dewey showed up and made a scene." Lester cackled. "The bastard was drunk as a skunk and wavin' his gun around like he was some Wild West desperado, threatenin' to shoot me, or Helen, or himself, if she didn't come away with him. My father called the police, and they took Dewey to jail. But Helen insisted on going with him, and I knew I'd lost. For me, it was just a lark anyway, a chance to spend a day with a beautiful woman and get a little jab in at my good buddy. But I didn't realize it was so serious for Dewey.

"I tried to apologize and even wrote him a letter about it, but it didn't do any good. From that day on, he was my enemy, and he did all he could to make my life hell. My people might have been here longer, but his had more money and the influence where it counted. I was just setting up shop as an architect at the time, but thanks to Dewey, nobody wanted to hire me. And to make a long story short, the sonofabitch ran me out of town."

He shook his head, grinned, and sipped his Bloody Mary. "Now, you might think that would give me reason to want to see Dewey dead," he went on, "but I don't feel that way anymore. Haven't felt it for a long time. The truth is that moving to Atlanta was the best thing that could have happened to me. It put me in on the ground floor of the boom and made me one of the most successful builders in the country, as well as a very rich man. So," he concluded with a wry grin, "if Dewey was here right now—much as it would pain me to do it—I'd have to thank the sonofabitch."

"How much does this 'New Knoxville' project mean to you?" I asked.

"Well, I don't have too much capital tied up in it," he said, "if that's what you mean. Not yet, anyway. Just a little development money, and that's a write-off if the project falls through. But . . ." He nodded. "It's important to me, *yes*. I want this to work."

"Why?"

He waved around. "It's my hometown, Mister Cochran, and this is my chance to make a mark on it."

"And Dewey was standing in your way."

He gave me a wry grin and shook his head. "I had him this time. Shamrock is on its last legs, and he knew that. He fought me because that was the way he was, but when the time came, I figured he'd give in and sell. And if he didn't, the other brothers would do it for him."

"You couldn't *know* that," said Molly.

"Darrell and Duncan were with me from the start," he said, "and they were convinced your father was in the bag as well."

"They may have been premature on that," she said.

"Maybe," he said mildly.

"But with Dewey dead," she said, "there's no question, is there?"

"No, there isn't," he agreed. "Without him, who's going to run Shamrock? Darrell and Duncan don't want it. Helen and your father don't have the energy. And how about you? Are *you* willing to leave your detective job to run a failing coffee business?"

"No," she conceded.

"I didn't think so," he said. "Helen will resist, of course, because Dewey would have wanted her to, but she'll smarten up before the board meeting and vote for the sale."

"And you'll have your final victory over Dewey," said Molly.

"Oh, I already have it," he said sadly. "I'm alive, and Dewey's dead. In any logical scoring system, that means I win."

We stood and thanked him for his time. As we shook hands, two young men in spiffy white stewards' uniforms appeared—one with his arms full of table linens, the other

226

pushing a cart loaded with china and crystal. We left as they started setting up the table for Lester's luncheon.

We had an hour before our appointment with the bookie, so we killed time by driving through the sprawling University of Tennessee campus. To my eyes, the students looked more like high schoolers than undergraduates, but I'd had the same reaction on other visits to college campuses.

Arms full of books, they stood or walked with members of the opposite sex, or hurried alone to class. Others jogged, or tossed Frisbees, or played a pickup game of basketball at an outside court. Except for changes in fashion and hairstyle and the prevalence of Walkmans, it could have been a scene from my own college days. I envied their possibilities and pitied their disillusionments. They had yet to learn that life was a killer.

30

We met Darrell's bookie in the parking lot of Bill
Meyer Stadium, Home of the Knoxville Smokies,
an AA franchise in the Southern League. The Smokies
were part of the World Champion Toronto Blue Jays'
minor league system, and the concrete-block stadium was
freshly painted in the Blue Jays' colors: blue and white.

A dark blue Mercedes was waiting for us, and two men
got out as we pulled up. The driver was my height, six-two
or so, but twenty years younger and a lot more muscular,
with no neck and overdeveloped trapeziuses ruining the
line of his Armani suit. A second man got out of the backseat on the other side and came around to stand by the back
door. This one was in his fifties with brush-cut hair and a
rock-hard face. He was a head shorter than his comrade and
wasn't dressed as well, but the Armani suit waited for a nod
from him before opening the back door.

The man who emerged was in his mid-thirties with dark
hair and Mediterranean good looks. He was sleek and trim
and maybe six feet tall, dressed in casual yuppie gear: penny
loafers and no socks, khaki chinos, and a forest-green polo
shirt.

He grinned at us and said, "I'm Frank Brazzi, and these
are my associates." He nodded at the older man—"Mister
Bolla"—and the younger—"Mister Cardini." His speech
retained only a hint of his New Jersey heritage, overlaid
with the mid-Atlantic diction taught at good New England

228

prep schools. To Molly he added, "And you're Miz Flanagan. Or should I call you Detective Flanagan?"

"Molly's okay," she said.

"Then Molly it is." He explained to his bookends, "Molly's a Galveston Police detective, gentlemen, so keep your jackets buttoned." Then he turned to me and said, "You must be Bull Cochran."

"That's me," I agreed, and shook his hand. His grip was casual, like his attire.

"And here we have a former major league pitcher," he said to his men, "one who actually stood on the mound at Yankee Stadium."

"Only once," I said, "and briefly at that. Until the Yank hitters shelled me into the dugout."

Frank laughed. "At least you made it into the history books." He turned to his guards. "You see before you, gentlemen, only the second pitcher in the history of professional baseball to kill a man with a pitched ball."

Thanks for reminding me, asshole. "That's right," I admitted.

"As a matter of fact, I understand you've killed three men." He sounded like he was discussing my golf handicap, and I thought to myself that Frank was one passive-aggressive slimeball.

"Two, actually, Mister Brazzi," I told him.

"I thought it was three," he said. "And call me Frank, please." Including Molly with a smile, he added, "Both of you."

"All right, Frank," I said. "But I'm pretty sure it was only two."

"What about the guy on the boat?"

"I didn't kill him. That rumor was started by a Houston reporter, but rumors are hard to stop."

"Indeed," he said. "Denials are useless, and saying 'no comment' only makes you look guilty."

Molly said with just a soupçon of impatience, "We appreciate you're agreeing to see us, Frank, but we don't want to take up too much of your time. We have just a few questions."

"Of course you do, Molly," he said pleasantly. "But there's no rush, is there?"

"Well, no, but—"

"It's a lovely afternoon," he went on, "and I've been running around all morning. I haven't had a chance for lunch, and I thought we'd have a picnic, if that's all right with you two."

I didn't particularly want to eat with the man, but sharing a meal with him appeared to be his price for answering our questions, so we agreed that a picnic sounded okay with us. He led the way to a gate in the right field fence, then his associate, Mr. Bolla, unlocked it, and we stepped through into foul territory.

The smell of grass and line chalk was achingly familiar, as were the faintly lingering (or, no doubt, imagined) odors of beer and roasted peanuts, sweat and liniment, resin and pine tar.

On the grass behind the plate, in the shade of the covered stands, a table had been set for three. As we approached, I could see it was only a card table and folding chairs, but the table was draped with white linen and set with fine china, crystal, and silverware. Mr. Brazzi was going to a lot of trouble to impress us, and I couldn't help wondering why.

"How'd you get a key to this place?" I asked.

"The groundskeeper's assistant is a friend of mine," he said, which I assumed meant that the groundskeeper's assistant was a betting man. "He slipped me the key, on the condition that I clean up after myself and not tear up the sod."

The younger bodyguard/chauffeur poured champagne, and the older one tossed a Caesar salad, as Frank said, "I have to tell you, Bull, that I envy you." He jerked a thumb toward the stands. "I have a box over there, and I'm in it every game—that's how much I love this sport. I know that everybody around here is supposed to bleed orange and root for the Volunteers, but my game is baseball, and my team is the Knoxville Smokies.

"When I was a kid, my team was the Yankees, of course, and I used to dream of taking the mound at the Stadium, or putting one over that short left field fence. But the fact is," he said with a shrug, "I wasn't good enough. But you. You made it. You were there." He shook his head. "I can't imagine a bigger thrill than that."

"No," I reluctantly agreed.

After staring at me expectantly for a moment, he said with smiling disbelief, "That's all you have to say on the subject?"

"I don't really like to talk about it, Frank."

"Why not?"

"Because I fell on my face, damn it!"

Both guards turned and took a step my way, but Frank raised a hand, and they went back to what they were doing. "Now you're angry at me," he said unhappily. "It was the digs about how many men you've killed, wasn't it?" He shook his head. "It's Sicilian humor, but not everybody understands that, and I went too far, as usual. I apologize for offending you."

"That's okay."

"If you don't want to talk about what it was like in the majors, that's okay, too. It's just that I'm a fan, and I don't often get to talk to somebody who's actually been there."

I sighed and thought, *Oh, what the hell.* "It *was* a thrill, Frank. I just wish I'd done something to keep me up there a little longer."

He nodded sympathetically. "You don't know whether to feel blessed for the chance, or cursed for the failure."

We all stared at him in amazement until Mr. Bolla broke the spell by serving the salad. It was followed by a cold cucumber soup, then a main course of steamed asparagus tips in a hollandaise sauce, artichoke hearts vinaigrette, and any combination of cold lobster claws, broiled lobster tails, and lobster thermidor.

"It's from 'Frank's,' my restaurant," said Frank. "Original name, huh? What do you think of the food?"

"Delicious," I said, and Molly nodded, her mouth too full to speak.

He was pleased. "I'll tell the chef. He's French and a real fag princess bastard, but he can cook." He said to Molly, "Ask your uncle Darrell. He's a regular. Eats lunch there every weekday."

Molly nodded. "I heard you knew each other."

Frank grinned. "I can imagine what you've heard," he said. "That I'm his bookie, that he owes me money, and that I'm putting pressure on him to pay up?"

Molly nodded. "That's the gist of it. Is it true?"

His grin softened into a smile. "If I asked if you were wearing a wire, you'd say no, wouldn't you?"

"Of course," she agreed.

"And I'd believe you," he said, "because you're an honest person. Besides, you're not interested in me. You just want to know what's happening to your family."

"Does that mean you *know* what's happening?"

"I know what I hear," he said.

"And what do you hear?"

"I heard about your uncle's death, of course. That was front-page news. But I've also heard about shootings and burglaries, cars being run off the road, and people being pushed down stairs."

"How do you know all that?" Molly asked him, not liking it.

"As I say, I hear things," he said. "The trick is figuring out how much of it to believe." He turned to me. "Since you're new to this part of the country, Mister Cochran, I should tell you that, when these people give you the glad hand, the slap on the back, and the good-ole-boy grin, you better duck, because the bullshit is about to fly. If you're not from here, you're an outsider, and once an outsider, always an outsider. Except that they don't come out and tell you that. Up North, they might curse you to your face, but down here they wait till you leave the room. That's what's meant by Southern Hospitality."

I thought there was some truth in what he said, but Molly objected, "Then how do you, as an outsider, rate such good information?"

"You have to break down the barrier on an individual basis, Molly, then rely on a chosen few for the inside scoop."

"Including a friend or two among the cops?" she suggested.

"Well," he said with a modest grin, "law enforcement officials are an important source of information. Wouldn't you agree?"

"Handy, too," she said, "for someone in your business."

"Restaurateur, you mean."

"That, too."

Getting back to the point, he said, "Concerning your family's troubles, I know at least one thing that you *don't*."

"What's that?"

"That whatever is happening to you has nothing to do with me."

Oddly enough, I believed him. On the other hand, I'd been wrong before.

Molly thought about it, wiping hot sauce off her fingers. "You haven't denied that you're Darrell's bookie."

He smiled into his wineglass and took a sip. "What if it were true? What if, on occasion, I happened to place a friendly wager for your uncle, as a favor to a valued customer? It's illegal, yes, but it's a crime at which the law only winks. You know it, and I know it." Molly nodded. "As for putting pressure on Darrell, I think that a man should pay his debts, but I'm not Michael Corleone, and I've never found it necessary to use strong-arm tactics."

233

Molly glanced at Bolla and Cardini, and Frank laughed. "You might find this hard to believe, but in spite of my charm, there are people who actually wish me ill." He nodded at his guards. "That's why these gentlemen are here."

I wondered if Frank could be in the Witness Protection Program. It would explain a few things, including his being in Knoxville. He was keeping a high profile for a man in hiding, but from what I'd heard, that wasn't unusual. I considered asking him about it, but if it was true, then he would only deny it. Instead, I took out a copy of the Com-photo, unfolded it, and laid it on the table in front of him. "Do you know this man?" I asked.

He took a look. "Don't believe I do." Then he held it out to his bodyguard. "Mario?"

Bolla finished pouring my coffee before examining the picture. He indicated that Cardini should look, too, and when the younger man shook his head, Bolla said, "We ain't seen him." Unlike Frank, he sounded straight out of Newark.

"Who is he?" Frank asked me.

"Does the name Lonnie Deets mean anything to you?"

"No," he said. "Mario?"

Bolla glanced at Cardini, who shook his head. "Never heard a him."

I nodded and said, "If you don't mind my asking, Frank, why did you agree to see us?"

He took a sip of coffee, then turned to Molly. "I met your uncle Dewey about a year ago, when he showed up at my restaurant one night and told me who he was. He said he needed to talk to me, so I took him into the office. He told me he was there to pay off his brother's debt, but said he'd wanted to see what sort of man I was first. When I asked him what he thought, he said he hadn't decided yet, but he wasn't impressed so far." Frank laughed. "He was a hard man, but I liked him. I was sorry to hear that he was dead, and I was surprised it was suicide. He didn't seem like the type."

"I don't think it *was* suicide," Molly said.

He looked interested. "I heard he opened his veins."

"Or somebody opened them for him."

"That's inventive," he said.

The driver nodded, and the older man seemed to consider the logistics.

"You know, Frank," Molly said, "you could probably help us, if you wanted to."

He blotted his mouth and dropped his napkin on the table. "Help you?"

"As you say, a man in your business hears things. If you happened to hear anything that might be relevant to my family's troubles, you could call me."

He smiled. "I just *know* you're not asking me to spy on my customers."

She looked him straight in the eye and said dryly, "You might think of it as doing your civic duty."

Frank liked that. "Well, I'll keep it in mind," he said with a grin, "in case I hear anything. Meanwhile, you two have to promise to come to my restaurant some evening. Dinner, of course, will be on me."

I glanced at Molly, who said without a trace of sarcasm, "We'd love it."

31

That evening, we went with Helen and Cyrus to visit Ida at St. Mary's. After an hour of her surliness, we drove downtown to see Donald at Fort Sanders. Every effort had been made to create a positive atmosphere on the cancer ward, but sadness hung over the place like a cloud, and the smells took me back to the time I'd spent watching my father die. I was happy to leave there.

After we got back to the bighouse, Rooker called to tell us that Duncan had been attacked and beaten this evening in the Shamrock parking lot and had been taken to Fort Sanders. We didn't bother Helen with the news, but twenty minutes later, we were back at the hospital.

Duncan had a concussion, a dislocated shoulder, three broken ribs, and he'd lost a tooth. He wore a bandage over his left eye for a scratched cornea and had a shaved area the size and shape of a playing card on the right side of his head, where a C-shaped flap of skin had been reattached to his scalp. His face was lumpy and lopsided, the worst of the swelling on the left side (indicating a right-handed assailant). The bruises on his arms and face were mostly red, but the worst were already beginning to darken.

He had told the police his attacker was a black man in his early twenties, but we didn't believe it.

"It was Lonnie, wasn't it?" asked Molly.

Duncan was sitting up in bed, his good eye staring straight ahead, but he wasn't talking. Not to us, at least.

Molly said, "He killed your brother, Duncan, and now

he's trying to kill you. Are you going to let him get away with that?"

The eye blinked; otherwise, nothing.

"We're talking about saving your life," she said.

Still nothing.

"It's all going to come out, Duncan," she said. "It's too late to stop it. If Lonnie survives, he'll tell them you hired him. And if he doesn't, they'll still make a case against you. All they have to do is put you two together, then it's only a question of *what* you hired him to do. Are you going to let *him* tell them, or would you rather get your version of the story on the record first?" He blinked a couple of times, but that was all. "You're an accomplice to murder. You know that, don't you?" Duncan shook his head. "Oh, yes, the police are reopening the case, and it's only a matter of time before they prove that Lonnie killed Dewey."

"No," he said.

"Is that what you wanted, Duncan?" she asked. "Did you really want Dewey dead?"

"Of course not," he said, and stopped. The one good eye stared hard at Molly, then finally closed, and his body seemed to go slack. After a moment, he said in an exhausted voice, "He was supposed to get the photos, that's all."

"The ones Dewey was using to blackmail you?"

"Yes."

"To get you to vote against selling Shamrock?"

"Yes."

"When were the pictures taken?"

"On a Monday about three weeks ago."

"That would make it the Monday before Dewey chased Darrell out of his office."

"Right."

"When did Dewey tell you about them?"

"He called that Wednesday. Said he was having some of them blown up, and they would be ready for me by the weekend." The eye closed, and he gently shook his head.

237

"Dewey could be a real bastard when he wanted to."

"When did you call Lonnie?"

"I didn't," he said. "He came to see me that Thursday at my office."

Surprised. "*He* came to you?"

"Yes."

"Did he drop in often?"

"I hadn't seen him in years."

"Did he know about the photos?" I asked.

"No." He stopped. "I don't *think* he did." His eye tracked my way. "How could he know?"

"It just seems like quite a coincidence that he should happen to drop by the day after Dewey tells you about the photos. What did Lonnie say to you?"

"That he needed money, and he wondered if there was anything he could do to earn some."

"And what did *you* say?"

"I told him Dewey had something of mine, and he said he'd get it back for me."

"But it wasn't that easy, was it?"

"No," he agreed. "He broke into Dewey's study that night, but he didn't find anything."

Molly asked, "How did you contact him?"

"There was a number where I could reach him sometimes."

"What number?" asked Molly.

"For the phone at a bar out in Fountain City," he said. "But I spoke to the bartender yesterday, and he hadn't seen him in a week."

"I'd like that number," said Molly.

"In the drawer there," he said. "The black appointment book, look under *L* for Lonnie."

Molly took out the appointment book, found the number, and wrote it down. "Do you know where he's staying?"

"No, I'm afraid not."

She nodded. "So what happened tonight?"

"I went out looking for Michael."

"Michael Nixon?"

"Yes."

"Why?"

He looked away. "I wanted to talk to him."

"About what?"

"Can you believe I missed his company?" He shook his head. "In spite of what he did to me, I was lonely for him."

"He was coerced, you know," said Molly.

He turned back. "What?"

"The private detective threatened to ruin his career if he didn't get you to that motel room."

"I didn't know that," he admitted, "but that still doesn't excuse what he did. He should have told me. I could have done something."

"He made a stupid mistake," she agreed.

"Yes, he did."

"But I thought you should know."

"Yes, thank you."

"So, anyway," she said, getting back to business, "you went out looking for Michael, and . . ."

"I tried his apartment, but he wasn't home, so I checked the bars in the Old City. When I still didn't find him, I had a drink and went back to the car. I'd parked in the fenced-in lot at Shamrock, and I had to unlock the gate to get back in, but Lonnie was waiting for me inside. He didn't say a word; he just started hitting me. And when I fell down, he kicked me."

"You're lucky he didn't kill you," she said.

"He was trying to," he said with a shiver. "I'd be dead now if some people hadn't walked by and seen us. A man yelled for Lonnie to stop and shook the fence, and his friends joined in. When one of them cried that he was going for the police, Lonnie gave me one last kick and ran off."

I asked, "How did you know the photos would be in the office that Friday?"

"I didn't," he said. "But Dewey got to work late that morning, and if he picked them up on his way in, it made sense that they'd be there."

"When did you make the date for lunch?"

"That morning."

"No wonder he was suspicious," I said. "He shows up late with the photos, and you suddenly call to invite him to lunch."

Molly asked him, "How did you know Dewey was late for work?"

"We got a call from Darrell's spy," he said.

"A spy at Shamrock?"

"Of course."

It surprised both of us. "I didn't know Darrell was that cunning," she said.

His good eye settled on her. "There's a lot you don't know about us, Molly."

"I'm starting to think I don't know much of anything," she agreed. "To start with, why is Lonnie waging war on us? Why does he hate us so much?"

We'd talked it over, and we believed we knew the answer to that, but we needed confirmation.

"You'll have to ask Helen," he said.

"I don't want to ask Helen," she said impatiently. "I'm tired of playing games. I want *you* to tell me."

But he wouldn't. All he would say was, "You'll have to talk to Helen."

We did, but we had to wait until Friday evening to do it, because Helen had a doctor's appointment that morning, and we had a meeting with the M.E.

Dr. Cleveland, the Knox County Medical Examiner, was in his late fifties, had a long, dour, hangdog face, and stretched about a hundred and eighty pounds over a six-foot-six-inch frame. He looked and even sounded a bit like the late film actor John Carradine, making him central casting for the role of undertaker or pathologist. His dialect was deep

South, his speech cultivated, and his courtly manner that of an old-style Southern Gentleman.

When he bent over Molly's hand, I half expected him to kiss it, but he didn't. Not quite. He escorted her to a chair and said, "I knew your uncle well, Miz Flanagan, and I have found it difficult to accept his death. My profession doesn't encourage illusions about immortality, but for someone of Dewey's energy and passion for life, dying seems not merely unfortunate, but sadly inappropriate."

Molly nodded.

"However," he went on, "as I said on the phone, I really can't imagine how I can help you. I'm afraid the evidence clearly dictated a ruling of suicide."

She nodded. "Your ruling mentioned the presence of psychotropic drugs. Would you mind telling me which drugs were detected?"

"Not at all." Opening a file folder, he said, "Frankly, I was surprised that Dewey was able to work himself into a suicidal state, given the amount of Thorazine in his system."

Molly sat forward. "Thorazine?"

He nodded, consulting a sheet of paper. "Fifty milligrams, at least. Individual response varies greatly, but at that dosage, in combination with Prozac and Xanax, most of us would be tranquil as lambs. The presence of Thorazine probably indicated a recent bout of agitation."

"But Doctor Fredericks said Dewey was calm and lucid that morning. He also told us what medications Dewey was being given, and he made no mention of Thorazine."

Dr. Cleveland pursed his lips. "Perhaps a mistake was made in the dispensing of medications. It's been known to happen."

"I don't believe that was the case here," Molly insisted. She told him about Lonnie Deets—what we knew and what we suspected.

He took a moment to absorb the information, then picked up the phone, touched a button, and said, "Missus

Wilkinson, would you get Doctor Fredericks at Riverside Center on the phone for me, please?"

As he replaced the receiver, Molly asked him, "How did you know Dewey?"

"We were both members of the Holston Hills Country Club, and we played golf there regularly for forty years. In fact," he said, "we played the Sunday before he was admitted to the hospital."

"Did he seem troubled?"

"Not noticeably," he said. "Distracted, perhaps. I seem to recall him muttering to himself once or twice that afternoon, but we all do that occasionally, and I thought nothing of it. It didn't appear to affect his play. Even with his handicap, he was low man in the foursome."

The phone beeped, and he picked it up. It was Doctor Fredericks, and they spoke for several minutes. After putting the receiver down, he took a moment to consider his words. "I'm satisfied," he said finally, "that none of Doctor Fredericks' nursing staff administered the Thorazine."

"And Lonnie Deets?" Molly asked.

He steepled his long fingers under his chin and conceded, "It would appear that Mister Deets had the opportunity. Doctor Fredericks confirmed that Thorazine is available at his facility in all its forms. I saw no evidence of a recent intramuscular injection, so it would appear that the drug was administered orally. The bitter taste of Thorazine is difficult to mask in foods, but Doctor Fredericks suggested that it could have been divided between his cereal, coffee, and orange juice. It wouldn't have improved his oatmeal," he added, "but Dewey was never known for his discerning palate."

Molly smiled. "Then you're willing to reconsider your ruling?"

"It would appear that I have no choice," he said solemnly. "If necessary, I'll move to have the body disinterred."

"Thank you, Doctor," said Molly.

"Not at all, my dear," he said, in his courtly fashion. "Dewey was my friend, and the very least I can do is to accurately determine the cause of his death."

We went straight from Doctor Cleveland's office to Darrell's office, but Ms. Markham told us he wasn't in today. She graciously allowed us to confirm this by peeking into his office, and if he was there, he was hiding in the john. We got no answer when we tried calling his house, but we drove there anyway.

Darrell lived in a splendid Tudor on the north bank of the Tennessee River. It was in Sequoia Hills, west of the UT area, one of the oldest and most exclusive developments in town.

We rang the doorbell and tried the brass knocker, then walked around back to the patio and knocked on the French doors. We got no response there either, and the place looked deserted. The woman next door was pruning her rosebushes, and after Molly introduced herself, she was willing to talk to us. She'd seen Darrell's wife drive away with their children the afternoon before, and she hadn't seen anybody around the house since then.

When we called Frank Brazzi, he said Darrell hadn't showed up for his lunch reservation.

Before dinner that evening, we spoke to Helen in the front parlor. Had it been *after* dinner, it would have been the back parlor.

When Molly asked about Lonnie, Helen took a sip of wine and stared off for a moment. Then she put the glass down on the coffee table, sat up straight, and smoothed the skirt over her knees. "Dewey was their father," she said finally, "Lonnie's and Tim's. And Sybil Deets was his mistress."

So we had our confirmation, but Molly didn't look

happy about it. Among other things, it meant that she'd slept with her half brother—a hillbilly cliché brought to life.

Shaking her head in disgust, she asked, "What about Mitch? What did he have to say about it?"

Helen said with a sneer, "Mitch Leary was a shiftless drunk, who'd do anything Dewey asked as long as he kept him in liquor and chew. Mitch was living in a rooming house off Vine Street when Dewey found him and introduced him to Sibyl and suggested that she let him move in. He was there to serve as Dewey's cover, so nobody would suspect that the boys were his. Mitch was given a roof over his head, regular meals, and pocket money, and all he had to do to earn it was move into the shed out back of the house whenever Dewey came to visit."

"And you *knew* this?" Molly asked in disbelief.

"I learned about it after Rachel was born," she said. "That's why there were three years between Rachel and Ruth. Then, after Ruth, I couldn't have any more children, and Dewey couldn't have what he wanted more than anything."

"A son, you mean?"

Helen nodded and said, "He never forgave me for that."

"But he *had* sons."

She sighed and looked away. "Oh, yes, he had them, but they weren't *our* sons, and Dewey could never acknowledge them." Again she sighed. "He never forgave me for that, either."

There seemed to be two Dewey Flanagans. One was the generous spirit and bigger-than-life character loved by Molly, Helen, and his workers, by a Pulitzer Prize-winning novelist, by a famous country singer, and by practically everybody else who knew him. While the other Dewey blackmailed his brother, emotionally abused his loving wife, and denied his sons their birthright. The novelist described him as a man of contradictions, but he didn't know the half of it.

32

After dinner, Molly stepped out into the garden for some air, and I was alone in the back parlor, sipping a brandy, when the phone rang. Nobody else picked it up, so I answered. It was Frank Brazzi, phoning to say that Darrell had called.

"When?" I asked.

"Five minutes ago," he said. "He asked me to have the chef prepare something for take-out."

"Know where he was calling from?"

"No, but he told me he'd be by in half an hour. If you hurry, you should make it in time."

"Thanks," I said. "Where are you located?"

"Take the West Town exit off I-Forty, and go right on Kingston Pike. The restaurant's in the first strip center to the right. Look for a red neon sign saying 'Frank's.' "

"Thanks again," I said.

We were on our way in five minutes. Traffic was stop-and-go on I-40, due to a multicar accident, and we had to get off and take Kingston Pike. But we still pulled into the strip center just over twenty minutes later.

The restaurant had pale stucco walls and a fake thatch roof intended to give it the look of a French peasant's cottage. "Frank's" was written in longhand with red neon to the left of the entrance. The rest of the strip was closed for the evening, but the parking lot in front of the restaurant was jammed with cars, and we were lucky to find a space on the end, near the pike.

We were thirty feet from the entrance when I saw Darrell come out. He was ahead of schedule. A few minutes later, and we'd have missed him. He was all in black tonight, his jacket collar turned up and a wide-brimmed hat pulled low, but I recognized him. His furtiveness and the two plastic bags of takeout food gave him away. He stepped off the curb and started toward us, then spotted us and stopped.

We kept walking, and Molly said, "We just want to talk, Darrell."

He took a step back.

"Sooner or later," she went on, "you're going to have to talk to somebody."

An engine roared off to the left, and we glanced toward the sound. Tires squealed, and a dark sedan peeled away from the curb. A full-size Ford Motor Company car from the seventies, maybe an LTD.

Darrell barely had time to move. He threw the two plastic bags up in the air, took one step toward us, and the car hit him. The impact separated him from his hat and sent him somersaulting over the top. He thumped hard on the hood, the roof, the rear deck, and hit the pavement rolling.

I tore my eyes away and got the license number, as the car slowed with a screech to make a right. It accelerated toward Kingston Pike and shot straight out into traffic, causing considerable horn-blowing and a couple of fender benders as it straightened out heading west.

The police had the car's description on the air in minutes, but it turned out to have been stolen from one of Frank's customers. Lonnie was long gone by the time the car was found, and because the windows were darkly tinted, neither Molly nor I could positively identify him as the driver.

Darrell's heart stopped twice in the ambulance on the way to Park West Medical, and he was rushed straight into emergency surgery on his arrival.

*   *   *

Cyrus was at home when we got back. He'd spent the last three nights at St. Mary's with Ida, but she'd chased him out this evening, saying she didn't need to be watched over every minute like a baby.

We told him what had happened to Darrell, then Molly went to bed, and Cyrus and I took a couple of beers into the billiard room. We shot straight pool and talked, and I learned some things about the Wesners. Among other tidbits, I discovered that he and Ida had been taking care of this place for forty-six years, having been handpicked and personally trained for the job by Cyrus' predecessor, a Mr. Mallory.

"Then you worked for Dewey's father?" I said.

"That's right."

"And you remember Molly when she was young?"

"Sure do," he said, sinking a ball in a side pocket. "She was some little darlin'."

"Who'd she play with?"

"Well, with all the brothers livin' here; the house was full of children in those days."

"What about the Deets boys?"

He made a nice wide-angle cut, but scratched at the other end of the table. "Reckon they spent more time here when they was kids than they did at their own house."

"When did it stop?" I asked.

"It would have been after Molly's daddy took her off to Houston."

"Then you knew Lonnie pretty well?"

"Saw 'nough of him," he said.

I lined up a side-pocket bank shot, saying casually, "You knew it was him that first day, didn't you?" The object ball caromed off the opposite cushion and rolled back across the table, looking on target right up until the end. But the angle was off just enough for the ball to kick off one nipple, then the other, and end up sitting on the lip of the pocket.

Cyrus stared at the ball. "Like I tole you, I didn't see who hit me."

"I believe that," I assured him, "and I not calling you a liar. I wouldn't do that, Cyrus. I just had a hunch you might have guessed who it was, that's all."

He sank the ball I'd left hanging, then reluctantly admitted, "I thought it might be Lonnie."

"Did you know he was in town?"

"Yeah, he come by here one night a coupla weeks 'fore Dewey was took away. First time I'd seen him in ten years or more."

"What happened?"

"Dewey took him into his study."

"Did they argue?"

"Not that I heard," he said.

"Any idea what they talked about?"

"No, but Dewey tole me Lonnie'd give him an idea."

"About what?" I asked.

"He wouldn't say, but it sure made him laugh."

I nodded. "And this was two weeks before Dewey went into the hospital?"

" 'Bout that." He shook his head sadly. "That Lonnie took a wrong turn when he was little, and when they do it that early, they jus' never turn back."

Cyrus didn't talk much, but when he did, he generally had something to say. "If you don't mind my asking," I said, "why didn't you tell us about Lonnie at the start?"

" 'Cause Helen wouldn't a liked it."

"Why not? Because she was afraid it might get out that Tim and Lonnie were Dewey's bastards?"

"Guess that was it," he agreed. "But I never heard her use the word 'bastard,' and she always treated those boys like they was hers."

"What do you think Lonnie's up to, Cyrus? Why's he doing all this?"

He thought about it, rubbing his weathered face. "Could be he's after the gold."

"Sean Michael's treasure?"

"Yeah."

"Then you believe in it?"

"Oh, it's real enough," he said.

"You've *seen* it?"

"No, I never seen it," he said, "but Francis Eugene used to brag about fillin' his daddy's chest up with gold. And whenever Dewey needed money for the plant, he'd always make a trip up to the summerhouse."

Molly was still awake when I got upstairs, and I told her about my talk with Cyrus.

"Then you think Lonnie planned the whole thing from the start?" she asked.

"Maybe not all of it," I said. "But he talked to Dewey a week before Dewey had the pictures taken of Duncan, and Dewey said Lonnie had given him an idea."

She nodded. "So Lonnie was trying to create trouble between the brothers."

"And I'd say he succeeded."

"But why?" she wondered.

"Well, Dewey probably paid him for his blackmail idea, so money may have been part of it. But Lonnie also seems to enjoy torturing your family."

"Yeah," she conceded.

"And maybe he wanted to create confusion."

"Why?"

"To hide his real objective."

"Which was?"

"Cyrus thinks he's after the gold."

"Sean Michael's treasure?" She grinned. "You're not starting to believe in that stuff, are you?"

"Cyrus said it was real."

"He *did*?"

I nodded. "He said Dewey's daddy bragged about it, and you saw how much money he raked in during Prohibition. If even half of it was converted into gold, it would have made quite a pile." She nodded, and I had a thought. "You know, there's one place at the summerhouse we haven't looked yet."

"Where?"

"The day we arrived, Cyrus said the plumbing had never worked right up there, but Dewey always insisted that he patch it up rather than tear it out and start all over again."

"So?"

"So maybe Dewey wasn't just being cheap," I said.

33

Saturday morning, Detective Rooker called and asked us to drop by, so we had to put off checking out my theory about the plumbing.

When we arrived at the squad room, Rooker got us seated, poured us coffee, and said to Molly, "Sorry to hear about your uncle Darrell."

"Thanks," she said.

"I know this is a hard time for you, and I hate to disturb your Saturday morning—"

"That's all right," she said. "We want to help any way we can. What did you want to see us about?"

"I heard that you two actually witnessed the hit-and-run."

"That's right."

In his typically low-key manner, he asked, "How did you happen to be there at the time?"

"Frank Brazzi called to tell us that Darrell was dropping by," I said.

"Why did Mister Brazzi call *you?*"

"We asked him to let us know if he heard from Darrell."

"And he agreed to do that?"

"Uh huh."

"That was very obliging of him," said Rooker. "How do you know Mister Brazzi?"

"Darrell's a regular at his restaurant," I explained, "and we spoke to Frank a few days ago, thinking he might be able to tell us something."

"And did he?" Rooker asked.

"Nothing we didn't already know."

"I read what you told the cops last night," he said. "But would you mind going over it again?"

We did, and it didn't take long.

After giving him a moment to absorb it, Molly asked, "Have you talked to Duncan?"

Rooker nodded unhappily. "Yes, but he isn't being cooperative. The four witnesses agree that his attacker was a white male fitting Lonnie's description, but your uncle keeps insisting that the man was black."

"Any leads on Lonnie?" she asked.

"We have a positive ID on the Comphoto by practically everybody at Riverside Center. We pulled his driver's license photo and his mug shots, but the Comphoto's better. We also found a motel room he used for a while, and we talked to a woman who let him stay with her a few nights, but nobody's seen him in a week. I was hopin' *you* might know where he could be hiding."

She shrugged. "He knows this part of the valley as well as anybody, so it could be anywhere."

"That's the problem," he agreed.

"You speak to his mother?"

He nodded. "She told us she hadn't seen him, but I didn't quite believe her."

"We talked to her, too," said Molly. "She said Lonnie didn't come around much anymore, and I thought she was telling the truth about that, but she knew he was in town."

"Yes," he agreed. "When I asked how she knew that, she claimed to've heard it from somebody, but she couldn't remember who."

"Just talking about Lonnie made her nervous," said Molly, "and I had a feeling she knew he was up to something."

"Guess I better have another talk with her," he said.

"Good idea," she said. "Heard from Tim?"

"Not a word."

"He must be in trouble with the department by now."

Rooker nodded. "The Lieutenant covered for him the first day, putting him in for sick time. But somebody must've said somethin' to the Captain, 'cause he came by the next day wantin' to know where Tim was. We had to tell him the truth, of course, and he put him on suspension."

"You think Tim is out looking for Lonnie?" I asked.

"I imagine so," he said.

"I just hope he's up to it," said Molly.

"Tim's a good cop," Rooker told her, standing by his partner. "He knows what he's doin'."

Molly and I went back to the summerhouse to take a look at the plumbing. I thought we'd have to crawl underneath, but she showed me an easier way in.

There was a trapdoor under a throw rug in the bathroom connected to Helen's bedroom. The door opened upward and rested back against the edge of the tub, and a set of steep wooden steps led down into a square hole that had been dug to make room for the hot water heater and a tangle of pipes. The house was leveled on mortared columns of brick set about five feet apart, and the gap between ground level and floor level was wide enough to let in some daylight. With that and the light from the bathroom above, we didn't need flashlights.

A pipe carried dirty water from the sinks and tubs toward the front of the summerhouse, then ran under the front yard to a drain field down the hill. A thicker pipe carried sewage toward the back of the house.

We examined the water heater, thinking the gold might be stashed inside a concealed compartment, but we didn't find one. We looked for a hiding place among the patched-up pipes, then inspected the dirt walls and floor. Finally we followed the sewage pipe along a trench toward the back of the house, where it disappeared through a crack in the granite wall of the cliff.

"How do you reach the septic tank?" I asked.

"You have to go into the caves," she said.

"We should look there, too."

She agreed, and we climbed out. We closed the trapdoor and covered it with the rug, then went back along the porch to the entry hall. We grabbed our helmets from the rack, and Molly led me back into the caves.

Thirty feet along the main tunnel, we turned left into a narrow crack. We switched on our helmet lamps and shuffled sideways for about fifteen feet before the crack opened into a wider passage. It was half-filled by a mound of rubble, the air tainted with the first faint whiff of sewage. A knotted rope led up the side of the mound, and a second rope lowered us back to the floor, where the smell was considerably stronger. The way narrowed again, curving left, then right, and we stepped out into a roughly circular chamber, where the stifling stench of excrement dueled with the sharp tang of quicklime.

Molly threw a switch, and lights sprang on around the walls of the chamber. The sewage pipe emerged near floor level from a crack in the left wall, then made an abrupt right-angle turn as it dove into a circular hole in the middle of the floor. Fifty-pound bags of quicklime were stacked beside the pipe. One was open, and the handle of a metal scoop stuck out of the top. A trail of grayish-white powder led from the open bag to the hole.

I held my breath as I stepped to the edge. The hole was about ten feet across and went straight down for a hundred feet or more to an indistinct circle of darkness at the bottom.

"A volcanic chimney," she said. "The family's been using it for a hundred years now, and you can still barely see the sewage. Look up."

The chimney rose at a fairly constant width to a small circle of light maybe eighty feet above.

"Feel the breeze?"

Now that she mentioned it, I felt air moving out of the

tunnel behind us, faintly tickling the hairs on the back of my neck.

"Wind blowing over the top of the chimney creates an updraft that carries away the worst of the smell."

"Thank heaven for that," I said.

We circled the chamber, inspecting all the nooks and crannies for a hidden chest of gold. When we reached the other side, I took another look down into the chimney.

"What's that?" I asked.

"What?"

She stepped up beside me, and I said, "About twenty feet down. See it?" I showed her the spot with my helmet light. "An opening, almost square, covered with something."

"Looks like the same khaki canvas that's over the entrance to the secret room," she said.

"That's what it looks like to me, too."

"If there was a way down to it," she said, "I'd think we'd found what we were looking for."

"Yeah."

"You could rappel down," she said, "but it would be dicey getting through the opening."

"I can't picture Dewey swinging on the end of a rope anyway, can you?"

"No," she said.

"And what about Francis Eugene? Cyrus said he used to come up here frequently to add to his stash, and judging from his pictures, he wasn't the athletic type."

She shook her head. "No, they wouldn't hide it in a place this hard to get to."

"No," I agreed, "but somebody hung that canvas. Which must mean there's another way in."

"But from where?" she asked.

That, I had to agree, was the question.

On our way back to the main tunnel, I said, "While we're here, there's something else we should do."

"What's that?"

255

"We were so excited about finding the photos of Duncan that we forgot the ledger they were stuck in. But Dewey went to the same trouble to hide it as he did the photos, so maybe there's something in it we should see."

We retrieved the ledger from the secret room and took it back to the bighouse, where Cyrus was waiting with a message for Molly.

"They called about your daddy," he said.

She stood very still. "From the hospital?"

He nodded unhappily. "Said for you to call when you got in."

She nodded once, her expression grim, then headed for the phone in the front parlor.

I followed her, but hung back near the door to give her some space. She turned away as she made the call and spoke in a low voice, so I didn't hear much of what she said. But I could tell from her slumping shoulders that the news wasn't good.

She stood there for a moment after she hung up, then said numbly, "He's dead."

I'd expected bad, but not *that* bad. "How?"

She turned to me, white with shock. "Fell out of bed and broke his neck. The nurse said he must've tried to get up, but lost his balance and tumbled over the side."

"Lonnie," I said.

She nodded, as stunned as I was. It wasn't supposed to happen this way. The cancer was going to kill Donald, and he would die after an extended period of alternating agony and drugged stupor. But that plot hadn't included Lonnie.

He'd taken his revenge on the last of the Flanagan brothers, again leaving us dazzled by his audacity. He went where he wanted and did what he liked, and nobody saw him do it. If I were a believer in supernatural evil, Lonnie would have been a perfect candidate.

"I have to find him," Molly said.

"And then what?"

"Then," she said in a dry, flat voice, "I kill the sonofa-bitch."

34

After breaking the news to Helen and Cyrus, we drove in to meet Rooker at Fort Sanders. He agreed that Donald's death was probably Lonnie's handiwork, and he persuaded the police to treat the case as a possible homicide.

The staff of the medical center naturally resisted the idea that an unauthorized person could simply walk onto a closed ward, enter a room, and kill one of their patients. But the police learned that a male nurse had been assaulted and robbed on his way into work that afternoon. The man swore that he hadn't entered the hospital that day, that he'd gone straight home to call the cops and had phoned in sick. His charge nurse had logged the sick call and confirmed that he hadn't worked, but his security badge was found on the fire stairs nearest to the cancer ward.

When we got back to the bighouse, I made a pot of tea, and Molly sat down at the kitchen counter to make the necessary phone calls.

She started with those closest to her father, and she had a hard time holding herself together in the face of their grief. It had been bad enough with Dewey, but this was worse. After watching her struggle through the first few calls, I told her, "You don't have to do this, you know."

"Yes, I do," she said, picking up the receiver again.

"I understand that the calls have to be made," I said. "I just mean that I could make some of them for you."

"Thanks, Bull," she said, "but they need to hear it from me."

After another dozen calls, she finally gave in. "All that's left are business associates. Just give them the facts and tell them I'll call later." She made a list of names and numbers, then kissed me on the cheek and said, "Thanks." After she left the kitchen with a cup of tea, I took her place at the counter.

We put on some extra guards that night, and alarms were set and checked all over the house, but I still didn't feel safe. Molly went to bed early, but I couldn't sleep, so I took the ledger into the sitting room.

I expected to find columns of numbers, but discovered page after page of sloppy, often undecipherable handwriting. It started at the top of the first page with: "This be the true story of Sean Michael Flanagan," and went on to reveal in considerable detail how a young man from County Mayo, arriving in America with nothing but a handsome face and gift for blarney, could end up as the owner of a successful coffee business three years later. The scrawl was hard to read at best, and various liquids had been spilled on some of the pages, wiping out whole paragraphs, but what I could decipher was enough.

Somebody once said that behind every great fortune lay a crime, and it appeared that this was no exception. But with the Flanagans, there was a whole list of crimes, ranging from petty to capital. Sean Michael had picked a man's pocket for his passage to America and had won the land on Tazewell Pike cheating at cards, but he'd made himself rich with robbery and murder. He'd killed a man in Louisville, Kentucky, for a chest of gold coins, then had framed another man named Dwight Davis Deets for the murder.

After Deets had been hung for the crime, Sean Michael had generously paid for his burial, then had provided support and comfort for the man's young widow. He'd taken the woman as his mistress and had moved her and her children to Knoxville, where he'd bought into a partnership in a coffee company. He'd married his partner's only child, then had obtained sole ownership of the company by arranging his partner's death. But he'd kept the Deets woman as his mistress and had looked after her and her children until she'd died. He described her as "a pretty lass, if a tetch short in the leg, and terrible eager to please a gentleman of means and generosity."

The second half of the book was filled with the smaller, more elegant handwriting of Sean Michael's eldest, Francis Eugene Flanagan. I didn't read all of it, just scanned it for highlights, but I learned that Sean Michael had shared the secret of his crimes with his eldest son and that Francis Eugene had done the same with Dewey, each in turn taking responsibility for the Deets family's welfare and, in a strangely perverted tradition, taking a Deets female as his mistress.

Francis Eugene revealed two other secrets as well. The first was that he'd arranged the "fall from the horse" and the "boating accident" that had killed his two brothers and had given him total control of the family wealth on his father's death. The second was that Sean Michael's stolen chest of gold coins had never been emptied.

Buying into the coffee company had cost about half the gold, and building and furnishing the bighouse had been expensive, but Francis Eugene had refilled the chest to bursting during Prohibition, and at the time of his death thirty-five years before, it had contained several million dollars worth of gold. Even if Dewey had dug deeply in his efforts to keep Shamrock afloat, there should still be a fair amount left. Unfortunately, I could find no mention of where the chest was hidden.

When I looked up to see Molly standing in the doorway, I said I had something for her to read.

An hour later, lying on the bed, her elbows propped on either side of the ledger, she sighed and said, "I feel like

Cary Grant in *Arsenic and Old Lace*, when he learns that his sweet old aunties are serial killers."

"If Lonnie knows what your great-grandfather did to his great-grandfather," I said, "it might explain his hatred for your family."

"Yeah." She shook her head in wonder. "What we did to them . . . it's like slavery. Like the massuh taking care of his faithful retainers. It's disgusting."

"How could Lonnie have found out?"

"I don't know."

"But now he wants what's his."

She nodded. "The gold. But where is it?"

I pictured the secret room. It didn't make sense that it wasn't there. What was a secret room for except to hide your treasure? But we'd looked. We'd searched the chest and the desk and the filing cabinet, the couch and the throne, and the bookshelf wouldn't hide anything. Mostly empty shelves. Hardly any books.

"Where?" she repeated.

If he had no books, why'd he need a bookcase? And such a tall one at that? Sitting up, I said, "I think I know."

"Where?"

I grinned at her. "I'll show you tomorrow."

"Tomorrow?" she asked in disbelief. "You're going to make me wait till tomorrow?"

"Suspense is good for the soul."

"Who said that?"

"I did," I said. "Just made it up."

"You're really not going to tell me?"

"Not tonight."

"Okay." She put the ledger on the floor and slid under the covers.

"But I might be able to take your mind off of it," I said, running my hand up her thigh and over the curve of her hip.

"You think so?"

"I might."

She thought about it briefly and shrugged. "Worth a try, I guess."

I came wide-awake shortly after dawn and couldn't get back to sleep, too eager to see if I was right about the bookcase. I considered going up to the summerhouse alone, but I knew Molly wouldn't like it. I even briefly thought about waking her, but I figured she needed the rest. After lying in bed for another hour, I got up quietly, grabbed some clothes, and went downstairs. Cyrus had a pot of coffee ready, and he came in the back door as I was sitting down with a cup.

"Wanna show you somethin'," he said.

"What is it?"

"Gotta *show* you," was all he would say, and I followed him out the back door.

A cool front had moved in during the night, and it was a little chilly for jeans and a thin cotton shirt. I crossed my arms and jogged after Cyrus through the damp grass, passing the pool and the tennis court and the tree house.

"Where are we going?" I asked.

"To the barn."

"What is this, Cyrus?"

He wouldn't say, just kept going, and I followed. I didn't know what I was about to see, but I had a feeling I wasn't going to like it.

The big double doors were open, front and back, and I could see all the way through to the woods beyond. Cyrus hurried inside, with me close on his heels.

As I cleared the door, I heard something to the left and spun that way. I almost tripped over my feet as a figure moved out of the shadows in the first stall.

"*Lonnie!*"

I instinctively reached for my .38, even as I realized I didn't have it on me.

Then the shadow said, "No, it's me."

I gasped, "Tim?" as he stepped into the light. "Where the hell have you been?"

"Everywhere." He added to Cyrus, "Thanks."

Cyrus looked at me sheepishly and said, "Think I'll go make some breakfast."

As he left, I said to Tim, "Everybody's looking for you, you know."

"I know."

"You haven't even talked to Rooker, have you?"

"Had to talk to Lonnie first."

"And did you?" I asked.

"We had words."

"And?"

As he stepped closer, I saw that his left arm was hanging funny. "He wasn't happy to see me," he said.

"He *shot you?*"

"Just a flesh wound. Cyrus cleaned and bandaged it for me."

"When did it happen?"

"Couple of hours ago," he said. "I traced him to a woman he knew. He stayed with her last night, and I broke in on 'em this morning."

"But he got away?"

"Yeah," he admitted. "He got to the gun under his pillow and used the woman as a shield while we talked. After he had his say, he shot me, then threw her at me and took off." He shook his head and looked away.

"What is it?"

"I never realized before how much he hates us," he said. "Me and Mother and Mitch. Especially Mitch."

"Why Mitch?"

"Because of his weakness," he said, "and because he wasn't really our father." Again he shook his head. "He killed him, you know."

"Who?"

"Lonnie killed Mitch. He told me about it before he shot me."

I was surprised, though I probably shouldn't have been. "I thought it was a stickup."

"Oh, it was," he said. "Lonnie said he made him hand over all the money from the cash drawer first. A hundred and sixty-five dollars. Hardly worth the trouble. Then he made him empty his wallet and his pockets, for another twenty-three dollars and change. After that, he forced him to get down on his knees and beg for his life. He made him whine and plead and grovel like a dog. And when he got tired of that, he killed him." There were tears in his eyes, but whether for Mitch, or Lonnie, or himself, I couldn't say.

I gave him a moment, then said, "And you don't know where he is now?"

"He's somewhere around here," he said.

I jerked back, eyes darting from side to side. *"Here?"*

He grinned, enjoying my panic. "I followed him and saw him stash his car in the trees half a mile up the pike." The grin faded as he added, "But then I lost him."

"What's he doing, Tim?"

He stared at me. "You haven't figured it out yet?"

"Part of it," I said. "The question is: How much does he know?"

"Too much," he said. "When he was twelve, he heard Dewey tell Momma the whole story one night when he was drunk. All about how our great-grandfather was hung so the Flanagans could get rich and how Flanagan men have been fathering bastards on our women for three generations. A regular Flanagan family tradition."

"Did you hear it, too?"

"No, and Lonnie didn't tell me about it until I was in college."

"How did you feel about it?"

"How do you *think?*" he snapped. He stared off for a moment and said finally, "I grew up believing that my family was worse than poor white trash, that we were not only poor, but thieves and murderers. Only that turned out to be a lie. It was the Flanagans who were the criminals." He shook his head. "You see, I'd always been grateful for their generosity. How could I not be? Anything nice I ever had had come from them. But I realized then that they only gave me what was mine by rights. They stole our lives," he said bitterly. "They shut us out of the light, then turned us into beggars, so they could look charitable." He took a moment to calm himself, then said quietly, "To answer your question, Mister Cochran, I don't think much of the Flanagan clan."

"What about Molly?"

"She's different," he said.

"And you wouldn't want anything to happen to her?"

"No, I wouldn't," he said.

"Then you're not working with Lonnie."

His look was sharp. "Is that what you think?"

"No."

"Well, that's good," he said, "because I'm trying to stop him."

"From doing what?"

"From killing them all."

"Who's left, except Duncan?" I asked. "Darrell might as well be dead."

"There's Molly."

"I thought they were friends."

"And lovers," he said, getting in his jab. "But that was a long time ago. Now he says she's just another Flanagan and doesn't deserve what she has any more than the others."

"Is he crazy?"

"Yeah, you can say that. But I don't think it'll help you much, 'cause he's crazy smart, too."

"A dangerous mix," I said.

"Lethal," he concurred. "Tell Rooker what I said."

"Why don't *you* tell him?"

"I can't," he said. "Not yet. I think Lonnie's been hidin' out somewhere close, and if I can find out where, maybe I'll find him."

"Then what?"

"I ask him to surrender," he said.

"And when he refuses?"

He stared off for a moment. "Tell Rooker," he repeated, then turned and headed for the back door of the barn and the woods beyond.

35

I woke Molly and told her what Tim had said, and she got in touch with Rooker. As she spoke to him, I slipped a tee shirt on under my shirt to ward off the chill. Then she took a shower, and I went out to talk to the security guards. The one on the gate let in a patrol car, and the deputy said they were pulling in help from all over the county. "If Deets is around," he told me confidently, "we'll get him this time." I wasn't so sure about that, but I welcomed all the help we could get.

Molly drove us up the hill in Dewey's Lincoln with a security guard in the backseat. He went inside the summerhouse with us and looked around to make sure it was empty. Then he went back out to join the other guard, and Molly handed me the .38 from her purse.

She tucked her Glock into the waistband at the small of her back, and I did the same with mine, clipping the holster in place. I was wearing a white cotton shirt with an embroidered front that Molly had bought me in Mexico City back in the spring. It was designed to be worn loose outside the pants, so it was ideal for concealing a weapon.

In the secret room, Molly lit the Coleman lantern and held it for me as I examined the bookcase. There was a vertical strip of steel inset flush with the wood, running down the back edge on the right side of the case. The metal had been stained to look like wood, but it was obvious when you knew to look for it. At the base on the left side, concealed

267

at the back, was a vertical bolt that slipped into a slot in the floor.

When I lifted the bolt and tugged the bookcase away from the wall, it fairly flew out of my hand. It was well balanced and moved almost silently. Behind the bookcase was a dark opening barely covered by the case.

Molly handed me the lantern and said with a grin, "You got us this far, Bull, so lead on."

The tunnel beyond narrowed quickly to hardly more than a crack, then opened up again as it led down a shallow incline. As the slope started to flatten, my feet slipped out from under me on the muddy surface, and I went down hard. I would have kept sliding if Molly hadn't grabbed my hand.

Helping me back onto solid rock, she said, "Marl."

"Beg your pardon?"

"M-a-r-l," she said. "A mixture of clay and sand and limestone that's slippery as ice when it's wet."

The wall of stone to our left glistened with moisture, and the marl lapped up to the rock on which we stood. The tunnel maintained a shallow slope, as it narrowed toward a dark archway about fifty feet straight ahead.

"Probably the entrance to a marl chute," she said.

"What's that?"

"Trouble," she said. "Like a toboggan run, with you as the toboggan."

"Sounds dangerous."

"Extremely."

She led me along the dripping wall toward a smaller opening to the left. The opening and the tunnel beyond were almost perfectly circular.

"A lava tube," said Molly.

"No longer in use, I assume."

"Not by lava."

She had to duck to enter, and I had to bend nearly double, but luckily, we didn't have to keep it up for long.

Fifteen feet in, we squeezed past a boulder and stepped

into the open. The lava tube lay in shards all about us, shattered by the boulder. The tube continued about ten feet in front of us, but here the ceiling was far over our heads. A sandy path led uphill to our left, with walls of stone sloping outward and upward on both sides. At the top of the rise was an ancient infall, where a great slab of granite was wedged at an angle, supporting a mound of rubble on its back.

The slab sloped upward from left to right, and I caught a whiff of sewage as I ducked under the high end. I trailed Molly through a litter of broken rock toward an opening at the rear. It was about door-high and roughly triangular in shape, and the stink grew stronger as we approached. The opening led into a small natural chamber with a folding chair to the right, a wooden chest to the left, and a piece of khaki canvas hanging from a two-by-four frame straight ahead.

The stench of sewage and quicklime was strong, and when Molly pulled the canvas aside, it was overpowering.

"Yeah," she said, "it's the opening we saw in the side of the septic tank."

"Great," I said, holding my nose.

"You want to see?"

"I'll take your word for it."

"Suit yourself."

I was relieved when she dropped the curtain back into place. The smell wasn't much diminished, but every little bit helped.

The chest was old, stood about two and a half feet to the peak of its barrel top, and was made of dark-stained wood strapped with rusted steel. There was no padlock on the front, so Molly just lifted the latch and pulled up the lid.

The interior was lined with tarnished copper, and the cavity was half-filled with gleaming gold coins. Most were about the size of quarters, but there were a few as large as silver dollars and some no bigger than dimes. I picked up one of the silver-dollar-size coins and knew immediately it had to be gold. Nothing else, but regret, was as heavy.

Molly stared into the chest for a moment, then said, "Take a handful, and let's go. If this is what Lonnie's looking for, maybe we can use it to trap him."

I slipped several of the silver-dollar-size coins into the pockets of my jeans and followed Molly out of the chamber. We retraced our route to the secret room, and I was conscious of the weight of the coins the whole way back.

I stepped into the room and let Molly go past, then handed her the lantern and turned to the bookcase.

"Jus' leave it," a voice said.

I jerked around as Lonnie flicked on his helmet light. He sat on the red velvet throne in the alcove, and he was pointing a gun at us.

"Don't, Molly," he said, in the same cold, raspy voice I'd heard outside the grape arbor.

Her hand froze on the way to her weapon, then slowly dropped back to her side.

He got to his feet and stepped out of the alcove, saying, "Move away from there, pothead. Set your ass on the couch." I did. "Put the lamp on the desk, Molly." She did. "Now, reach for your piece with your left hand. Slowly. Good. And put it next to the lamp." She did that, too.

I was insulted that Lonnie didn't think enough of me to check for a weapon, but it was a mistake, and he hadn't made many.

"Okay," he said to Molly, "sit down next to him."

She sat. "What are you trying to do, Lonnie?"

"Jus' takin' my rightful place, Molly," he said quietly. There was a cold stillness about him that was spooky. At that moment, he didn't seem quite real—more android than man.

"That's why you killed my father?" asked Molly.

"They all have to go."

"Why?"

"It's a clean sweep," he said. "But if it helps any, I don't think your ole man knew what hit him."

A muscle flexed in her jaw. "Not like with Dewey, huh?"

"No"—he gave her a level stare—"nothin' like that."

"I keep wondering why he didn't cry out," she said.

"Dewey?" he asked. "Hell, he was so doped up, he lost a quart of blood 'fore he felt a thing."

"How could he not feel it?" she asked. "Being cut with the plastic knife must have been excruciating."

He tilted his head quizzically. "Thought you would a figured it out by now, Molly, and I was more than half-afraid the Medical Examiner would catch it." He slipped a hand into his hip pocket and came out with a shiny strip of metal, then touched something, and a thin, mirror-edged blade sprung into position.

"You cut him with that," she said, "then covered your tracks with the plastic knife as he faded out."

He nodded, then closed the blade and slipped it back in his pocket.

"You planned it all, didn't you?" she asked.

"It was more like it fell into my lap."

"You went to see Dewey."

"Right."

"And you suggested that he take the photos of Duncan?"

"I didn't go there with that in mind," he said. "Jus' went lookin' for trouble and found him scared shitless of losin' his precious company. So I asked him why he didn't black-mail Duncan for bein' queer. And can you believe he didn't know?" He shook his head. "His own brother, and he didn't know. Or at least, *pretended* he didn't know. Anyway, I said he should get him some pictures of Duncan doin' the dirty, and that'd sew it up for him."

"Did he give you money?"

"Sure he did. The man thought I'd saved his ass, and he slipped me a thousand on the spot. I knew right then that I was on to somethin'."

"When he got himself thrown into Riverside Center," she said, "you had him just where you wanted him, didn't you? All you had to do was scare off the maintenance man and take his place. You went in to see him that Saturday. Nurse Lehr heard you arguing. What'd you threaten him with?"

"I said I'd tell the cops he was blackmailing his brother, if he didn't give me what's mine."

"That's good," she said admiringly, "especially since the blackmail was your idea."

"And if that didn't do the trick," he went on, "I said I'd go to the papers and TV with what I knew about the family. I told him it should be good for a best-seller, maybe even a movie of the week. But he just said to go ahead. He said nobody'd take the word of a lowlife ex-con like me, over a pillar of the community like him. And the worst part was that I figured he was right.

"So I ended up threatening to kill him, and even that didn't work. There he was, bleedin' to death, and he wouldn't say a word. I told him I'd call the nurse if he'd tell me where the gold was, but he wouldn't go for it."

"You were lying," she said.

"Course I was lyin'," he said. "But *he* didn't know that."

"Maybe he did," she said.

That stopped him for a second. "Well, even if he *did*," he said finally, "how could he not give in? He knew he was dyin', but he wouldn't plead for his life."

"He wouldn't give you the satisfaction," she said. "Dewey could be stubborn."

"How could anybody be *that* stubborn?"

"Look at *you*," she said.

"Are you sayin' I'm like that sonofabitch?"

"In some ways."

I thought for a moment he was going to shoot her, and I was preparing to go for my gun if he raised his weapon. Instead, he broke into a grin and said, "Guess I am at that. God knows killin' and stealin' runs in the family."

"And now you're going to steal his gold?"

"You can call it that, if you want," he said dryly. "But far as I'm concerned, I'm only takin' what's mine. The gold's s'posed to pass to the eldest son, which is me."

She said, "You can't get out of here with it."

"Maybe not all of it," he agreed. "But it should be safe where it is as long as you can't show them where to look."

She stared at him a moment, then said flatly, no pleading, "We were friends, Lonnie."

"No, we weren't friends, Molly," he said coldly. "We played together as kids, that's all."

"What about the summer when I was sixteen?" she asked. "I know you felt something then."

"Course I did," he said. "You were one prime young piece a tail."

"You said you loved me," she said.

That was a detail I could have done without, but I knew she was only trying to save us.

"In those days," he said, "I'd say just about anything for a pop."

"I don't believe that's all it was," she said.

He shrugged and said impatiently, "Believe what you want to, Molly, but I ain't never been much for long-term relationships."

She told him coldly, "Killing me won't help, Lonnie."

"Why not?"

"Because Tim followed you."

"Bullshit," he said.

"He said your car was hidden in the trees half a mile up the road."

He stared at her for a moment, then shook his head. "That's my little brother, a cop to the core."

"Just like you're bad to the bone, right?"

He'd had enough. "That's right. Now, show me the coins."

"What makes you think we took any?"

"Don't bullshit me," he said, stepping closer. "Nobody opens a chest of gold and leaves without takin' samples. Let's see 'em."

Molly didn't move for a moment, then sighed and nodded at me, and we pulled out our booty.

He examined the coins with satisfaction. "That's the stuff, all right. Now, stand up, both a you." He stepped back as we got to our feet. I pulled my shirttail down as I stood, trying to make the gesture look natural. He shoved Molly's Glock into his waistband, then said, "You, pothead, put the coins on the desk, and pick up the lamp. You lead, and I'll keep Molly with me. Do anything stupid, and I'll kill her, you hear?"

"I hear you," I said, picking up the lantern.

"Okay, Molly, put your coins on the table, and step away." She did, and he pocketed the gold. "All right, pothead, move out."

I stepped back through the bookcase opening, leading them through the narrowing passage and down the slope as it widened. I stayed close to the edge of the marl, hoping to lead Lonnie into the trecherous stuff, but he seemed to know what it was and gave it a wide berth.

We were crossing the thin strip of rock where the marl lapped almost up the wall, when a voice yelled from behind us, "Lonnie!"

We turned, and I caught a glimpse of Tim thirty feet up the slope.

He yelled, "Let 'em go, Lonnie!"

And Lonnie shot at him.

As he did, Molly stepped up close behind me, lifted the back of my shirt, and pulled the revolver. She turned as Lonnie spun to face her, and they fired at the same time.

She fell against me, knocking the lantern out of my hand and throwing me off balance. I caught her under the arms as I stumbled backward into the marl, then my feet slid out from under me, and I pulled her after me. I lost her as I landed and went sliding down the slope on my face. Unable to see where I was going, I pushed hard with my right arm and managed to flip myself over.

The Coleman lantern threw enough light to show me the dark opening ahead. I was going at a fair clip by that time

274

and still picking up speed. Like a scraper with soft paint, I was also picking up loads of marl with my feet, under my arms, and between my legs. It crawled over my limbs until I was covered with the stuff—cold and wet, stinking of mud and decay.

Glancing over my shoulder, I caught a flash of muzzle fire and saw Molly sliding after me. Then I turned to look ahead as I reached the opening. I slid over a rounded edge of rock, and my stomach dropped as I fell straight down into darkness.

36

I couldn't have fallen for more than a second, though it felt much longer. I landed on a steep, frictionless slope and continued my slide, unable to see anything. All I had was my sense of touch: the sensation of speed, the slick feel of the rock, and the wet ooze of the marl. It told me a lot about where I was, but almost nothing about where I was going. When the bottom dropped away again, I threw my hands up to protect my head and hit almost immediately. Moving fast now, all I could do was cover up and hope to survive whatever was ahead. Seconds later, I slid over another edge and fell again.

One thousand . . . two thousand . . . three thousand, I counted, getting scared now. The fall was too long, and I knew I'd never survive a collision with even the steepest slope at this speed.

I came down in something wet and shockingly cold. I landed on my back, and the impact knocked the breath out of me. As the wetness closed over me, I sucked in a mouthful of water. Water! That was it! I plunged deep, going down and down, needing all my will to stifle the urge to cough. Then my feet touched bottom, and I pushed off hard, kicking for the surface.

Going up took longer than going down, but I finally broke into the air spewing water, hacking and wheezing. I plunged back under, but quickly bobbed up again, gasping for air, still coughing at every breath.

My hand brushed something. Then it grabbed me, and I realized it was another hand.

I croaked, "Molly?"

"It's me," she said in a weak voice, as she flicked on her helmet lamp.

I tried mine, but nothing happened.

"The lens is broken," she said.

I slapped the side of the helmet, but didn't get a flicker.

"The bulb, too," she said.

"Oh, well," I said. "Are you shot?"

"Yeah."

"Where?"

"In the side."

"Is it bad?"

"It's not good." Seeing her push hair out of her eyes with the .38, I was impressed. Somehow, she'd hung on to it the whole way down the chute.

"Are you hurting?" I asked.

"Not much. I'm mostly numb." She lifted her head to show the lamp around, revealing facing walls of smooth rock rising straight up on both sides of the river.

"I don't see where we came out," I said.

"It's behind us," she said, and I realized she was right. The stream was carrying us along at a strolling pace.

"Then we can't get back out the way we came in," I said.

"Not likely," she agreed, "but we have to get out of this water."

"Can't climb these walls."

"Keep looking," she said. "There has to be a way out."

The cut was no straighter than the local roads, so we couldn't see far in either direction. Over the next few minutes, I spotted several openings above us, but nothing within reach, and I was starting to worry. I could no longer feel the cold, and I wasn't sure that was a good sign. But it was Molly who concerned me. Normally a much stronger swimmer than I was, she was now barely keeping her head above water, and she was too quiet.

"Are you hurting?" I asked.

"It burns," she said.

The current accelerated as the channel narrowed for a stretch, then slowed again as it widened, and she repeated in a shaky voice, "We have to get out of this water."

"Soon," I promised.

A quick, narrow channel bore sharply to the left, then back to the right. As it washed out into slower waters, I heard the roar of a waterfall ahead, and Molly's lamp picked out an arched opening about fifty yards in front of us—a faint mist hanging over the falls. She swung her lamp to the right, sweeping it across another vertical wall of rock, then back to the left. I didn't see anything at first, then Molly lowered the sweep of her lamp, and I saw a black gravel beach, much closer than the falls, maybe twenty yards away.

"The current's pulling us," she said.

"I feel it."

"Head for the beach!"

The pull got stronger by the second, and soon every foot toward the beach was costing me a yard toward the falls. I kept at it, stroking and kicking, but the roar grew too quickly, and the archway was suddenly closer than it should be. I buried my face and made like Mark Spitz, churning the water like a madman. When I came up for air, the beach was closer, but so, unfortunately, were the falls.

Molly was to my right, laboring now and gasping for breath. So I caught her arm and pulled her to me, saying, "Grab on." She slipped an arm around my waist, and I held her with one arm and stroked with the other, kicking for both of us.

I kept at it, and she provided what help she could, but my strength was giving out when my fingertips finally brushed gravel. Feeling a fresh surge of energy at the touch,

I dug in my nails and clawed my way forward, pulling Molly after me through the shallows. When we were both out of the water, I collapsed and lay there trying to breathe.

She said she was cold, so I wrapped my arms around her. When her trembling subsided, I got up and hoisted her to her feet, then helped her off with her shirt and saw the wound for the first time.

The slug had gone clean through. The entry wound was above her waist, a couple of inches from her left side: no bigger than a dime and almost fully closed. The exit wound was on her back: a little larger, more jagged, and already beginning to seep. The wounds had been closed by the cold water, but they would reopen as soon as we started moving.

"Does it hurt?" I asked.

"Not too much now, but . . ."

"Yeah."

I wrung out her shirt and handed it back to her, saying, "Hold this." Then I pulled off my shirt and undershirt and twisted the water out of them. I slipped my shirt back on and tore my tee shirt in half, then wet it in the river and used it to clean around her wound, wiping off specks of dirt and gravel. Afterward, I rinsed it out, twisted it as dry as I could, and wrapped it around her waist to serve as a bandage.

"Thanks," she said.

"You need a doctor."

"This'll do," she insisted.

After I helped her on with her shirt, she asked for the .38, which lay on the gravel where she'd dropped it. She flipped out the cylinder, picked out the spent cartridge, and tossed it. Then she poured the other cartridges into her hand, made sure the barrel and cylinders were clear, and tested the action before reloading.

"Five shots," she said, as she tucked the revolver into her waistband at the back. "Wish I had my Glock."

"You think Lonnie's coming after us?"

"Unless Tim killed him."

"Even if he does, how could he find us? Do *you* know where we are?"

"Only vaguely," she said. "But all he has to do is come down the marl chute."

I hadn't thought of that. "Just when I was beginning to feel safe," I said.

She showed her helmet lamp on the vertical walls to our right and across the lagoon, then turned and headed toward the waterfall. "I'd like to follow the river, if we can," she said. "It should eventually lead us out of here."

"To where?"

"To the other side of the ridge would be good," she said, "since Lonnie's somewhere behind us."

"Unless Tim killed him," I said.

"Too much to hope for," she replied.

The black beach ended at a bare hump of damp gray rock beside the waterfall, the base of the arch ten feet to the left. We climbed the hump and looked over the edge. The river plunged two hundred feet straight down, and the wall beneath us was almost perfectly vertical.

"So much for the river," Molly said, and turned to look over my shoulder. "Guess this is the only way left." She started in that direction, and I followed her lamp, the jittery circle of light showing rock and earth rising ahead.

She stopped at the base of the rise and slowly tilted her head back. The circle climbed a jumble of boulders, the crevices filled with sand and earth and gravel, ending fifty feet above us.

"A dry waterfall," she said.

"How can you tell?"

"See how the rocks are rounded? Only hundreds of years of water flowing over them can do that."

"Why did it dry up?"

"Something changed the river's course."

"Like one of those cave-ins or earthquakes you don't have around here?"

"I didn't say they never happened," she said, "just not in my lifetime."

She prowled the base of the old falls until she decided on the best way up, then started to climb. I let her go first, but stayed close behind her, ready to catch her if she fell. She picked her way gingerly from boulder to boulder, edging back and forth across the face of the falls, always looking for the easiest route.

Halfway up, her foot slipped, and as she twisted to catch her balance, she grabbed her side. I knew she'd reopened the wound, but she didn't need me to tell her that.

I offered a hand, but she said through gritted teeth, "Just give me a second."

"Take all the time you need," I said.

After a minute or so, she went on. But she moved more slowly and carefully, definitely favoring her side now.

We stopped at the top, so she could catch her breath, then started up the dry riverbed.

"Any idea which way we're headed?" I asked.

She shook her head, but kept moving. "We've twisted and turned too much for that," she said. "But it's either keep going, or sit down and wait for them to find us."

"*If* they find us."

She nodded.

"And it could be Lonnie who shows up first," I said.

That was so obvious she didn't even bother to nod, just kept walking.

We followed the winding course of the dry streambed for a couple of hundred yards, then came to the massive infall that had redirected the river. There seemed to be no way around, so we tried going over it. But thirty feet up, we came to a steep slope of fine gravel that proved impossible to climb. After scrambling upward and sliding back a half-dozen times, we climbed down and went looking for an alternative route.

Backtracking downstream, we found a dry tributary curving off to the left, and we followed it a couple of hundred feet to another waterfall. This one was as dry as the first and only a third its height, but a lot prettier. Molly's helmet light picked out glistening veins of red in the rocks.

"Rose quartz," she said.

Trailing her up the falls, I saw dark stains on her shirt and told her, "You're bleeding."

"Yeah."

"Want to stop?"

"If I do," she said wearily, "I might not start again."

From the top of the falls, we followed the meandering streambed to another infall. We clambered over this one without much trouble and found the same dry streambed on the other side.

It ended abruptly two hundred feet beyond in a great split in the earth. The streambed continued on the other side, but the split was too wide to jump, so we were again forced to retreat.

Halfway back to the infall, I spotted an opening high in the left wall of the tunnel. The wall was stratified in different shades—light gray, dark gray, green, and red—the exposed layers crumbled and worn into irregular steps leading up to the opening.

It was ten feet wide and about half that in height, and we had to move in a crouch. A hundred feet in, the ceiling began to drop, and we were forced to our knees. Fifty feet later, we were crawling on our bellies.

I could hear that Molly was having trouble. "You sure this is a good idea?"

Gasping for breath, she said, "No."

"Just hope it doesn't close up on us."

"Feel a breeze," she said. "Think it opens up."

She was right. The way got progressively easier. The ceiling rose until we could stand upright, and we came out on a white-sand beach.

Molly leaned against me, bleeding and exhausted and as entranced as I was by what lay before us. Her lamp provided tunnel-like views of a splendid underground lake—

pearly stalagmite-stalactite columns rising from snow-white sand, through water as transparent as air.

Her light wouldn't reach the other side, so I couldn't tell how big the lake was, but I figured we'd find a way around it or across when we had to. I wasn't worried about that right now.

Molly let me borrow her helmet lamp, so I could inspect her wound. It didn't look much worse, but she'd lost more blood. Her jeans were stained halfway down her left leg, and she'd bled through the tee shirt I'd used as a bandage. I rinsed it out in the lake—stirring up the sand, possibly for the first time since the basin had filled—then cleaned around the wound and applied direct pressure until the bleeding stopped.

After rinsing the tee shirt out again, I tied it back around her waist, saying, "It'll just open up again."

"I know," she said, "but we have to go on."

"Not yet." I dropped to the sand and pulled her down beside me. "Sit and rest for a moment. Put your head on my shoulder, and catch your breath."

She did as I said without argument, and we sat unmoving for all of a minute before I heard it. Faint, but distinct. The sharp ring of metal on stone.

37

C limbing to my feet, I said, "The sonofabitch doesn't give up, does he?"

"Never," Molly agreed; struggling after me.

She led us to the left along the edge of the water, as I kept watch behind us. The beach curved in a gentle arc around the lake, and after a hundred yards or so, I spotted a dark opening ahead.

"See it?" she asked.

"Yeah," I said.

I glanced back, caught a faint glint of light, and whispered, "Turn off the lamp!"

She didn't ask why, just did it.

We were in total darkness for moment, then the light was back, a little brighter, maybe. We watched it approach, until it stopped at the edge of the water, maybe fifty yards away. The beam settled into the lake and tracked across it from left to right, then it rose and panned toward us. As it got close, I remembered that I was wearing a white shirt.

It was too late to take it off, or try to get out of the way, so I froze and closed my eyes. Not sure why I closed them, but maybe a part of me thought he couldn't see me if I couldn't see him. After a few seconds, I cracked an eyelid to see what was up, and the beam had moved off to our left. Realizing he hadn't spotted the shirt, it suddenly occurred to me that, after crawling all over this cave, the shirt was probably closer to gray or brown than its original white.

As Lonnie's light turned to the beach, I whispered,

"Let's go," then took Molly's hand and led her toward the wall to our left. I couldn't see it, but I knew it had to be there. When my hand touched rock, I started feeling my way along. I lost contact a few times, as the stone jutted away from me, but I always found it again. At one point the rock face jumped out in front of me, and I almost slammed into it head-on. But I caught myself just in time, then felt my way around the protrusion and kept going.

When I glanced behind us, I saw we were in trouble. Lonnie's light was aimed at the sand, and he was following our tracks! I pulled Molly after me and stumbled straight into ankle-deep water at the edge of the lake.

At the first splash, I froze, and Lonnie called out, "I hear you, pothead!"

His helmet light bobbed after us as he broke into a jog.

Molly snapped, "Come on!" and tugged me out of the water.

Lonnie fired at the sound, but we kept going. Back on the sand, we moved silently, except for the sound of our breathing and the blood pounding in my ears.

We found the rock face and quickly stumbled upon the opening, then ducked into it and felt our way far enough inside to be shielded from Lonnie's sight before Molly switched on her lamp. I caught a glimpse of a sandy track leading up a gentle slope, then she grabbed my hand, switched off her lamp, and pulled me into a run.

We miscalculated our speed in the darkness and hit the top of the rise sooner than expected. As the ground fell away, Molly lost her footing and pulled me after her, tumbling down a steep sandy slope.

We arrived uninjured at the bottom and disentangled ourselves. Then I helped her up, and she gave us another quick look at what was ahead. The sand turned to clay a few feet in front of us, and the tunnel led straight to a slanted opening a hundred feet away.

She doused the light and jogged on. I followed her footfalls, shortening my strides and trying to match her rhythm. She was favoring her injured side, so one stride was shorter than the other. She flicked on her lamp again when we were about ten feet from the opening and kept it on as she moved under the leaning slab.

As I followed her, I heard a shot and ducked as a slug ricocheted off the slanting rock to my left.

Molly's light went out, then she fumbled for my hand and led me ahead. After a dozen paces, she used a quick flash to reveal a large boulder in front of us, and we felt our way around it in darkness. On the other side, the light went on again, and Molly gave a low whistle.

We stood at the top of a shallow, rocky slope leading down into a tumbled mass of enormous boulders. Haphazard stacks of them extended as far as we could see.

"What's this?" I whispered.

"It's a climbing cave." She raised her lamp toward the ceiling, but the light wouldn't reach. "If I had a flare, I'd show it to you."

"So tell me."

"On the way," she said, starting down the slope.

Knowing Lonnie was close, we hurried toward the nearest gap in the boulders and hoped it led somewhere. We moved along a narrow passageway, over loose drifts of shattered rock, circled one boulder and ducked under another that hadn't quite made it to floor level.

Molly explained that climbing caves were caverns in the midst of creation. "Somewhere up there," she said, raising her light, "the ceiling is climbing by shedding these boulders."

"Sounds dangerous."

"Not necessarily," she said. "It could have been centuries since the last boulder fell."

"On the other hand—"

"On the other hand, the whole thing could come crashing down around our ears at any second."

"Cheerful thought."

After winding through the boulder field for another five

minutes, she led us upward. We climbed another drift of crushed stone to the top of a relatively low chunk of rock. From that one we climbed atop another, higher boulder, and from there to the top of one still higher.

Then Molly turned back to our starting point as she switched off her light, and we stood there for a minute or two, searching the darkness, until we caught a phantom glimmer of reflected light maybe two hundred feet behind us, right at the edge of the field of boulders.

Having located Lonnie, Molly turned around, flicked her lamp on again, and took a look at where we were headed. All we could see was more of the same. Boulders on boulders, like an ant's-eye view of a driveway. The opposite wall of the cavern was out there somewhere, but it was beyond the range of her helmet light.

We took the high road as long as we could, stepping or jumping from one massive rock to another, but we finally came to a gap that was too wide to jump and had to climb down. And once down, we had to stay down for a while. The boulders were crowded, but steep-sided, and we couldn't find a way up. We were forced to backtrack several times, and detours were common, so it was impossible to maintain anything like a straight course.

After an hour of this, I asked, "How can you be sure we're still heading in the same direction?"

"Instinct," said Molly.

"In other words, you *can't*."

"Right."

We hadn't seen Lonnie's light since that one time back near the entrance, and we surely would have spotted it if he was close behind us. But he could be *anywhere*. He could have veered off on a tangent, or stumbled in a circle, or found an easier route and passed us by. We might never see him again, or he might be waiting just ahead.

As the boulders grew more widely scattered, the covering of crushed rock became thinner, and I could see that we were walking over another layer of boulders that had fallen long before. It had settled into a fairly even surface, but in places, gaping fissures made progress slow and treacherous. Then the boulders began to grow thicker again, and we quickly found our way back up onto high ground. A few minutes later, we stumbled upon a craterlike depression with sloping walls to shield us from view, and we stopped and took a break.

Molly's wound was redder and puffier, but it was the loss of blood that worried me. Her pants leg was stained to the cuff now, and I knew she couldn't have much more blood to spare. Her face was bone-white, her freckles standing out darkly against the skin, and she looked exhausted. Her mouth hung open, and there were black shadows under her eyes.

The bandage was stiff with blood over the wounds, and I had no water to rinse it in. All I could do was adjust it so that a fresh part of the tee shirt was over the wounds.

"Tie it tight," she said.

"Won't it hurt?"

"I need it. Feel like I'm coming apart."

"Tell me when."

She nodded. "Tighter."

"How's that?"

"That's good."

She buttoned her shirt and started to get up, but I held her in place. "Sit a moment," I said, "and give yourself a break. I can't see how Lonnie can follow us through this."

"Wouldn't put it past him," she said, but she didn't get up.

I tried not to think about Lonnie, but when I succeeded, I thought about other unfortunate subjects instead, such as Molly bleeding to death, or how thirsty I was. We hadn't seen water since the lake, and with all the rock dust I was eating, on top of the unaccustomed exercise, I was parched.

After five minutes rest, Molly said, "Gotta go."

As I helped her up, she slumped against me, and I said, "Sure you wouldn't like to lie down for a while?"

"No." She pushed away and stood there weaving. "Gotta go *now*, while I can."

With my help, she made it up the sloping wall of the crater and trudged on, laboring and unsteady, but still moving. I didn't know how she kept it up. In her place, I would have been flat on my back.

After another couple of hundred feet, we came to another wide gap and had to climb down again. It was a long way down this time, but at the bottom, we found a stream and drank our fill.

I took off Molly's bandage again and saw that she hadn't bled as much, but I wasn't sure if that was good or bad. After rinsing out the tee shirt as well as I could, I tied it back on her.

"Make it tight," she said again, and again I did as she said.

We waded across the stream and attacked the hill on the other side, but it was a slope of loose rock chips and proved unclimbable. So we retreated to the stream and walked along the bank until we found a better route.

Better in that it was possible, but it wasn't easy. A rocky slope rose to the base of a mountain of boulders, and from that point, there was no way but up.

Molly was weak now and more unsteady than ever, and I kept close behind her as she climbed, ready to catch her, or fall with her, if she fell. She had to take frequent breaks, but she kept them short, clearly afraid that she wouldn't be able to get up again if she sat too long.

We were resting in a cleft formed by the intersection of three huge stones when she said hoarsely, "This could be it."

"It?"

"The other side of the cavern."

Still catching my breath, I said, "You think so?"

"Might be."

I looked up. "All we need now is a way out."

"We'll find one," she assured me.

A couple of breaks later and fifty feet higher, she dropped exhausted onto a broad flat ledge. I stayed on my feet, my knee twinging, my back aching, and stared out into the darkness for a moment. As I turned back, I simultaneously heard a shot and the slug *spang!* off rock to my left.

Echoes rolled across the cavern like thunder as I dropped to the ledge beside Molly. She killed her light and whispered, "Come on!" and I followed as she crawled toward the back of the ledge.

Her light came on again as she slithered into a crevice, and I joined her, whispering, "Did you see where it came from?"

"Above us, I think."

"*Above* us?"

"Think so," she said.

"How'd he get above us?"

"Don't ask me."

"This guy's amazing."

She handed me the .38. "You better have this. I can't trust myself to shoot straight."

She switched off the lamp again, and we lay in the darkness, listening and waiting for Lonnie to make his move. After several minutes with no further activity, Molly turned her lamp back on and looked toward the rear of the crevice.

"I think we can get out through there," she said.

The crevice sloped upward at a forty-five-degree angle, and Molly showed me how to climb it. She sat with her back to the slope and worked her way up by pushing with her hands and feet against the sides. I soon got the hang of it and followed her.

We came out under another boulder, but we were able to squeeze through a gap beneath it. I heard Molly gasp, and when she moved aside, I saw why. I scrambled after her, forcing my way through the last tight space. Then I climbed to my feet and stared silently at something I thought I'd never see again.

Daylight.

38

We weren't outside yet, but we were close. We stood at the edge of a smaller cavern with a shaft of golden afternoon light slanting down from the middle of the distant ceiling. The opening was far out of reach, but the great outdoors was just on the other side of this cavern. All we had to do was get across and find an exit.

But first we had to get down. We were on a ledge about thirty feet above floor level, and just in front of us, the ledge dropped off sheer into another river. The water emerged from beneath the floor to the left and flowed off to the right. The channel was wide and looked fairly deep, but several boulders peeked through the surface.

I glanced behind us, looking right and left along the wall of rocks, but didn't see Lonnie. No surprise there. He never exposed himself for long. There was a gravel slope a short hike to the left that offered a way down, but the ledge looked a bit iffy in places. I helped Molly up with my left hand, holding the .38 in my right. As always, I felt like a fraud with a gun in my hand, but I had to play it for real this time, had to pretend that I actually knew what I was doing. Molly had brought us this far, but she was as pale as a ghost now and half-asleep on her feet. This beautiful, smart, capable—even dangerous—woman, who'd saved my life a number of times, now needed *me* to save *her*. I wasn't certain I was up to it, but I damn sure had to try. I was all we had.

"Go on." I nudged her to the left. "I'll cover you."

She didn't nod or speak, just started toward the rock slope. We went single file, sometimes sideways, along a rounded, rolling, irregular lip of stone, rarely more than a couple of yards wide, with a mound of boulders rising on one side and the precipice falling away on the other. I stayed close behind her, shielding her with my body, as I simultaneously tried to watch her, my footing, and the rocks.

Molly moved slowly and carefully, like an old person, or a closet drinker. But cautious as she was, when the slope abruptly steepened, she lost her balance and stumbled toward the edge.

I leapt and caught her arm, pulling her back as she was going over. She held on to me weakly and gave me a shaky look of thanks. I smiled encouragingly and glanced behind us as Lonnie stepped out of the rocks.

He stopped twenty feet away with Molly's Glock at his side and a look of satisfaction on his face.

As his arm came up, I shoved Molly toward the edge, then fired wildly in his direction and jumped after her. If Lonnie fired, I didn't hear it.

As soon as I jumped, I remembered the boulders—the boulders I'd seen sticking out of the river, the river into which I was currently jumping. I couldn't recall where the rocks were located, and it was too late to do anything about it anyway, so I just didn't look down. Fortunately, I wasn't held in suspense for long.

We came down in water. Deep and icy cold. Molly entered a beat ahead of me, and I landed almost on top of her. I caught up with her underwater, saw the closed eyes and the bubbles streaming from her open mouth, then shoved the gun into my pants, grabbed her, and kicked for the surface.

I broke into the air with her hanging limp in my arms, her face blue, her eyes rolled back, and her mouth spilling water. Fighting to keep both our heads above the surface, I spun her around and wrapped my arms around her, made a fist with my right hand—thumb side to her belly—then gripped it with my left and jerked upward. I wasn't sure the Heimlich maneuver would work on a drowning victim, but I couldn't think of anything else to try.

Water gushed from her mouth, and I kept at it until she started coughing and gasping. When she caught her breath and let out a groan, I asked, "Are you with me?"

She nodded.

"*Are* you? Talk to me!"

"Yes," she said hoarsely.

I pressed my face to her wet hair and said, "God, you scared me."

"Sorry."

I laughed in relief and looked around. Daylight was only a faint glimmer upstream, and we again had to rely on Molly's helmet lamp. I thought I heard the faint roar of a waterfall ahead, and I decided it was time to get out of the river, but the prospects didn't look hopeful. To the right, the rock face rose straight for more than thirty feet, the first ten worn smooth by the river. To the left, the rock face ended at floor level, ten feet above us.

The river followed a gentle curve to the left, then back to the right. As the channel straightened, I saw a boulder ahead, wedged against the left bank, the top sloping up from the water to just below floor level.

"See it?" I asked.

Nothing.

"Molly?"

"Wha—?"

"Ahead to the left. The rock? See it?"

She squinted and said, "Yeah."

"Swim for it."

She made it to the boulder on her own, but I had to help her out of the water. As soon as I got her on her feet, she went down again, dropping to her knees at the edge of the river and upchucking what was left of her breakfast. Not much there, but that didn't stop the heaves. I knelt beside

293

her and did what I could to help, rubbing her back and whispering useless things like "there-there," as the spasms came and went.

When they passed, she washed her mouth out and splashed some water onto her face. She took a moment to catch her breath, then put a hand on my knee and tried to push herself up, but she just didn't have the strength. I practically had to pick her up, and once on her feet, she leaned against me, shaking all over.

I was shaking, too, but it was nothing like the quaking she experienced. I pressed my wet body to hers, trying to warm her, holding her so tightly that her trembling felt like my own.

When it finally subsided, she pushed away and said through clenched teeth, "Gotta go."

"I should check your wound."

She shook her head, said, "He's too close," and started up the slope. The first few strides were okay, then she began to stagger, and I was half carrying her by the time we reached the top. At the highest point, we were barely three feet below floor level, so I boosted her over the edge without much trouble and climbed after her.

The river had carried us out of the cavern into a broad passage, with a rock ledge running along the left bank and the ceiling arched like an old subway tunnel. Because I would be leading, I switched helmets with Molly. And since Lonnie was behind us, we kept heading downstream.

Except for an occasional minor infall or modest mudslide, the floor was rock. The width of the ledge ranged from a promenade fifteen feet across down to one stretch like a windowsill less than a foot wide. But for that narrow stretch, the tunnel wall sloped away from the river, and we had the lean on our side. I held on to Molly and didn't rush her, and we made it across with minimal excitement.

After that, the wall to our left was broken twice within a short distance. The first opened into another tunnel and the second into a smallish cavern. I considered trying the tunnel, but neither it nor the cavern offered any glimmer of daylight, so we passed them by.

The second dip in the river had clearly taken a lot out of Molly, but she kept on going: shuffling and staggering; stumbling and sometimes falling. But when she went down, I would help her up, and she would plod on. I occasionally had to steer her in the right direction, or she would have walked into the river. But it was her grim, willful determination that carried her through.

As the river veered to the left, the sound of the waterfall became unmistakable. The curve sharpened, the roar growing louder at every step. Then the passage ended, and we came out beside the falls. The river fell forty feet into another deep channel that cut across the floor of another cavern and continued on its merry way, but the ledge simply stopped, leaving a straight drop to the floor thirty feet below. It was too far to jump, but a rockslide fell away to our left, offering an easier way down.

Easier, but still a challenge for Molly. She was okay as long as the floor was reasonably level, but her balance was shot, and on the slope, I had to hold her to keep her from falling.

We were about halfway down when we were hit with a flash of light from above. I snatched the revolver out of my waistband and fired at the light, a little surprised that the gun still worked after two dunkings in the river, especially since neither of us had thought to test it the last time. I gave Molly a shove toward a large boulder as I fired, then followed, hustling her behind it. The way down was harder from there, but at least we had some cover.

We slid the last twenty feet or so down a slope of pea-sized gravel, then I scrambled to my feet and hurried on, dragging Molly after me. The floor was a flat expanse of stone, littered with rock from the slide, but none of it was big enough to hide behind, and I felt awfully exposed. When I spotted a towering rock formation ahead, I looked back and saw Lonnie's light at floor level.

I pulled Molly into a jog, and she did her best to keep up. But after a few strides, she stumbled, and would have fallen if I hadn't caught her. We couldn't stay there, so I picked her up and kept going. That might sound easy, but it wasn't. Molly was no ballerina, and I was no Arnold Schwarzenegger. Exhausted and feeling terribly out of shape, I gritted my teeth and struggled on.

As we neared the base of the rock formation, I grunted, "Wake up!"

"M awake," she said.

"Gotta put you down."

"Kay."

I waddled to a stop and put her on her feet, then slapped off my helmet light and turned to take the Weaver position: right shoulder back, left hand cradling the gun hand, sighting along my straight right arm at Lonnie's bobbing helmet light. Both arms were shaking so badly, I couldn't hold the target, but he was getting too close, so I fired.

The light fell to the right and went out.

Did I hit him? I didn't know, but I doubted it. I couldn't see him in the blackness, but I could imagine him crawling this way, so I took Molly's hand and whispered, "Let's go."

Knowing my helmet lamp would only give him a target, I blindly felt my way around the rock formation to the left, moving as quickly and silently as I could, afraid to stop, not knowing how close he was behind us. I pushed Molly hard, probably too hard for her condition, but we had to find a hiding place, or a way out, or something, anything, to give us an advantage.

Instead I felt my way around a wide skirt of rock, then flicked on my light and saw that we were at a dead end. Smooth walls of granite rose straight up on three sides. No way up, around, over, or through. A trap, in other words.

"Ooops," Molly said quietly.

"Couldn't have put it better myself," I agreed.

I turned and listened for Lonnie, but I couldn't hear him.

Then I backed Molly into a shallow alcove and left her leaning there. I whispered, "Don't move," then tiptoed to the
other side of the cul-de-sac, about fifteen feet away. I raised
the .38 and sighted at the edge of the skirt of rock.

After holding that pose for a few seconds, I lowered the
gun and looked around. There was a shelf of rock about
head-high to my left, so I took off my helmet and put it
there. Then I faced the lamp straight ahead, switched it off,
and moved an arm's length away, keeping a finger on the
switch.

Phantom lights played across my vision. Otherwise, the
darkness was absolute. I listened hard, trying to tune out
the pounding of my heart. Adrenaline was giving me the
shakes, so I tried a technique I had used in my playing days.
Before going out to pitch a game, I would find a private
place, then stick my tongue out and pant like a dog. I had
picked up the ritual from a nightclub singer, who'd claimed
that the panting helped to relax the diaphragm, thereby de-
creasing the muscular tension that caused the shakes. It
wasn't easy to pant without making a sound, but it seemed
to do the trick, even in this modified form.

Minutes passed, and I considered the possibility that I'd
killed Lonnie, or incapacitated him. I considered it, but I
didn't believe it. I doubted I'd even hit him.

In a sudden spurt of panic, I realized I didn't know how
many shots I had left. When I hurriedly added it up, I got a
total of four firings: one for Molly, and three for me. That
left me with only two shots, so I had to make them count.

I'd never been crazy about the dark, and this adventure
in the underworld hadn't altered my feelings. The combination of darkness and stillness was disorienting, and after a
time, I could no longer feel the floor under my feet. I felt
like I was floating and gradually lost all sense of up and
down. Only when I pressed my back hard against the rock
did I finally regain orientation.

At the same moment, I realized that Lonnie was with us.
I didn't see him, hear him, or smell him. At least, I wasn't

aware of doing any of those things. I sensed him, and I knew he was close, though precisely *where*, I couldn't say.

I held my breath and listened. Then I forced myself to breathe, but kept it slow and as silent as I could make it. I heard nothing at first. Then, no . . . yes . . . something. A breath. An exhaled breath. Somewhere in front of me.

I fingered the switch. *Should I?* If I did, there was a good chance that Lonnie would kill me. And then he'd kill Molly. He was good at it. He'd already killed Mitch and Donald and Dewey. He would have killed Duncan if he hadn't been interrupted, and he'd put Darrell in a coma. What chance did I have against somebody like that? I could hold still and hope he would turn around and go back the way he'd come. But what if he found me? Or, worse, found *Molly*. I couldn't let him do that. Then I heard a piece of gravel skitter across the floor and flicked on the light.

The beam caught him in profile, and he threw himself forward, turning and firing as he moved. The helmet popped off the shelf and spun in the air, the lamp lighting him in strobing flashes as it fell. I held my ground, waiting for a clear shot, thinking, *Aim for the middle of the body. Make it count.* The helmet hit the floor and flipped onto its top, then rocked back and pinned Lonnie in its beam, as he bounced off the wall.

And I fired.

He took it in the stomach and stopped dead in his tracks, but he didn't go down. I was moving to my right when he fired, and I felt the breeze from the slug. Then I punched the .38 back up to firing position, thinking again, *Make it count!*

He was close now, only a few feet away, so I raised my sights and shot him point-blank in the middle of the forehead.

And he dropped like a rock.

39

J ust like that. No wavering. One second he was up, the next he was down. I couldn't believe it.

I kept him covered as I kicked the Glock away from his hand. My gun was empty, but he didn't know that. Then I stepped in, trying to stay out of the spreading pool of blood, and laid the barrel behind his ear, as I felt with the fingers of my other hand for a pulse in his neck.

I didn't find one, and he didn't move, so I picked up the Glock and tucked the .38 into my pants. I ejected the clip from his weapon and saw that he had three bullets left, not that they did him much good now.

I'd killed him. My third man. My first with a gun. Did it feel different? Not that I could tell. Frankly, I didn't feel much of anything, only a lingering sense of disbelief.

When something hit the rock floor behind me, I jerked around and saw that Molly had finally collapsed. I dropped beside her to search for a pulse and thanked God when I found one. I didn't believe in the old faker, but I needed somebody to thank.

I knelt there, utterly spent, too tired to think or move. As the Glock slipped from my hand and clattered the floor, I let everything go. I had to get Molly out of there and knew I couldn't afford to fall asleep, but I also couldn't go on any longer without a break. I thought it would be all right as long as I kept my eyes open. Just a minute or two, then I'd get up and do what I had to do.

Just don't close your eyes, I told myself.

But it didn't help.

Next thing I knew, I was curled on my side on the floor. My mouth was dry, and I realized with a vague sense of guilt that I'd fallen asleep. I wasn't supposed to do that, though I couldn't remember exactly why. I was about to doze off again when I felt a pat on the shoulder and turned to look into the face of a demon.

Shiny dark skin; oversized ears standing erect; an upturned nose with fat quivering nostrils; tiny black eyes; a mouth full of small sharp teeth; and leathery wings opening and closing like an umbrella. *Pat-pat-pat*, they went on my shoulder.

I shot upright, as though electrocuted, even before my sluggish, sleep-fogged brain registered that it was a bat. I threw the vile thing off and scrambled away, pumping my legs and driving my heels until my back slammed into the wall.

The bat lay flat where it had plopped, glaring up at me from under those leathery wings. On a rational level, I knew it had to be a fruit or insect bat, not a vampire, but I sat there with my heart pounding, waiting for it to come for me.

When it suddenly sprang up onto the tips of its wings, I jerked back, cracking my head against the rock hard enough to make my eyes water. But instead of coming for me, it lifted its nose in disdain, staggered into a U-turn, and capered around the skirt of rock into the darkness.

As it vanished, I caught sight of Molly on the floor and remembered why I wasn't supposed to fall asleep. I crawled over and laid a hand on her cheek, then sighed with relief when I felt her warmth.

If the bat hadn't awakened me, I realized, I would still be curled up on the floor, and who knows how long I would have slept. There was some irony there: that I, of all people, should owe a debt of gratitude to a bat. No wonder it had stalked off in a huff. The least I could have done was say thanks.

I struggled to my feet and walked over to pick up my helmet, then strapped it on and squatted back at Molly's side. It took me three tries to get her up in my arms, then I had to lean her against the wall for a moment to catch my breath. I started back around the rock formation, stopping every twenty feet or so to take the weight off my arms. Each break got a little longer, and every successive advance was shorter than the one before.

After a dozen or more pauses, I rounded a stone buttress, then squeezed the two of us through a crack in the rock and was stopped again, this time by the sight of daylight. Not much of it, only a small patch reflecting off a dull stone surface a hundred yards away. But this time it was at floor level.

After another brief rest, I hefted Molly again and started for the light, making one last all-out effort to get her out of there. My knee was stiffening up, and my back was aching, and I was afraid to turn, or bend, or stop, for fear of seizing up or triggering a spasm.

I don't remember much of that final trek. It was all I could do to put one foot in front of the other, and several times I almost gave up and let myself fall. But I knew I'd never get Molly back up in my arms again. So I plodded on, living from step to step, pretending that each was the last. *Just one more*, I kept telling myself.

I was on autopilot by the time I staggered into the light, but I felt its heat and turned like a sunflower toward the source. *Just one more step.* The light grew into a bright blur that surrounded me and finally engulfed me. But as it did, I stumbled and felt myself falling. On the way down, I cursed my failure, knowing that Molly would die now, and Lonnie would win.

A greenish haze resolved into blades of grass, seen close-up, translucent in the sunlight. Then I saw the boots. Scuffed black square-toed boots, standing before me. I craned back and looked up past faded jeans and a blue work shirt to see

301

Tim staring over my head toward the caves. I knew what he was looking for.

"Sorry, Tim."

A muscle flexed in his jaw, as he looked down at me. "Who killed him?"

"I did."

He nodded, then turned and walked away a few steps.

I sat up and saw Molly sprawled in the grass about six feet in front of me. I crawled to her side and felt her pulse. It was light and a little fast, but steady. Her breathing was regular, and she seemed to be sleeping peacefully, but I knew I had to get her help soon.

Ten feet beyond her, treetops rose over a steep dropoff. Behind me, grass stretched toward the mouth of the cave, and woods pressed against the sides of the clearing.

Then Tim was back, standing over me again, as he said bitterly, "They take it all in the end, don't they? And when they can't do it themselves, they always find somebody to do it for them!"

Seeing his hand resting on the butt of his gun, I tried to reason with him. "He did it to himself, Tim."

"I *know* that, but . . ." He shook his head. "They drove him to it! Can't you see that?"

"I see you," I said. "You live with the same knowledge, and it hasn't turned you into a killer."

"But *I* didn't learn about it when I was just a kid, either."

"That's what Cyrus said," I told him. "He said it happened when Lonnie was too young, and when they turn that early, they never turn back."

Tim stared at me—angry, hurt, and grieving—and I considered trying to get up. But I wasn't sure I could make it, and as long as I was down, I was no threat to him.

When he finally looked back at the cave, I said as gently as I could, "We have to get Molly to a hospital, Tim."

He turned and looked at her, as if seeing her for the first time, then nodded and said, "Of course."

Then I saw Rooker. He was behind Tim, maybe thirty

feet away, half-hidden by a tree. I caught him putting his weapon away, apparently having decided that Tim wasn't going to shoot me after all.

As Tim reached for his radio, Rooker strolled out of the trees, asking casually, "So what's up, partner?"

Rooker and I tailed the ambulance to St. Mary's, and Tim followed in his car. They rushed Molly into the emergency room, and I hurried in after her, but they wouldn't let me into the treatment area. After the Lieutenant showed up and took Tim outside to talk, Rooker said it might be a good time for me to tell him what had happened.

He borrowed a conference room on the administrative floor and took my statement, taping it with a pocket recorder and making notes on a pad. He had questions, and it took a while to satisfy them. Food was brought in, but I couldn't eat much. By the time we were finished, he knew everything I knew, except about the chest of gold, the photos of Duncan and Michael Nixon, Duncan's hiring of Lonnie, and the sinful doings detailed in the ledger. It wasn't up to me to make any of those things public, so I didn't mention them. As for the shooting, Rooker said it was a clear-cut case of self-defense, but he explained that there would still have to be a grand jury hearing. A man had been killed, and a jury of my peers would have to decide if charges should be brought. It was just a formality, he assured me, but I'd been through it before, and I didn't look forward to it.

I was in Molly's room when they brought her up, and she was relieved to see me. When she'd regained consciousness, nobody had been able to tell her how I was, or how she got there. She had missed the exciting conclusion of our drama, so she had as many questions as Rooker. I gladly answered them, but I knew I was tiring her, and when she finally nodded off, I called Cyrus to come get me. I left a note saying I'd be back in the morning, then went downstairs to wait for my ride.

I was leaning against a brick wall near the visitors entrance, wishing I had a joint, when a high, twangy voice said, "Guess it's all over, huh?" and I turned to see the tall, gawky form of Oliver Fryman.

"God, I hope so," I said.

"How's Molly?"

"Doctor says she'll make it."

"That's good," he said, sounding sincerely relieved.

"I suppose you want an interview," I said, and his smug expression told me I'd guessed right on the first try. "You did us a favor, and now you expect one in return."

"That's how it works, Mister Cochran," he agreed with a grin.

I gave him the interview in the back parlor of the big-house, while sipping good brandy. I still hadn't found time for a joint, so I had to make do.

The interview was printed in the Tuesday edition of the *News-Sentinel* and was picked up for reprint all over the country. It concluded with me saying, "I'm glad it's over. A man tried to kill us, and I killed him instead. Simple as that."

But it wasn't, of course.

Donald was buried on Monday afternoon at Calvary Cemetery, crowded in shoulder to shoulder with Dewey in the Flanagan family plot.

Helen sat to Molly's left, watching for the second time in a week as a man she loved was lowered into the ground. Molly was in a wheelchair, feeling weak and taking antibiotics for her infected wound, which was bandaged now with something more sanitary than a dirty tee shirt. Ida, also in a wheelchair, sat with Cyrus to my right. She'd been allowed to attend the service, but would return to St. Mary's afterward to continue rehabilitative therapy. Tim and Rooker stood off to the side, at the edge of the crowd. Tim was still on suspension, but they had come together. Duncan stood near them, his head bandaged and his arm in a sling. He was out of the hospital now, but the police had asked him not to leave town. His brother Darrell remained in a coma at Park West Medical and wasn't expected to recover. Lonnie would be buried tomorrow.

As Donald's casket dropped out of sight, I thought of what Tim had said to me one dark morning up at the summerhouse. He'd noted that people did a lot of dying around me and had suggested that maybe I was a carrier. I'd resisted the idea, but maybe there was something to his theory. There was no question that death and misery had a way of following me wherever I went.

The grand jury was convened on Tuesday, and I testified, along with Rooker, Doctor Cleveland, the patrolman who first saw the body, and the forensic technician who'd examined the scene. My peers decided that I had acted lawfully in defending myself against an armed attacker.

Lonnie was buried that afternoon, and Helen paid for the funeral, but none of us attended the service. Molly had felt that a Flanagan should be present, but there were no Flanagans who would have been welcome.

By the end of our third week in Knoxville, Tim's suspension had been lifted, and he was back with his squad. Shamrock's fate was still officially undecided, but it would almost certainly be sold. As Lester Prine had said, without Dewey, the company was finished. Of the original board of directors, only Duncan was left. Darrell's wife and Helen would vote their husbands' stock, and Molly would vote her father's. I assumed that Duncan's view was unchanged and that Darrell's wife would vote as her husband had intended, and I knew that Molly and Helen had reluctantly decided to accept Lester's offer. So it appeared that he would get his land.

The following Friday, two weeks after Molly was shot, the Celica was finally released from the shop. She decided she felt up to a cross-country drive and said we would leave the next morning. I offered to drive the car back to Galveston and let her fly, but she insisted on going along for the ride.

That afternoon, we dropped by to see Ida and found her unhappily trudging down the corridor on a walker. She nodded at us as she passed and silently led us to her room. I was flattered to see my three books stacked on her bedside table. She gave them a glance as she lowered herself to the side of the bed, but all she said was, "So you're goin', are you?"

"Tomorrow," said Molly.

She nodded. "You comin' back?"

"Soon."

"You, too?" she asked me.

"I'll bring her," I promised. Her eyes brushed over the books on the bedside table, but I knew she wouldn't ask, so I said, "Would you like me to sign them for you?"

"That'd be all right," she allowed, thrusting a book into my hands. When I returned the last one, she told me, "Thank you."

And I said, "Don't mention it."

That evening, Molly and I had dinner at "Frank's." In gratitude for our keeping him out of our troubles, our host provided a private dining room, away from the curious public and the prying press, and was there in person to make sure we enjoyed ourselves. The service was impeccable, the food delicious, and with a different wine being served with each course, I was thoroughly lubricated by the time they pushed up the dessert cart.

Over a wedge of Kaisertorte and a cup of coffee—after Frank had graciously bowed out with his waiters—I asked Molly, "Will you marry me?"

And she said without hesitation, "Yes."

Oh, boy!

"What did you say?" she asked.

I swallowed hard. "Nothing."

She smiled. "Having second thoughts already?"

"No," I said quickly, "I'm not."

"Then why don't you sound happy?"

"I *am!*"

"You sure?"

"Positive."

"But?" she asked.

"But what?"

"Thought I heard a 'but.' "

"No, but—"

"See!"

"No, I just mean that . . . well, you're a rich woman now, and I guess I can't help wondering why you would want somebody like me when you could have anybody."

"I love you," she said quietly.

"That's a plus," I had to agree.

"And you saved my life," she added, putting her hand on mine. "I know that killing Lonnie bothered you. And it *should* bother you! But you were only doing what you had to do, and you did it as well as *I* could have done."

"I doubt that," I said. "And I haven't the foggiest idea *how* I did it."

"That's okay," she said with a smile. "Luck is important, too."